Newport, New Hampshire

ALSO BY CATHERINE TUDISH

Tenney's Landing

American Cream

A Novel

CATHERINE TUDISH

Scribner

New York   London   Toronto   Sydney

SCRIBNER
1230 Avenue of the Americas
New York, NY 10020

First Scribner hardcover edition August 2007

SCRIBNER and design are trademarks of Macmillan Library Reference USA, Inc. used under license by Simon & Schuster, the publisher of this work.

For information about special discounts for bulk purchases, please contact Simon & Schuster Special Sales at 1-800-456-6798 or business@simonandschuster.com.

Designed by Kyoko Watanabe
Text set in Bembo

Manufactured in the United States of America

1   3   5   7   9   10   8   6   4   2

Library of Congress Cataloging-in-Publication Data
Tudish, Catherine, [date]
American cream : a novel / Catherine Tudish.
p. cm.
1. Self-realization in women—Fiction. 2. Psychological fiction. I. Title.

PS3620.U34A83 2007
813'.6—dc22
2006102463

ISBN-13: 978-0-7432-6769-4
ISBN-10: 0-7432-6769-9

For my mother and father

The present falls, the present falls away;
How pure the motion of the rising day.

—THEODORE ROETHKE,
"THE TREE, THE BIRD"

American Cream

CAROLINE

I died on a bright morning of Indian summer. Neither old nor sick, I stepped out into a day of maples blazing on the hilltop, frost lingering in the shade of the barn. I carried a pan of vegetable peelings for my hens. They saw me and started coming—headlong, wings tucked back as if holding up their downy skirts. I called to one lagging behind, and in that instant all the light of the morning narrowed down to one tiny point, winked like a star, and was gone.

Swimming out of darkness, I heard my husband call my name. He knelt beside the fallen body, cradling the head, pressing his fingers to the wrist. I was close by, hardly more than a held breath. Not afraid, but sorry for Nathan, who took the body in his arms and ran with it. I watched as he lay her across the backseat of the car and drove away. I was sorry for the woman, too, the woman whose hens scratched and pecked at the potato peelings and carrot scrapings flung from the pan when she fell, sorry for the shape of her left behind in the damp grass.

Over the following days, I stayed close to Nathan, wishing I had hands or a voice to comfort him when he sank down sobbing on the floor of our bedroom. In substance, I was something like a whisper of air, the silent notes of a flute. While he slept, I practiced sailing about the house. I could make the curtains flutter but could not slam a door. I could whisk a fly from the windowsill, snuff the lighted candle Nathan left on the bedside table. I could not see our son or daughter, who were grown and gone. Late at night, I rested on the roof as the moon traveled across the sky, as the mist cooled and fell again as frost.

After the funeral, I tucked myself into the branches of an oak as they gathered beside the open grave in the hilltop cemetery. A cold wind came rushing down from the mountains, driving dark clouds before it, scattering leaves. My family drew closer together, buttoning their coats. I smelled the damp, mildew scent of freshly turned earth as my uncle Herman, the old minister, said the words "ashes to ashes, dust to dust." It brought back the greasy feel of his thumb on my forehead, the words of Ash Wednesday that foretold cold and darkness. But I am here, I wanted to say, here in this tree.

They took turns with the sad business of shoveling a spade of dirt into the grave. Nathan went first, then my brother, Dan; my son, Larry; my daughter, Virginia. Her son, Randall, a tall boy of twelve, linked his arm through hers and leaned against her. Larry's two girls, a little younger than Randall, amused themselves collecting leaves and acorns, picking up handfuls of the soft, golden needles that fell from the pines swaying in the wind.

At last Virginia stepped forward, bowing her dark head. How lovely she was, fingers of sunlight breaking through the clouds above her, dancing across her hair and shoulders. Unfolding a piece of paper, she began reading the words of the Shaker hymn I had read for Aunt Ida years before, the one that ends with the promise of a little boat to carry us beyond this vale of sorrow. It was a comfort to me, for I knew that soon I would not be able to see or hear them any longer.

West Moffat had come to the cemetery without his wife. He stood opposite Virginia, the grave between them, his eyes on her as she read. They had loved each other as children, and I confess I played a part in Virginia's leaving him, even though he was like a second son to me. I wondered sometimes if I had been wrong to keep them apart, but I was happy for her when she fell in love with Robert. He was a good man, too, a doctor. Seeing West's gaze, he went to Virginia and took her in his arms when she had finished and led her to the waiting car.

At the house, my friend Sissy and my sister-in-law, Hillary, had everything ready. The dining room table was covered with plates of sandwiches and cookies, bowls of green olives and tiny pickles. On the sideboard, cups and spoons, the big silver coffeepot. Sissy's husband, Jere, slipped his flask from his jacket and passed it among the men gathered in the living room. From time to time, a bark of laughter rang out, and the voices would quiet before picking up again. In the kitchen, Sissy was telling how I had started to give her a permanent one night when we were young but couldn't finish because the fumes made me sick. She had gone to school the next day with half her hair curly, half straight. "I was so mad at her," she said, her voice catching. Her niece, dear Henny, pushed herself down the hall in her wheelchair, returning with a box of tissues, the hint of a smile on her face. She passed it around, and there were more stories, more laughing and crying.

Then it was evening. The last of the guests had left; the

dishes were washed and put away. I was tired, my airy spirit nearly spent. But I saw Virginia going through the door to sit alone on the back steps, and I wanted to wait with her awhile. She was wearing my green sweater, pulling it tight against the chill. A kitchen window stood open; the smell of coffee lingered. From the living room the sound of muted voices drifted out to us—Larry and his family, Virginia's husband and son, Uncle Herman, occasionally a few words from Nathan in his new, husky tones. Of them all, I worried for Virginia. Nathan and Larry would grieve hard and be done with it, but my daughter held everything inside. Her grief would stay, and who could say where it might take her.

How sad to leave them, the house where I lived for more than forty years, the hills that deepened to purple in the twilight. And yet, like a traveler setting out on a journey, I awaited my little boat with growing curiosity.

The rain that had been threatening all afternoon finally started—softly at first, no more than a patter in the leaves. A cricket began to chirp, a melodic *chirr* from the grass near the corner of the porch. One summer, when we had a pair of crickets in the fireplace, my father-in-law told us they brought good luck. I listened for an answering chirp, but there was only the one. The season for mating was long past, his solitary song a mournful note in the descending night.

Chapter One

Startled by the cold clang of the bell, Virginia nearly smiled, remembering how her mother would say that something made her "jump out of her skin"—as if skin were a garment to be abandoned in case of emergency. She looked up at the steeple, where the paint was peeling away in ragged strips that fluttered in the biting December wind, and wondered who could be ringing the bell before the wedding. That was wrong. It was supposed to ring after, when the bride and groom came out together.

They used to have rules about the bell. On Sunday morning, at a quarter to ten, you rang it twelve times. If you rang it thirteen times, one of the deacons would give you the hairy eyeball and have a word with your parents during coffee hour. Hovering near the church steps alone, Virginia watched the old bell clang merrily back and forth—twenty times, twenty-one, free at last.

One of the bride's relatives, she guessed, picturing a boy of ten or eleven, the one wearing combat boots who had stared at her as he walked past with his parents. She could imagine him putting all his weight on the bell rope and then letting it fly, a fine dust of rotting wood and plaster drifting down on his hair.

Virginia had made Rob and Randall go inside without her. It seemed important to observe the arriving guests as they hurried from their cars and scooted past, cheeks reddened by the arctic chill that had descended the week after Thanksgiving. The people she knew waved a quick hello and ducked their heads. The others, the ones who would take their seats on the bride's side, regarded her curiously, then glanced away, whispering, wondering who she was.

The others. In Virginia's eyes, they might have come from a country beyond the hills, where they lived and worked and had their own customs. The women favored heavy makeup and hair dyed chestnut brown or bleached the color of bone. Heedless of the cold, they wore light, brightly colored dresses under their open coats, no gloves. The men appeared solemn, dressed mostly in black, with long sideburns and beards, as if they belonged to some religious sect. Then she remembered: It was the opening day of rifle season. Those were hunting beards.

As the last note rang from the steeple, she paused on the top step and took in the familiar street, the nearby white houses, scuffed and worn in the grim light of late afternoon. The yards and roofs of Tenney's Landing were dusted with a skiff of snow. In two or three front windows, Virginia could see the blinking lights of Christmas trees. Her mother used to say it was her favorite time of year, when the earth was still and waiting and the nights were long. Caroline would laugh a little, expecting everyone to disagree with her.

Reaching for the iron door latch, Virginia was reminded of

the itchy feel of wool kneesocks, the deathly cold of the narrow passage off the vestibule where she and Henny stood to
ring the bell, Henny so light the rope would lift her off her feet
if Virginia let go. Every other Sunday, when it was their turn,
they could read their names in the church bulletin, right under
the minister and the deacons on duty. Bell Ringers: Hennis
Eastman and Virginia Rownd. Henny always took a ballpoint
pen from her mother's purse and crossed out their first names,
wrote in "Henny" and "Ginny." They pretended not to be
sorry the year they turned twelve and two younger girls took
their places.

Val Kramer, the organist, turned and nodded when she
noticed Virginia, relieved to see her at last. Rob walked calmly
down the center aisle to meet her and put her arm through his,
escorting her to the front pew on the right. He betrayed no
uneasiness, but Randall's expression was worried, in case she
might do something to embarrass him. The instant Virginia sat
down, Val leaned hard on the organ, drawing out the opening
notes of Beethoven's "Ode to Joy." Transfixed by the overflowing basket of flowers on the altar—an improbable mixture of
chrysanthemums, tiger lilies, and white roses—Virginia wondered why everything was backward.

When Rob pressed her hand, her eyes flicked involuntarily
to the door to the right of the altar, where she saw her father
in his good gray suit behind the minister. Someone was holding his hand, too. Mrs. Will, from the school cafeteria. The
bride.

As they passed in front, Virginia's father let his gaze rest on
her face for a moment. His look was benevolent, as if she were
the one needing forgiveness. It did nothing to calm her thumping heart, the rushing sound in her ears. The little group
squared off in front of the altar, her father and Mrs. Will and

the two witnesses—a man and a woman she'd never seen before—standing before the Reverend Gleason. At the words "Dearly beloved," Mrs. Will gave her father's hand a squeeze before letting go.

Dearly beloved. No other church service starts that way, the minister addressing the congregation as "beloved." The word is on her mother's gravestone: Caroline Rownd, Beloved Wife of Nathan, February 16, 1939–October 19, 2005. Not such a long life.

A solid-looking woman from behind, Lydia Will was wearing a navy dress and jacket. Though she had none of Caroline's willowy grace, she did, Virginia conceded, have fine posture.

Mrs. Swill they used to call her, she and Henny, whispering the name as they moved through the cafeteria line. Her face would be flushed from working in the kitchen all morning, a contrast to the snowy white of her bleached-out aprons. Her hands were rough and red, scratched. Maybe she scraped her knuckles while grating cheese for their lunches. She barely glanced at the children as they came along with their clattery silver trays. A serving spoon in each hand, she dished up watery beef stew and applesauce or chili mac and pineapple chunks. "Disgusting," Virginia and Henny would agree, probing the food with their forks.

Every other Friday, though, was sheet cake day, when Mrs. Will baked her enormous one-layer cakes with chocolate frosting, the sweet chocolate applied so thinly it barely covered the surface. The two girls couldn't get enough of that cake, the way the frosting, so stingy on the top, magically trickled down into the little hollows. They would volunteer to stay in from recess to help scrape the trays and rinse the silverware. As Mrs. Will loaded the dishwasher, the girls swabbed the tables with green, antiseptic-smelling sponges, then turned the benches upside down on top of them and swept up crumbs with two big push brooms.

"It's no mystery why you're being so helpful all of a sudden," Mrs. Will would say, drying her hands on her apron and looking critically at the spotless cafeteria before giving each of them an extra piece of cake wrapped in a paper napkin. They would wolf it down in the hallway before their classmates came in from the playground.

At the words "take this woman," Virginia shifted in the pew, enough to make her father's shoulder twitch. He started to turn his head in her direction, then clasped his hands behind his back. Only a year before, he had stood there reciting a psalm at Caroline's funeral. Not her favorite, as everyone expected, not Psalm 100 with its joyful "Enter his gates with thanksgiving and his courts with praise." No. Ashen, his hands trembling, he got up and said he was going to read Psalm 137. Virginia didn't know that one, but she remembered how it surprised Uncle Herman, who had come out of retirement and put on his minister's robe one last time. "Ah," her mother's uncle had said, standing aside, bowing his head to listen.

"By the rivers of Babylon we sat down and wept when we remembered Zion." Nathan had memorized the text, and he kept his eyes on the back of the church, his voice holding back a river of sorrow. "There on the willow trees we hung up our harps, for there those who carried us off demanded music and singing; and our captors called on us to be merry: 'Sing us one of the songs of Zion.' How could we sing the Lord's song in a foreign land?" He looked down at Virginia, and at her brother, Larry, and then, gripping the sides of the podium with his two hands, he went on. "If I forget you, O Jerusalem, let my right hand wither away; let my tongue cling to the roof of my mouth if I do not remember you, if I do not set Jerusalem above my highest joy." When he sat down beside Virginia again, she was afraid to touch him.

The day after the funeral, Virginia had retrieved the family Bible, its pages spotted with salt spray from the nights their ancestor Thaddeus Rownd had carried it up on deck during his crossing from Blackpool, praying for safe passage. In the light of the kitchen, the pages crisp in her hands, she discovered that her father hadn't recited the entire psalm. He'd left out the last part, about "Babylon the destroyer," the wish that the children of Babylon be dashed against the rocks. It still shocked her, the fierceness of the Old Testament, even though Uncle Herman had led them through it in his days as pastor of the First Presbyterian Church. Psalm 137 was a strange choice, Virginia and her brother had agreed.

"What has happened to you?" Virginia wanted to shout as her father stood at the altar in his wedding clothes.

Her brother did not come to the wedding. He lived too far away, he said, without embarrassment. When he and his wife and daughters had made the trip from Sioux Falls for Caroline's funeral, it was the first time in several years.

Larry remembered Lydia Will from the school cafeteria and her husband from the service station, but he claimed to have no objection to the marriage. "It's none of our business," he told Virginia on the phone. "He must be lonely, on the farm by himself."

Rob defended Nathan, too, repeating Larry's words. Henny understood. She had also chosen not to come—though for her it would have been only a short drive.

The man standing next to Nathan grinned as he fished in his jacket pocket and handed over the gold band. To avoid watching her father put the ring on Lydia's finger, Virginia turned to Randall, brushing invisible lint from his sleeve. He ignored her, absorbed by the scene in front of him. Lydia Rownd. It was a pretty name, actually. Virginia had expected to cry during the ceremony. Instead she felt dry, hollow.

The rest went quickly, and before Virginia had steeled herself for the end, Reverend Gleason was extending his arms as if enfolding the couple before him. "Those whom God has joined together," he intoned, "let no man put asunder." And in the silence that followed, he added, "You can kiss your bride, Nathan."

Flustered for a moment, Nathan glanced at the ceiling, then bent to Lydia's waiting lips.

The organ wheezed, came to life again. Val was playing something Virginia didn't recognize, something happy. As the newlyweds proceeded down the aisle together, there was a perceptible divide—on the bride's side, approving smiles, and on the groom's an awkward hesitation. Virginia noticed several people watching her to see how she was taking it, but all she could do was blink at them. Gradually, the church filled with chatter as the guests began to move toward the back to deliver their good wishes. Rooted to her spot in the front, Virginia realized that Rob was waiting for her.

"Go on," she told him. "I'm going to help out with the refreshments."

"I'll come with you," Randall said quickly, turning away from the sanctuary.

At least they had planned a simple reception. No fancy meal, no dancing, just some finger food and punch in the parish hall behind the church. Not even a wedding cake. Virginia's father had upset her the day before, wanting to know if she would bake lemon tarts.

They were a favorite of her mother's, and she couldn't believe he'd asked. She wondered if he was losing his mind.

In the end, she had stayed up late to bake a second batch because she burned the first. It was well past midnight when she poured powdered sugar into a tea strainer, as her mother had taught her, to dust the cooled tarts. Everyone else had gone to bed, scared off by her rage when she flung the three pans of charred pastry against the wall.

She had heaved the baking pans one after the other with all her strength, watching as chunks of blackened crust and sticky filling dropped to the floor, as Rob and Randall appeared in the doorway. They had been in the living room playing gin rummy with her father, entertaining the nervous groom.

"Don't touch it," she warned Randall as he made a move to clean up. They backed out the door quietly, and in a few minutes she heard them calling good night.

Virginia had begun to scrape at the mess with a spatula when she sensed her father nearby. "I'm sorry it didn't work out, Ginny," he said, and then he, too, left her alone.

By the time she had scrubbed down the wall and the floor, washed the baking pans, she was ashamed of herself. So she started over, slicing lemons, squeezing out the juice, measuring flour and sugar and butter. It felt companionable, almost as if she and her mother were working together, preparing a treat for her father. In the day and a half she'd been back at the farm, she hadn't been able to shake the image of Lydia Will everywhere—sitting in her mother's chair, fingering the collection of cream pitchers in the dining room cabinet, rearranging things.

With the new batch of lemon tarts in the oven, their citrus fragrance filling the downstairs, Virginia went around turning off lights. She stood at the kitchen window, looking at the chicken house and the barn, the dark shapes silhouetted against the hillside. Her mother had decided one spring to paint the chicken house apple green. She got Larry to show her how to use the jigsaw so she could make curlicue ornaments to hang over the door and the windows. As the final touch, she painted the decorations a dark purple. "A Painted Lady," she'd announced, flushed with pleasure. She had kept it up, changing the colors every few years, claiming her Rhode Island Reds liked the variety. Virginia couldn't guess how many times she had waited at that window, watching as her mother came toward the house with a basket of eggs.

In the parish hall Sissy Harding, her mother's best friend, rushed to embrace her, kissing her on both cheeks. "You dear thing," she said. Then she kissed Randall, who was thirteen and too old for it, on top of the head.

Sissy had skipped the wedding, choosing to tend to the percolator and the punch bowl, arrange and rearrange the plates of sandwiches and cookies. She had garnished the lemon tarts with mint sprigs and placed them in the center of the table.

"Everything looks nice," Virginia assured her as Sissy turned away to wipe her eyes with the hem of her apron.

"I never thought I'd see this day," Sissy said. "I don't understand it."

"They're starting to come in," Randall said and offered to help her with the coffee cups.

About to follow them, Virginia was stopped by a hand on her shoulder.

"The reverend left out the part about 'Speak now or forever hold your peace,' " West Moffat said in her ear. "Why do you suppose he did that?"

"I wouldn't know." She could feel her cheeks grow warm, and she looked down at the tips of his newly polished shoes.

"I thought you might have a word or two on the subject."

Facing him, Virginia was aware of his hand still on her shoulder. He had grown a beard, too, a neatly trimmed beard that, together with his dark suit, made him look settled and reliable.

"Did you get out this morning?" she asked him.

"What do you think?" He took his hand away. "I've got my eye on a ten-pointer, two hundred pounds at least. But this morning my older boys and I were trying to drive a spike horn past my youngest. It's Cody's first season. He says he never saw it, though. Your boy hunt? Kendall?"

"Randall. No, not much deer hunting in suburban Maryland." She spotted West's wife, Theresa, out of the corner of her eye, wearing a slinky dress, showing some cleavage. As Theresa moved closer, West caught her with one arm and drew her in next to him.

"Hey," Theresa said, glancing over Virginia's shoulder.

"I was telling Ginny we should take her boy out hunting. Maybe next year."

When West reached inside his jacket, Virginia noticed he was wearing striped suspenders, which, for some reason, made her want to press her palm against his white shirtfront. He handed her a business card, and the jacket fell closed again.

"Call us next time you come up," he said. "We should get our kids together."

"You think?" Theresa asked, leaning closer to him. "I don't know—our boys are pretty wild. Like their father."

"Speaking of which, they're home alone. We should get a bite to eat and head back soon." He paused. "Go ahead, Tess. I'll be right along."

"I haven't seen you since your mother's funeral," he said as his wife moved away. "How are you?"

"It's hard. Every day I think of something I want to tell her." Virginia noticed Sissy watching them from the far side of the room and felt another wave of heat creeping up her neck.

"You look good," she told West. "Even with the beard," she added, as if she were joking.

His hand darted out, but he pulled it back at the last second and scratched his neck. "Well, take care of yourself." And then as he started to go, "Hey, how's your sidekick? I thought she might be here."

"Henny? I'm going to stop by and see her after this."

"Tell her hi from me."

The card he'd given Virginia had a rainbow trout in the center, with "Weston Moffat and Sons" printed at the top, and under that, "Trout Farm." Beneath the fish were the address and phone number, also a web address. Another new venture. She vaguely remembered some story about a fallow deer farm that was going well until . . . what? She would have to ask Henny.

Jere Harding, Sissy's husband, walked up to her, extending his hand. "Let me take your coat," he said. "You look like you're about to run away."

When she finally saw Rob, he was walking between her father and Lydia. *Traitor,* she thought, trying to assume a neutral expression as the three of them approached. There was only one thing to do, she decided. Nothing had ever felt so peculiar as hugging Lydia Will, though Virginia's arms scarcely touched her and it was over in a second. Lydia no longer smelled of bleach but had some new, flowery scent. Nathan squeezed his daughter hard, then held her at arm's length, looking at her the way he once did when she learned to swim, when she won her first 4-H ribbon. She wanted to tell him not to make too much of it.

"Sissy made her planter's punch," she said instead. "I'll go get you some."

She was filling the little glass cups when she noticed her

cousin Carrie standing close by, arm in arm with her new husband, the two of them watching Virginia uncertainly.

"This must be dreadful for you," Carrie whispered and then, in a normal voice, "You remember Gerald, I'm sure."

"I certainly do." Their wedding had created something of a sensation. Not only was Gerald a car salesman but he was a Dibbs to boot—a combination that horrified the MacKemson clan and the Rownds, too. Now here they were a year later, trying to suppress their high spirits for Virginia's sake. "Is it my imagination, or are you two up to something?"

"We are," Carrie agreed, placing her hands flat on her stomach so Virginia would notice the swelling beneath them. "And in another three months and twenty-four days, or thereabouts, there will be a new Dibbs in the world. A boy. I saw it on the ultrasound."

Gerald was taller than Virginia remembered, with a friendly, youthful face. "We're trying to find a name we both like," he told her. "One of my cousins has been called Baby her whole life because her parents couldn't decide between Lillian and Joyce. 'Baby Dibbs' it says on her birth certificate."

"I've never been crazy about being named after a state myself."

"Oh, but Virginia is so beautiful," Carrie said. "Wasn't it your great-grandmother's name?"

"Yes, and her mother's and her great-aunt's. Quite a few Virginia Rownds."

"But none like you," Carrie insisted. "How long are you staying?"

"Just until tomorrow afternoon."

"Stop by and see us," Gerald said. "We're still out on Blaze Hollow Road."

"We'll try."

They moved down the table, filling one plate between them. Though Carrie was a close relative, she had grown up in Philadelphia, and Virginia never got to know her well. She did meet the first husband a couple of times, a good-looking but sour fellow in whose company Carrie seemed to fade. It was brave of her to marry Gerald, Virginia considered, with the family so dead set against him. The irony of that sentiment didn't escape her. But her father's situation was completely different.

As Virginia set off, balancing two cups of punch in each hand, the sight of Reverend Gleason clapping her father on the back stopped her. The wedding was his fault. It would never have happened, Virginia was certain, if he hadn't started meddling. She could imagine his idiotic delight when the idea first occurred to him. A widow and a widower in his congregation, about the same age. Let's invite them over for dinner, honey. So what if it's not a match made in heaven? It's the next best thing.

Rob appeared in front of Virginia, reaching for the punch. "What is it? You look as if you're about to faint."

"It's that man, Gleason. I won't speak to him."

She started looking for Sissy and Randall, nodding absently at the guests who greeted her before she found them in the kitchen. They had begun washing up already, Sissy wearing an oversize pair of rubber gloves. Randall had slipped out of his sport coat and tied a dish towel around his waist.

"I'm here to help," she announced.

"There aren't that many dishes yet," Sissy said, swirling a cup in the soapy water. "Really, I wish I still smoked."

"Me, too."

Randall looked at her. "You used to smoke?"

"Not that much," she assured him. "Now and then, with Henny."

"Everyone smoked," Sissy said. "We weren't as smart as your generation."

"I wouldn't mind going outside and having a few puffs right now," Virginia admitted.

"Maybe Theresa Moffat has a pack in her purse," Sissy said. "Why don't you go ask her?"

"Very funny." Virginia leaned against the counter, stifling a sigh. "Randall, have you said anything to your grandfather yet?"

"Not since breakfast."

"Do this, will you? Shake hands with them and say 'congratulations.' Otherwise, you're going to feel sorry later on."

"She's right," Sissy agreed. "You don't need to say you're happy for them."

"Why did you say 'funny' about Theresa Moffat and the cigarettes?" he asked his mother, stalling.

"I don't know." She untied the towel from his waist. "It's just that I used to go out with West. When we were in high school."

"Really?" Randall stood in the doorway to get a better look at him.

West was talking with four other men, one arm draped around Theresa's neck. Virginia knew they were discussing deer—where they were bedding down, what browse they preferred, whether they were moving north or south. West looked up and smiled.

"Huh," Randall said. "I wouldn't have picked him."

"He's learned a lot about you in the last five minutes," Sissy remarked as Randall crossed the room toward his grandfather.

Randall looked especially spruce that day, his hair trimmed short, his shirt and tie still crisp. At the last minute, he turned to look back at them and squared his shoulders.

"He's more like Rob every time I see him," Sissy said.

"He certainly tries." Virginia was touched by Randall's narrow waist, the way his pants hung on his hips because he had forgotten to bring a belt. "But he's got a sweetness all his own."

"Your father's that way. Gentle for a man." She watched Randall offering his hand to Lydia. "I expect that's what got him into this."

"There must be eighty people here," Virginia said to Sissy. She didn't know why she mentioned it, except that she was thinking it looked like a normal reception, the older women sitting together in one corner on metal folding chairs, drinking their coffee black, the children starting to get rambunctious. She saw the boy in combat boots toss a piece of cookie in the air and catch it in his mouth, and two or three younger children trying to imitate him. Here and there, the bride's guests and the groom's guests were striking up conversations. The parish hall—a long, narrow room with the kitchen at one end—looked the way it had for forty years, the worn linoleum floor, the brown veins in the acoustic ceiling tiles where the roof used to leak, the folding tables covered with embossed white paper cloths. Those tables pinched your fingers if you weren't careful when you put them away.

"Would you be mad at me if I slipped out?" she asked Sissy, drying the few cups in the dish drainer and setting them on the counter. "I don't want to abandon you here, but I have a powerful urge to see Henny."

"When did you see her last?" Sissy peeled off the big yellow gloves and draped them over the edge of the sink, looked at her fingernails. Henny was her sister's only daughter.

"Not since August, when we came up for Dad's birthday."

"Henny's not doing too well." Sissy lowered her voice, although no one else was nearby. "You'll notice a difference."

Chapter Two

————— ·◆◆◆· —————

Outside the church, the town was still—people in their houses watching the Penn State football game, wives deciding what to cook for Saturday night supper. In the hills across the river, cold seeping through their wool jackets, the deer hunters would be pausing to blow on their fingers, gauge the remaining light. As Virginia headed north, toward Rownd's Point, the lowering sun cast a golden pink haze across a stubbled cornfield. One dry stalk still standing in the middle appeared to wave frantically as she drove past. Even with the windows up, she could hear the clatter of wind in its ancient leaves.

Henny's father had inherited the original Eastman farm, the one old Prosper and Steadfast began farming before the Revolution. It was a choice piece of land, about halfway between Tenney's Landing and Rownd's Point, wooded hills rising gradually above acres of fertile bottomland adjacent to the river.

Virginia's first glimpse of the house always pleased her, the way it was sited on a gentle rise—the main house built of tan and gray fieldstone with two wooden additions, the ample front porch with its rocking chairs left out all winter, the huge oaks on either side.

Though she and Henny always referred to the ancestors as "old," they were young men when they pried loose the stones to build the house—much younger than she and Henny were now, she reflected, turning her car in to the long driveway. True to their names, Prosper married and had many children, while Steadfast remained a bachelor, living and working on the farm until he died at eighty-four, letting go of the plow and falling into the warm earth behind his team of mules one spring afternoon.

Seeing a light in the room off the kitchen, Virginia didn't bother to knock but called Henny's name as she went in the front door. Even after so many years, it was always hard at first.

Henny had been waiting for her, she could tell. A book lay open on top of the wool blanket that covered her legs.

"Hey, Hen." She leaned over the wheelchair to kiss her friend's pale forehead.

Henny's smile was impish. "Did he actually go through with it?"

"I'm afraid so. He's now officially Mr. Swill."

"Lord." Henny closed the book and placed it on the small bedside table. "Come on," she said, taking hold of the wheels and rolling herself forward. "I'll put the kettle on."

Virginia was glad to leave the airless room, with its smells of stale sheets and Mentholatum. Furnished with a hospital bed, a table, and two chairs, located between the kitchen and a specially fitted bathroom, it was where Henny spent hours of her life every day. An enormous bookshelf along one wall, crammed with books and magazines, looked as if it was about to tip over. Every surface was covered with knickknacks and souvenirs her friends and relatives had brought in over the years: a miniature Statue of Liberty, a bobble-head doll wearing a Pirates uniform, a windup toy alligator, six or seven snow globes, stuffed animals of various sizes and species, baseball caps of many colors, piles of snapshots and postcards. Virginia once gave her an amaryllis for Christmas, but it never bloomed because Henny kept the shades down.

"West says hi," Virginia told her, watching as Henny negotiated the space between the kitchen sink and the stove with a kettle of water. She knew better than to offer help.

"West says a lot of things." Henny banged the kettle down, expertly struck a match on the hard rubber wheel of her chair, and lit the gas burner.

"He's raising trout now?"

"So I hear."

"Didn't something awful happen to his fallow deer?"

"They got some disease or other. I can't remember what." Henny glanced expectantly at Virginia's coat folded over one of the chairs.

"I didn't bring that much." Virginia had sneaked out of the reception with only half an egg salad sandwich and two cookies. When she took the food, wrapped in a paper napkin, out of her coat pocket, West's card fell onto the tabletop. Henny's thin hand covered it immediately.

She looked at the card for a minute before sliding it back. "If you'd been here a little earlier, you would have seen his two oldest. They came over to do the afternoon milking so my folks could go to the wedding."

"They're old enough to drive?" Virginia was remembering the four boys at a Fourth of July barbecue a few years before, all of them except the youngest with neatly clipped black hair, chewing bubble gum and spitting on the grass during the baseball game, slamming their fists into their gloves. One of them had called "easy out, easy out" when Randall got up to bat.

"West Junior—the one they call Weston—got his license last year." Henny polished off the sandwich in four bites, reached for a cookie. "The roads aren't safe anymore. And neither are the girls. I'm not joking, he is one good-looking guy."

"Sounds like Theresa's got her hands full."

"Did she talk to you today?"

"Not so you'd notice." Virginia recalled the way Theresa had pressed herself against West, diverting his attention. "I'm trying to remember how old she is. How many years was she behind us at school?"

"Six. She was one of the sixth-graders who carried the flag at our high school graduation. About the size of a hummingbird back then."

"So she was what, eighteen, when she and West got married?"

"Nineteen. Everyone in town assumed she was pregnant. The old biddies were so disappointed when it took two years before she started to show."

"And now they have all those handsome boys."

"Theresa doesn't like you. In case you hadn't noticed," Henny said, pouring the boiling water.

"Why wouldn't she like me?"

Henny brought the cups of tea to the table one at a time, went back for spoons and sugar. "Do you know what Theresa does?" she asked. "She makes greeting cards. Really nice ones, watercolors mostly. Woodland scenes, flowers, that sort of thing. They sell them at the Good Food Market down in the Landing, two for five dollars. Also at that bookstore in Fayette, the one near the college. She has a natural talent."

"Good for her." Virginia tasted the tea, stirred in a little more sugar.

"Now she says there's a gift shop in Pittsburgh that wants to carry them, too."

"She'll be busy then."

"Theresa's not just some bimbo, you know. She also designed West's business card, the one you're clutching there."

"I never said she was."

"That's what you think, though." Henny looked away.

"I know it's been a long time since I came up to see you, Hen."

"I thought you'd be over yesterday."

She had lost weight, Virginia noticed, but there was something else, too, a look of weariness when she let her guard down. "I meant to," Virginia assured her. "But the day got away from me. Dad asked me to sort through some of Caro's things. It was a sad business—a pile for me, a pile for Larry, a couple of boxes for Goodwill."

"Didn't he keep anything for himself?"

"Not much. He put her really special things in the casket, remember? Her Elizabeth Barrett Browning, the jade necklace he gave her for their twenty-fifth anniversary."

"I thought it was very romantic of him," Henny said. "Do you know what Randall told me after her funeral?"

"What?"

"He said Caro was like an Egyptian princess, going off on the death journey, and those things your father put in her casket would help keep her safe until she got to the other side."

"The other side?"

"They were studying ancient Egypt in school. They'd just been on a field trip to the museum or something."

"Well," Virginia said, a little envious. Randall and Henny

had some connection she didn't quite understand. "Anyway, I saved one of her bracelets for you. It's the silver one, with the engraved violets and the amethyst stone." She reached for her coat again and then remembered leaving the bracelet on the dresser. "I forgot to bring it. We'll stop by on our way out tomorrow and give it to you."

"You're leaving so soon?"

"We have to. Randall and I have school on Monday. Rob's got surgery."

"I was wondering," Henny said, breaking into a smile. "Are the newlyweds going on a honeymoon?"

"They are. My dad got some package deal up at Lake Ligonier. I heard him telling Rob, 'All our meals and unlimited use of the spa for four hundred dollars.'"

"The spa," Henny repeated. "I can see Mrs. Swill in one of those rubber bathing caps, yelling at everyone to mind their manners and keep their voices down." She chuckled, swallowed the last of her tea. "So if you're leaving, who's going to look after the farm while they're gone?"

"A couple of her nephews. They'll stay at the house and milk the cows."

"Your dad should watch out. Her family's going to take over if he's not careful."

"Henny, that is so paranoid. It's only for three days."

"If you say so."

Virginia wished Henny would drop her insinuating tone and sit up straighter in her chair. "What are you doing for exercise these days?" she asked, to change the subject.

"You mean besides the marathon training?" Henny's laugh trailed off quickly, and she confided that she had a crush on her new physical therapist. "He's about thirty," she said. "Married, with a baby on the way. He comes to the house on Mondays

and Thursdays, so those days, at least, I have a reason to get out
of bed in the morning."

When Henny talked that way, Virginia was tempted to argue
with her, though she knew it would be pointless. She remembered how Henny had frustrated Uncle Herman, who was used
to people taking his advice.

"Stubborn as an old tortoise." That was his pronouncement,
four years after the accident that put her in a wheelchair. Not
only had he been urging Henny to try a job training program
but he'd gently suggested that Chick Mason's marriage proposal
was not a sign of pity.

"It's pride," Caroline had said. "Henny would rather hide
herself away than risk looking foolish. Don't you think so,
Virginia?"

"Another person in Henny's circumstances might be proud
of getting on with her life," Uncle Herman had declared, drawing himself up. "Another person might take on the challenge."

"She will," Virginia had said. "In her own good time."

Virginia and her mother had been sitting on the front
porch—the good porch, reserved for special guests—with Uncle
Herman, waiting for her father and Larry to come in from the
milking. It was early September, still warm. Virginia was visiting for a few days before going on to Los Angeles to join Rob,
who was starting his surgical residency. They wouldn't have
much time together in the months to come, and she was nervous about the move to a strange city, the hours alone.

Her mind had drifted away from their talk of Henny. She
had seen West that morning, nearly colliding with him as she
left the market with a bag of groceries. They stood frozen on
the sidewalk, a few inches apart.

"So," Virginia said finally, noticing the bits of hay clinging
to his T-shirt. "You must be haying."

"I ran into town to pick up a few things for my mother. She's making dinner for the crew." He brushed a hand over his clothes. "I guess I might have changed my shirt."

"Don't be silly." She assumed he meant on her account.

"I hear you and your husband are off to California," he said abruptly, moving toward the steps of the market again. "Good luck to you."

"It's just for two years," she said, watching the door close behind him. West wasn't married yet, but Virginia had heard a rumor about Theresa.

"Do you remember my uncle Herman's hands?" Virginia asked Henny, watching her pick at the cookie crumbs on her plate.

"Enormous."

"I was thinking of all the children he baptized. You and me, my mother, Randall. Three generations." When he placed one of his big, clean hands on her head, Virginia felt blessed, even if he was only telling her to stop mumbling her Bible verses in Sunday school.

"He must have been close to a hundred when he died."

"Ninety-four." He had outlived Caroline by eleven weeks.

"When he came to visit, he used to pull a chair right up and put his hands on my knees. If it had been anyone else, I would have told him to get lost." Henny moved closer, covering Virginia's knees with her hands, looked her in the eye. " 'Now,' he'd say, 'have you given any more thought to what we talked about last week?' " She leaned away again. "*We* never talked about anything. He would go on forever about the mysterious ways of the Lord—so sure of himself. It wouldn't have fazed him if I'd stood up and walked one day."

Virginia heard the slamming of car doors, Henny's parents back from the wedding. Rinsing their cups at the sink, she remembered how Uncle Herman had locked himself in his study after his wife's funeral. He came out after four days, in time to give his Sunday sermon. "The Lord tests us," he said from the pulpit. His robe was unpressed, and he'd left a dab of shaving lather beneath one ear, but his voice carried to the far corners of the church. "And we stand or fall according to our lights. We show Him who we are." He was sixty-six then, a magnet for the spinsters and widows from his congregation and beyond. He was so courteous, and so oblivious, that one by one they turned their attentions elsewhere.

"I thought you'd be here, Ginny," Mrs. Eastman said from the doorway, "when I couldn't find you at the reception." She told them about the best man's toast, the laughing girl who had caught the bride's nosegay of pink and white roses.

"Say what you will," Mr. Eastman added. "We gave them a proper send-off, tossing the rice and all. Someone even painted 'Just Married' on the back window of your father's car."

Henny and Virginia exchanged a look. "See you tomorrow," Henny reminded her.

When Virginia stooped to give her a good-bye hug, her friend felt as skinny as a bundle of sticks.

HENNY

I learned bookkeeping through a correspondence course, partly to get Ginny's uncle Herman off my back, and started keeping the farm records. Turned out I liked working with numbers, the stories they told. I would write "300 bales," and that was three days in the hayfield—cutting, raking, praying the rain would hold off. It was the sweet scent of alfalfa with the morning dew still on, the tractor starting up in a blue cloud of diesel fumes. It was the shimmer of heat in the afternoon, the baler thumping along, the haying crew calling out to each other as they loaded the trucks in the evening. All things I remembered. The numbers were dozens of eggs and gallons of milk and bushels of grain—and behind them, invisible, untold hours of work. At the end of each month, they were two neat columns that balanced out, as if I had weighed everything on a scale.

My father bragged that his girl had a head for numbers, and

it wasn't long before people started bringing me their account books, the pages smudged, the columns snarled and snagged like so much fishing line. They would set a cardboard box full of receipts down on the kitchen table, glad to get it off their hands. My first customers were mostly our farm neighbors, and then a few merchants from the Landing and the Point. Pretty soon, I had a regular clientele. I kept their books, did their tax returns. I worked magic, they said.

It was patience, not magic, I might have told them. Because if there's one thing living in a wheelchair teaches you, it's patience.

Maybe, because I already knew so much about their business, because I wasn't a gossip, they started telling me things. Personal things. The first time it happened, Bernie Bishop walked into the kitchen one evening with an armload of papers and sat down at the table. He was thinking of opening his own real estate office, he said, and wondered if I could help him with a business plan. We were sorting through some figures when he stopped talking and looked at me for a minute. I heard the sound of a laugh track from the living room, where my parents were watching television.

"Henny," he said. "You know I've been working over in Archerville for a few years, and now I want to make a good start here at home."

"That's what you've been telling me, Bernie."

"The thing is . . ." He paused, rubbing his thumb over his chin. "There's a woman in Archerville. She wants to get married."

"And you don't." I could see how that might throw his calculations off. He had about enough money to pay two months' rent and buy himself a decent pair of shoes.

He shook his head.

"But you don't want to break it off?"

"No, I do," he said eagerly. "If I could figure out how." He seemed embarrassed, as if I might be thinking less of him. "She's not the right person for me," he added, dropping his eyes.

I'd known Bernie in an offhand way since we were kids, and for the first time I felt a kind of tenderness for him, sitting there with his earnest face and his shiny hopes. He was probably talking about the only woman he'd ever slept with.

"You want to be a gentleman." I said the first thing that came into my head. "So you tell her in person. Invite her out for a drink, say she'll always be special to you, et cetera."

"Et cetera?" He looked alarmed.

In the end, I had practically written a script for him. We became friendly after that. I did his bookkeeping for no charge the first few years, and he asked my advice about the two or three women he dated before he married Gwen Short. If he had asked me about Gwen, I would have told him to keep looking, but there's no accounting for love. Bernie is still a regular client. Every time he makes a big sale, he sends me a dozen roses.

There were others. I'd be hacking my way through a thicket of numbers, and the people sitting across from me would be worrying about something else, I could see. After a while, they would bring it out. I have a pain in my side that's getting worse, one might say. I get dizzy every time I stand up. I think there's something wrong with my sister's baby girl. My son is a bully. My wife won't sleep in the same room with me. My husband gets drunk every night. I'm in love with that new priest down in Fayette, really in love.

They handed over their troubles the same way they handed over their messed-up account books. I let them talk, all the while punching numbers into the electric calculator my father had bought me. I used to wish it had special buttons: Cheating Spouse, Impossible Child, Body Gone Haywire, Forbidden Love. Sometimes the stories took my breath away. But I just listened. And I learned that in their hearts people already knew what they had to do. Make a doctor's appointment. Apologize. Tell the truth. Stop seeing him or her. Stand up for themselves. Sooner or later, they'd get around to admitting that, too.

When the old minister came to visit, I was tempted to tell him we were in the same business. He would have gotten a kick out of that. Sometimes I was dying to tell Ginny about Bernie Bishop's latest girlfriend or Dennis Carter's frigid wife. I didn't, though. Those people trusted me.

Ginny was here a few days ago, after her father's wedding. I don't know what perverse impulse made me sing Theresa Moffat's praises when Ginny asked me a question about West, but I could tell it hurt her feelings. And we never made it right, but talked around in circles and cracked a joke or two about Lydia.

Chapter Three

Virginia pulled one of the lawn chairs into a patch of sunlight, sank down in the canvas seat, and closed her eyes. She had awakened that morning with a stiff neck, curled up tight against Rob's back, and she imagined the sun's warmth melting away the little knots of pain.

Earlier, as they were making the bed together, she had asked Rob if he thought it might be a sign of arthritis. Virginia remembered the way her grandmother Hattie's knuckles had begun to swell, the way she would hold her hands over a steaming pot on the stove and rub her fingers to limber them up.

Pulling up the blanket on his side, Rob had paused and smiled at her, shaking his head. "You just slept funny. It should be gone by the afternoon." And then, straightening the pillows, he'd said, "You were talking in your sleep."

"Really? What did I say?"

"It sounded like 'go away.' You were thrashing around, as if someone was chasing you. When I said your name, you got quiet and snuggled up against me." He had smiled again, and she'd followed him downstairs to make breakfast.

Six months after her father's wedding, Virginia sprawled in the backyard of her house in Laurel Springs, savoring the scent of damp grass and passing flowers. Having tended them for years, she was pleased by the perennial beds surrounding their half acre of lawn. The tulips and daffodils had gone by, but the purple flags of the Japanese irises remained. Her mother had dug up the irises with a pitchfork one windy afternoon in April as Virginia and Rob were packing the car to return home.

"Wait," Caroline had called, running outside in her Sunday dress. "You have to take some of these flowers. They're out of control." She sent Randall to the barn for a couple of old milk pails and the pitchfork. Virginia helped with a spade as they tried to separate the green clumps growing on either side of the back door. Though both of them poked and prodded the massive root web until they were breathing hard, the roots were hardly budging.

"This is ridiculous," Virginia complained, leaning on the spade handle. "For heaven's sake," she said to her mother. "You're not even wearing shoes."

Caroline glanced down, as if surprised, and started laughing. "Throw your back into it," she said. "We can do this."

Virginia had traveled the next four hours holding the muddy pails between her feet as they leaked onto the newspaper she'd put down to protect the carpeting of Rob's car. Even though it was already dark when they got home, she had turned on the back porch lights and planted the irises in her own flower beds.

She sat up in the lawn chair, squinting at the brightness. In a few minutes, she would have to get moving. It was a Friday, her day off from school, and she had a long list of things to do, starting with a trip to the vet for Cleo, their aging golden retriever. The dog was stretched out at her feet, sleeping soundly.

On an ordinary Friday, Virginia would have been busy by then, negotiating an oversize cart through the supermarket aisles, grocery list in hand. It was June 4, though, which meant only one more week of school. She was feeling leisurely. The summer opened before her like a book of empty pages, as if she, too, were a schoolchild and the weeks ahead an idyll. This year, she had decided, she was going to paint again.

She had already carried the easel down from the attic and dusted it off, bought new tubes of oils and brushes to fill the paint-splashed wooden case she had saved from college. She had in mind a romantic image of herself, driving into the countryside with a lunch of fruit and cheese, setting up near a tumbledown barn or a field of wildflowers. *En plein air*, delicious phrase. Although she had kept a sketching journal, she hadn't attempted a real painting since Randall was a baby.

Despite some mild protests on her son's part, she had spent hours arranging the summer for him—day camps, music workshops, excursions to the museums downtown. She had set up car pools, bargained with other parents, called in favors. It was all in place, the schedule of days blocked out on three separate sheets held in place by magnets on the side of the refrigerator. Monday through Thursday would be her own.

Until the last week of August, when they would drive to Pennsylvania for a few days to celebrate her father's seventieth birthday. She had been taking Lydia in homeopathic doses since the wedding, trying gradually to increase her tolerance. In the weekly phone calls to her father, Virginia routinely spoke with Lydia, too—working up from three or four minutes to nearly ten. They were both ill at ease, starting off with polite questions about the weather. Then Virginia would tell her something about Randall, and Lydia would report something about the cows or the chickens. Virginia was trying to convince Larry to bring his family for the birthday celebration, thinking that would help.

Virginia's family had gone back once, for Easter, arriving late Saturday afternoon and leaving soon after dinner on Sunday. On Easter morning, Virginia decided to visit Henny instead of going to church with the others. It was a sunny day, though the air was chilly, and she pushed Henny's chair out to the front porch. Henny complained that the light was too bright; she wanted to go back in. But Virginia found a pair of Mrs. Eastman's sunglasses for her. They were old, with scratched lenses and swooping, aqua-colored frames.

"I look like an idiot," Henny objected.

"You look glamorous, actually." She did, too. Virginia had taken a handful of foil-wrapped eggs from Randall's basket, and she gave half to Henny.

Now she felt glad, anticipating the feel of the brush in her hand, wondering where the first strokes would lead. When she reached down to scratch Cleo's back, the dog thumped her tail on the warm grass. "Come on," Virginia said. "We have places to go."

They were headed out the door when the phone rang. The unexpected sound of Lydia's voice made her stomach clench, even before she grasped the words.

"Your father," Lydia repeated. "I said he's been hurt. Can you hear me?"

"Yes." She let go of the dog's leash. "How bad is it? What happened?"

"It's bad enough. He rolled the tractor, and he's going to be in the hospital a few days. He broke his left arm, dislocated his shoulder, cracked a few ribs. Bruised his hip, too."

Virginia glanced at her watch—just past eight-thirty. "This morning?"

"Yesterday afternoon."

"Yesterday? Why didn't you call right away?"

"I wanted to, but Nathan said to wait. Until we had some things sorted out."

"What things?"

"Don't get upset now," Lydia said, her voice pleading and commanding at the same time.

Virginia knew that tone from her school days, when Mrs. Will would order her and Henny to clean up some mess they hadn't made. "Don't waste time getting upset now," she'd say, towering over them, hands on her white-aproned hips. "Just go and do what I tell you."

Virginia watched Cleo flop down by the door with a sigh. "You're sure he's going to be all right?"

Ten minutes later, she was in the car with the dog, haunted by the image of her father falling, the crushing weight of the tractor. She knew exactly where it had happened. Not where Lydia said, but higher up on the hill above the hay barn, where the shoulder of a hummock bulged suddenly, pushing up out of the high grass. If you didn't approach it at the right angle, the rear tire on the high side would lose its purchase. Nobody knew that better than her father.

He had rolled the tractor in that very spot, more than thirty years ago, on a morning when she and Larry were out working in the garden. They heard a sharp cry and looked up in time to see him leaping away as the tractor fell on its side and started down the hill. It rolled over four times, like some huge toy, until it stopped in a gully, right side up, the engine still running. Her father came striding after it, cursing, and savagely kicked one of the big tires when he reached it. "Son of a bitch," he muttered before noticing them. "And don't tell your mother I said that."

Now he was in the hospital with broken bones.

"He's going to be laid up all summer," Lydia had said. "That's a problem we have, how to keep the farm going. I can't do it by myself."

Virginia pulled into the parking lot of the veterinarian's office with a minute to spare. Cleo would get her shots, at least. Otherwise, it felt as if the day was crumbling into chaos. What she wanted to do more than anything was see her father. But Lydia had asked her to wait. One of her nephews could stay at the farm for the next week, until Nathan was home from the hospital, until school was out.

"This is an awfully big favor, I know," Lydia had said on the phone, and then she had started making odd clicking sounds in her throat, as if she were trying not to cry. "Nathan doesn't even know I'm asking you, but if you could see your way clear to come and stay with us this summer and help out—well, that would be a relief."

Lifting Cleo onto the cold metal examining table, stroking her ears as they waited for the vet, Virginia was ashamed of how she'd answered. "I'll have to talk it over with Rob," she had said, her mind darting about. "Randall has a lot of plans for the summer. Not that they're so important, really." She had forced herself to stop talking, imagining what Lydia would think—that she was the same selfish girl who was nice to her only when she wanted an extra piece of cake.

Back at home with the dog, she went upstairs and started sorting laundry. Not for the first time, the sight of Rob's dirty socks puzzled her, the way he tied each pair together in a knot. Did he think one sock would run away? When she'd asked him about it once, he'd said it was just a habit. She sat down on the edge of the bed and untied them. As she was stuffing the first load in the washing machine, she remembered that she had meant to go to the supermarket after the vet. But grocery shopping seemed overwhelming.

She picked up the phone and called information to get the number of the hospital, then waited through several rings after speaking with the switchboard operator. At last, someone answered, a woman who identified herself as Jean Kaminsky. She said Nathan was sleeping, still knocked out by the painkillers, and suggested Virginia call the nurses' station in the future, to avoid disturbing him.

"This is his daughter," Virginia told her, repeating her name.

"I know," Jean Kaminsky said. "We went to school together."

Her voice was cool, with an edge of irritation. Virginia had no idea who she was. "Can you tell me how he is, at least?"

"Lucky to be alive." Virginia heard her speaking to someone else, and when she came back on, her manner was slightly warmer. "The doctor says he's going to be okay, but he has some rough weeks ahead. He's pretty banged up right now."

Virginia asked her to tell Nathan that she'd called. Wondering whether Jean Kaminsky was having a bad day or whether she had once offended her, Virginia began tracing circles in the dust on the windowsill. Even before Lydia came along, it had been painful for her to spend time at the farm. Without her mother, the place seemed desolate, and as much as she loved her father, Virginia dreaded going back.

She went into the kitchen and looked through the calendar, counting the weeks between the end of school and Labor Day. Twelve. That would be eighty-four days of Lydia. Randall wouldn't want to go, either. And it would leave Rob on his own most of the summer.

She called Rob at his office and asked him to phone Nathan's doctor to find out the real story. The familiar calm of her husband's voice was partly a doctor's trick, she knew, a way of soothing people in distress, but after all those years, it still worked. Rob advised her to take a long walk. He promised to come home with pizza for dinner and news of her father.

Instead of a walk, she decided to rake the front lawn, which was still littered with the twigs and dead leaves that had come down during the winter. She and Rob had been amused to discover that the neighbor across the street had recently hired a gardener. But watching the slender, elderly man at work in his baseball cap and faded jeans, Virginia began to feel intimidated by him and focused all her efforts on the backyard, which he couldn't see.

It was satisfying, though, the scratching of the bamboo rake, the simple job of making neat piles to pick up later. She considered going to the nursery to buy petunias for the border along the walkway. Randall could help her put them in when he got home from school. She was overcome by a surge of affection for their house, a modest white Cape with black shutters and a generous front lawn that sloped down to the sidewalk. Randall had learned to ride his bicycle on that sidewalk.

Rob had started thinking of where they might live next. He had wakened her in the night not long before, wanting to know if she ever considered the future.

Virginia had turned over sleepily, trying to see him in the dark. "What are you talking about?"

"Our future, once we get our boy through college. Don't you ever think about selling this house? We could buy a sailboat. A chalet in Switzerland." He laughed. "Raise goats. Eat cheese."

"Is this your midlife crisis coming on?"

"Maybe," he said, sliding his arms around her. "But if it is, I'm taking you down with me."

They had made love with such intensity that afterward, her hand resting on his stomach as he fell asleep, she wondered what was really on his mind.

Pausing in her raking, Virginia bent down to examine a cluster of tiny gray feathers in the grass. Every so often her husband reminded her of another person—of Robert MacLeod, age twenty-one. Gathering the feathers in her hand, she felt she was weighing out a measure of sorrow. A dead phoebe most likely, a fledgling caught by the neighbor's well-fed cat. She held the longest feather up to the light. A miracle. Watching it flutter back to the ground, she heard a gate opening. Across the street, the gardener was coming around the side of the house, unrolling a hose. Noticing her, he nodded and touched the brim of his cap. Virginia waved back. He had a pleasant, coffee-colored face and looked about the age of her father. Maybe she would walk over in a while and ask his advice about something. Perhaps he could tell her why the purple clematis looked so droopy, or why men are never satisfied with the status quo.

Virginia didn't discuss Rob with other people, the way he unsettled her sometimes. She had, at first, with Henny, but that had seemed natural because it was Henny who'd introduced them.

She'd looked so lovely when she stepped off the bus in front of the Greenfield College administration building, Henny with her shiny auburn hair cut short, dressed in a pair of slim black pants and a pink shirt with the cuffs turned back. "You're even wearing lipstick!" Virginia had blurted, hugging her.

"Well?" Henny asked, looking across the street at the quadrangle shining in the late afternoon sun and hoisting her small bag over her shoulder. "Now what?"

"You're finally here." Virginia had been trying for nearly two years to get her to come.

"Drew wasn't that crazy about the idea, but the fact is he wanted to go on a fishing trip with his father this weekend. So it worked out."

Drew was Henny's longtime boyfriend, a person Virginia didn't trust. Resisting the urge to comment, she took her friend by the arm as they crossed the grass and entered the cool interior of Grover Hall.

Nervously, Virginia switched on the lights in the gallery where her paintings hung. The official opening and reception were scheduled for the following afternoon.

Henny approached the three pictures and stopped suddenly, letting her bag drop to the floor. "Holy gods," she said. "I know these people." She walked up and peered closely at each one, then stepped back again. "I surely do."

Virginia watched as Henny studied the small printed card that described her paintings. "*Pennsylvania Triptych* by Virginia Rownd," Henny read out. "Combining elements of realism, impressionism, and fantasy, the paintings emphasize the vertical plane. Each twenty by thirty-two inches, oil on panel."

She was wishing Henny would say something else, but the gallery remained silent.

In the painting on the left, West, dressed in buckskin, carried an old flintlock rifle. Wrapped around his neck was a sleeping fox, its front paws primly crossed. In the background, crows with bloodred beaks swirled through the branches of bare trees. West's hair streamed in the wind, turning into drops of blood at the tips.

On the right, her mother stood beneath an apple tree, its blossoms falling on her head and shoulders. She held her hands folded in front of her, as if she were praying. At the top of the canvas, puffy clouds scudded across a purple sky. Inside one of the clouds floated a cherub, brandishing a butcher knife.

In the center was Bob Will, standing in front of Mason's Garage, wearing his greasy trousers and a striped shirt, looking as if he'd just come off a bender. His face was haggard, with several days' growth of beard. Matted with dried grass and twigs, his hair had been woven into a bird's nest. He was holding his hands out, palms up. On one of them sat the jar of pickled eggs that had stood untouched by the cash register for as long as Virginia could remember. On the other a sparrow opened its wings, about to fly away.

"Bob Will won a prize," she told Henny. "They'll put a ribbon on it tomorrow."

"Does Mrs. Swill know you've been painting her husband?" Henny asked, still studying the canvas. When she turned around at last, her eyes glistened. "How come your parents aren't here this weekend?"

"I told them it was no big thing," Virginia said, shrugging. She was uneasy about the butcher knife in her mother's picture and planned to paint over it. "Besides, I really wanted to spend this time with you."

"You're afraid they'd take one look at these and drag you back home."

Later, when they joined a table of art and theater majors for dinner in the student union, Virginia introduced her friend as Hennis. Nodding slightly, sitting down with her tray, Henny seemed not to notice everyone watching her. When someone asked where she went to school, she replied breezily that she was a farmer.

"I would have guessed dancer." The young man across from her smiled shyly.

"Hardly," Henny told him, her cheeks flushing. "Though I suppose farming does build muscle tone."

As they drank sour red wine in Virginia's room that night,

just the two of them, Henny confessed that she'd been worried about the trip all week. "I made Aunt Sissy take me to Pittsburgh," she said, "so I could get a decent haircut. And then I tried on clothes the whole day. I had no idea what to wear."

"You look fabulous," Virginia said. "I think about fifteen guys fell in love with you at dinner."

"Fabulous? I guess that's how you'll talk when you get famous." Henny reached over to clink glasses. "So, when are you going to paint me?"

———

Henny talked to Rob before Virginia did. She spotted him at the reception, standing in front of *Pennsylvania Triptych* with his arms crossed. She went and stood beside him, crossing her arms, too. Virginia lingered nearby, pretending to be involved in a conversation with her professor.

"What do you think?" Henny asked Rob after a minute.

"I think this woman"—he glanced over at the card—"Virginia Something, is seriously disturbed. And I would love to meet her."

"You must be a psychology major."

"Please. Biology."

"Perfect," Henny said. "Let me see if I can find her."

"My name's Robert MacLeod," he said, shaking Virginia's hand. "And I don't have the slightest idea how to talk about paintings. The truth is, I wandered in here to get some free food."

"Slim pickings," Henny said, drifting toward the table of cheese and crackers.

"You're not what I expected." Rob was sizing Virginia up, as if she were part of the exhibition. "I mean, you're ridiculously young, aren't you?"

"You were hoping for a crazy old lady with a bird nest in her hair."

"Yeah, at the very least." He turned back to the paintings. "Davy Crockett, there, that's your boyfriend, I'm guessing."

"Was." Virginia bristled.

"Uh-huh. And that fellow in the center—not your father, I hope?" He talked quickly, as if he were afraid of losing his nerve.

"Just a guy who lives in our town."

"I have a motorcycle, you should know."

"That explains why you're walking around with a helmet under your arm."

"Well, yes, and it's supposed to impress you, too." He glanced down at his boots, which were coated with dust. "It's actually kind of a sorry-ass motorcycle. I spend way too much time working on it. Why don't we go somewhere and get some real food, by the way?"

"Can't," Virginia said, flattered and disconcerted at the same time. "I have to stay until this is over. And besides, my friend is here visiting."

"All right, then." Rob checked his watch. "I'll go shower and meet you and your friend back here in an hour." He winked at Henny as he picked up a handful of crackers on his way out.

Virginia couldn't help wondering why Rob had never noticed her before. Greenfield was a small school. She had seen him lots of times on his motorcycle, often with a woman riding on the seat behind him. She had even stopped to watch him at lacrosse practice once or twice, on her way to the library.

———

Thank goodness for Henny, who kept the female side of the conversation going as Virginia picked at her cheeseburger and fries. The three of them shared a booth at Stoney's Pub, where Virginia noticed a group of lacrosse players at a table in the back.

Still wet from the shower, Rob's hair, a deep rust red, began to spring into curls as it dried. He caught Virginia staring and brushed a hand through it, smiling. Gradually, she found herself leaning closer to him and laughing a little too much. She wondered if Henny was feeling it, too. When he started talking about going to medical school in the fall, she was sorry to think he would be gone in a few weeks. She could imagine herself on his motorcycle, the feel of his leather jacket as she clasped his waist.

"He's full of himself, but he'll age well," Henny told her afterward.

"Maybe, but I'll never see him after he graduates."

"Don't be so sure. I mean, how far away is the University of Cincinnati?"

Henny was right. Rob had aged well. He was the sort of person to trust with your life. He was not a person to take for granted, though, and he reminded Virginia of that from time to time. What had made him think of selling their house?

A song drifted across the street, muffled by spray from a hose, and she recognized a few Spanish words. The gardener. Virginia wondered where he was from, whether he was happy in his new country. She thought of her father in the hospital, the awful sensation of the tractor falling away beneath him, and of the empty space her mother had left in the world. She set the rake aside and went around back for the wheelbarrow.

Chapter Four

There was no talking in the car. Randall, listening to his iPod, looked steadily out the passenger-side window. Virginia had packed a small cooler with drinks and snacks, but more than two hours into the trip, he still hadn't touched it. She was grateful for Cleo, who woke from her spot on the backseat and nuzzled Virginia's ear. The dog tried to squeeze into the front to sit next to her.

"Stay back, sweet girl." Virginia blocked the space between the seats with her arm. Her voice sounded unusually loud.

Randall reached for the dog's collar and settled her again, laying a comforting hand on her back, as if she had been unfairly scolded.

He looked unkempt, part of his protest. His hair, a lighter shade of red than Rob's, was flattened on one side from sleeping, and he was wearing a pair of torn sweatpants. Virginia guessed he hadn't brushed his teeth. She couldn't imagine what he had packed in his duffel bag. As she was arranging things carefully in the trunk of the car, Randall had come out and shoved his bag into one corner. At the last minute, he'd returned to the house and come out with his saxophone case, placing it gently on the backseat.

Less than forty-eight hours before, after his eighth-grade graduation, Randall had been standing on the school lawn in his coat and tie, talking with his friends. He had seemed suddenly older. It was all too easy to picture him going off to college, leaving them behind. So it was something of a relief to have the awkward boy in the car with her, unhappy as he was.

Virginia had expected resistance but not anger. She and Rob had broken the news together. "Think of it as an adventure. Summer on the farm. It could be one of the best times of your life."

"What do you think?" Randall asked, his voice cracking. "I'm like five years old?"

"You've always loved going there," Virginia said.

"Why can't I stay here with Dad? I mean, you already made all those charts of what I'm supposed to be doing every minute." He leaned forward, elbows on his knees. "I wouldn't even have time to get in trouble."

"That's not the point," she started to explain.

"It's settled," Rob told him. "My hours are too unpredictable, and besides, your mother needs your help."

"This sucks. You're taking away my whole summer." Randall got up and left the room. At the top of the stairs, he turned. "I'm not going," he said, very coolly.

"And we've always been conceited about how well behaved he is," Rob remarked as they listened to him closing his bedroom door. "Do you think I should go up there?"

"I say let him blow off a little steam. Meanwhile, the parents could probably use a glass of wine." Rob objected to the idea, too. They had argued about it the night before, but by morning he had decided it was Virginia's decision to make. And by then she felt she had no choice.

The following day, Randall told his mother he didn't want to lose a whole summer of music lessons, just when he was starting to sound decent. Then he reminded her about the lacrosse camp in August. He had already sent in a deposit, with money he'd saved over the winter. "Please," he said. "Don't make me go with you."

"I feel bad for you, I really do," she told him. "I know how much you want to spend the summer with your friends."

"You know?" Randall sneered. And then he stopped talking to her.

Halfway up the steep grade of King John's Mountain, the car behind them blinked its headlights at the same moment Virginia felt the engine skip a beat. As she pulled into the slow lane, Randall sighed deeply. Virginia downshifted, pushed harder on the gas. When the car started bucking, she eased off the pedal, and they sputtered to the top of the mountain between two heavily loaded log trucks. She hadn't planned to stop at the summit, but noticing the temperature gauge climbing, she turned in to the parking area.

As she was fiddling with the hood latch, Virginia heard someone ask if she needed a hand. Two young men, both wearing bright orange T-shirts, approached the car, their expressions amused and dreamy, as if they'd been smoking dope. The shorter one smiled at her. One of his front teeth was missing.

"That's all right," she said. "My son can help me."

Randall seemed to be engrossed in something on the floor of the car, however. Only Cleo was paying attention, standing up on the seat, swishing her tail.

"Pretty dog," the taller man said.

They were moving in too close. "Really, it's nothing," Virginia said. Their small red truck was parked nearby, its rear fender patched with duct tape. Otherwise, the lot was empty. Finally, Randall got out, stretching and yawning before he came around to the front. He pulled a crushed insect off the headlight, studied it on his palm.

"I thought it was a cicada," he said.

The two men watched him, as if they were deciding what to do next. Maybe they wanted money. Virginia's purse was on the front seat, in plain sight.

The hiss of air brakes diverted their attention—another log truck, and it was pulling off the highway. Virginia stepped into its path, waving at the driver. When he stopped, the young men turned away, and she heard them laughing softly as they walked off.

"Trouble?" The log truck driver hopped down from his cab. There was something reassuring about his solid bulk.

"I'm not certain." Out of the corner of her eye, Virginia saw the red truck backing out. "I stopped to check the radiator, but I can't open the hood."

Randall reached into the grille, releasing the latch, then got back in the car.

"We have three at home," the driver said. "Teenagers." He added water to the radiator and advised her to let the car sit for a few minutes. After telling her to get the spark plugs checked, he said he was going to park in the shade for a nap. "Bang on the cab if you need anything," he added.

When Virginia asked Randall if he wanted to get out and walk around, he shook his head. It seemed to be a point of honor to remain in the car.

With Cleo on her leash, Virginia passed the bronze plaque

that told how the mountain got its name, letting her hand brush across the raised letters. She knew what it said. King John's Mountain, elevation 2,095 feet. Named for a black soldier killed there in 1756, during the French and Indian War, as he helped a small band of frontiersmen fight off an Indian attack. When the battle was over, King John was buried on the summit in an unmarked grave. The sketchiness of his story troubled her.

A few years before, when Randall wrote a report for school, she had helped him do research on King John. It was hard to find enough to fill even two pages. In one account, he was said to be an African American scout, in another a regular soldier, and in another a slave. He was described as a large, powerful man, a valiant fighter. Virginia kept hoping they would discover the origin of *his* name, or a last name, but they never did. One story referred to him as Samson, the servant of a Captain Josiah Flynn. Bewildered by the inconsistencies, Randall ended his third-grade report this way: "If Samson was his true name, then we would call it Samson Mountain, and we don't. His name was King John."

It had become a family tradition to stop at the summit of King John's Mountain, the last of the Alleghenies to cross on their trips from Maryland into Pennsylvania. There was a scenic view, as a sign on the highway informed motorists. They liked to stand at the height of the mountain and take pictures of each other with the view in the background—the great, sweeping valley of Pennsylvania farmland. In the near distance, narrow white farmhouses and wide barns stood in green fields; farther on, a patchwork of small towns and rivers, woods and streams, the farms becoming mere bands of color; and finally, a silvery blur at the horizon. At home, they had many snapshots taken from that spot, mostly pictures Rob took of Virginia with Randall and Cleo. And the first picture Randall ever took, of Rob bending to kiss Virginia on the forehead, his arms held out behind as if he were about to dive.

This day she watched high clouds sailing overhead, their shadows gliding across the valley floor. Virginia used to love the anticipation of driving down the other side of the mountain, especially in the early evening, the roads growing narrower and more twisted, until finally they would see her parents' farm in the distance, light spilling from the house and the barn. Her mother would hear the car and come out to meet them, calling, "Here you are, at last. Just look at you."

And Randall would fly out of the backseat. "Yes, we're here."

Going downhill, the car ran fine. Virginia was hoping the change of scene, once they'd gotten into the countryside, would lighten Randall's mood. She was remembering the summer he played scout. Having decided King John was a scout rather than a regular soldier, Randall would pack himself a lunch in the morning and go off with Cleo, roaming the woods in search of danger. He would return in the afternoon, tired and sunburned, to report his sightings: a deer carcass, black bear tracks, and once a copperhead swimming across the creek.

She hadn't noticed before how many farms sat empty by the side of the highway, the windows of the houses covered with plywood, the fields grown up with weeds.

"Hey," Randall said in a small voice as they passed the Shady Grove Farmstand. It was closed up, too, long boards nailed across the shutters, its red paint faded. Shady Grove was the place where they stopped to buy fresh lemonade, pulpy and tart, in big glass jugs beaded with moisture. They would get a paper cup full for each of them and a gallon to take to Nathan and Caroline. From there, it was less than an hour to the farm.

When Virginia drove into the dooryard, the place looked deserted, except for the cows drowsing in the shade of the sycamores beside the brook. Heat shimmered off the metal barn roof, and a slight breeze ruffled the long grass on the hillside. She could see where her father had started cutting hay up on top, as well as the swath that ended suddenly. Sliding out of the car, she noticed Lydia just inside the kitchen screen door. Lydia stood there quietly while they took their bags out of the trunk and then held the door open as they went inside.

"I have lunch ready," she announced, "but I expect you'll want to see Nathan first." She was wearing an apron over her cotton dress, and she twisted a handkerchief in her hands, frowning as they set their things down in the hallway.

"You mean he can't come down?" Virginia said to Lydia's heels as she led them upstairs.

"Heavens no."

Nathan was groggy and seemed confused for a minute, but his face lit up when he recognized them. "It's the drugs," he said, pushing himself up from the pillows with his good arm. "All I do is sleep nowadays."

"That's what you need to do," Lydia said as Virginia sat beside him on the bed and kissed him cautiously on the cheek. "Rest without a lot of disturbance."

"Don't be afraid," he told Randall, who was hanging back. "You won't break me." His voice sounded scratchy.

Bending over his grandfather for an awkward hug, Randall looked at Virginia uncertainly, the first time he'd acknowledged her in days. "You look like hell, Granddad," he said.

"You don't look so good yourself, young man," Nathan replied. "You sleep in those clothes last night?"

"Yeah, I did." Randall sat in the open window, plucking at a hole in the knee of his sweatpants.

"Now that you're awake, Nathan, I'll go get you something to eat." Lydia gave Randall a stern look, then they heard her shoes clicking back down the stairs.

"How are you feeling, Dad?" Virginia brushed her hand lightly over his cheek and felt the prick of stubble against her palm. Through his thin T-shirt she could see the elastic bandages wrapped around and around. He held his left arm, bound in a sling, tight against his chest. "Your face is all scraped."

"It feels like the worst rug burn you can imagine. I got it sliding over the grass. All down my good arm, too." He turned his arm to show them.

"Why are you in Larry's room?" Virginia got up to open another window. "Don't you think it's hot in here?"

No one answered.

"Wouldn't you like a fan?" she suggested. "We could pull this hot air out."

"I'm fine," Nathan insisted. "Lydia's taking good care of me."

When he asked about their trip, Randall told him they'd had a little trouble with the car. "You should have seen these two rednecks," he said, "up on the mountain, trying to flirt with Mom."

"They weren't flirting," Virginia said. "Just being creepy."

Randall shrugged and looked away.

Lydia came back in a few minutes with a tray and set it on the night table. She had brought a bowl of vegetable soup, a plate of saltines, and a glass of iced tea. The soup looked canned. "Maybe you would like to freshen up while I help Nathan with his lunch," she said. "I'll be down in a few minutes."

"I expect Randall would like to freshen up," Nathan said, and Randall laughed as they left the room.

By the time they sat down at the table with Lydia, Randall was sulky again. He kept his eyes on the paper plate she had set in front of him, chewing methodically and taking frequent swallows of milk. Lydia had given them baloney sandwiches on white bread with mustard, along with sweet pickles and tall glasses of milk. Quite possibly, Virginia considered, her son had never eaten a baloney sandwich before. He covered his mouth with his hand, using his tongue to dislodge the sticky lumps of bread.

"Do you have maybe like an apple?" he asked Lydia after several minutes.

"Your mother can go grocery shopping, if you need anything extra." Offended, Lydia dabbed at her mouth with her handkerchief. "She knows what you like."

"We brought some apples in the cooler," Virginia told her. "But that's a good idea. We can go to the store this afternoon."

"I've been trying to keep things simple since Nathan's accident," Lydia said. "No time for fancy cooking." She got up when they heard footsteps on the porch. "Good. Here comes my nephew."

"Hey," he said, taking his cap off and using it to brush the dust from his pants. "I was out fixing some fence in the far pasture. I didn't hear you come in."

"It doesn't matter," Lydia said. "This is Fred, my sister's youngest boy. You met him at the wedding, you might remember." She took Fred's sandwich from the refrigerator while he washed up at the kitchen sink. "And this is Nathan's daughter, Virginia, and her son."

"Randall," Virginia added, wondering if Lydia had actually forgotten his name.

"Filthy work." Fred held up the grimy bar of soap to show them. "I can stay until after the milking this afternoon, then I have to take off. I've got a new job, starting tomorrow." He sat down, rubbing his wet hands over his shirtfront. "I figured I'd show you how the milking goes one time." He bit into his sandwich and gave Randall a long look. "It's not that hard. I've been milking at five and five, but I guess you could switch to six and six, if you like to sleep late."

"We don't need to go changing everything around," Lydia said firmly.

"At least your dad got his field corn planted before the accident," Fred told Virginia. "I was down in the lower field yesterday. It's looking pretty good."

In the car alone, heading for the Good Food Market in Tenney's Landing, she could feel the heavy lump of chewed bread and meat in her stomach. Fred seemed like a friendly, reliable sort, and Virginia was wishing he didn't have to leave so soon. Her father's condition was worse than she had imagined. She hadn't expected him to be in bed still, taking painkillers.

Randall had opted to stay and help Fred with the fencing, despite his mother's suggestion that they stop and visit Henny on the way. As she and Lydia watched him climbing into the cab of Fred's battered truck, Lydia said, "A little hard work will be good for that one."

"He might surprise you," Virginia told her. She hoped it was true.

Driving into town, Virginia saw two of West's boys cutting the church lawn, one of them riding the mower, the other running a weed trimmer around the base of a tree. There was no mistaking them. The boy on the mower waved as she went by, though he probably had no idea who she was. They seemed happy, as if there were nothing they'd rather be doing on a summer afternoon.

Except for the Good Food Market, which had a carved

wooden sign over the door and bright lights inside, the stores on Main Street still looked the way they had when Virginia was growing up. Four brick buildings with tall facades stood shoulder to shoulder on the north side, facing four nearly identical buildings across the street. The Market had taken over two of the original storefronts. The new owners, Mike and Claire Eastman, had knocked out most of the interior wall between them to create an airy, open space, so different from the old Wiggins Grocery, with its splintery floor and flyspecked windows. Virginia was about to detour over to the newspaper office to say hello to her uncle Dan, *The Messenger*'s editor, when she noticed Theresa Moffat coming out of Paula's Café. She darted inside the grocery store instead.

In spite of much sniffing and eye rolling on Lydia's part, Randall carried a card table upstairs so everyone could eat supper together. With Randall's help, Nathan had moved back to his own room, and he was sitting up in bed, interested in their preparations. Virginia had cooked a large meal—roast beef with mashed potatoes and gravy, green beans, salad, and strawberry shortcake.

"She must think you're not getting enough to eat," Lydia remarked as Virginia positioned a tray in front of Nathan.

"Oh, well . . . Ginny's quite a hand in the kitchen," he said.

Sitting at the rickety table in the middle of her parents' bedroom, Virginia remembered how they had saved for years to buy the maple bed and matching chests of drawers, how giddy they were the day the new furniture was delivered, as if they had never expected to own anything so fine. The candles she placed on the dresser cast thin shadows on the wallpaper Virginia and her mother had put up five summers before, the paper with the yellow flowers climbing green vines. Although it was only six-thirty, the room had begun to darken as clouds built up outside. The smell of rain blew in through the open windows.

"How did the milking go?" Nathan asked Randall. "Think you can manage it?"

Randall nodded. "They get kind of jumpy when you try to hook on those tit things, though."

"It's *teat*," Lydia said.

"Oh." Randall bit down on his fork to keep from smiling.

"Ginny can show you a thing or two," Nathan said. "When she was little, we milked by hand, and we had twice as many cows then. Later on, she learned to use the milking machine, too."

Virginia had expected to go along with Fred, to see how the newer machine worked, but when she started to the barn, Lydia had stopped her. "Hadn't you better be finishing up the supper?" she'd asked. "We like to eat earlier than you do, I expect. It used to be, when Nathan came in at six-fifteen, I put the food on the table."

"All right," Virginia had said. No point arguing the first day.

They ate in silence for a while, everyone except her father looking miserable to some degree. It was touching how much it pleased him that they had come.

"I hate to bring it up, Dad," Virginia said eventually. "But what kind of shape is the tractor in? I'm thinking about starting on the hay."

"She didn't make out so bad," he said, wincing as he shifted in bed. "Bent the front axle, broke a couple of hoses. Chick Mason's been over here working on it. Fred drove it around some yesterday, said it seems all right."

"Good. I want to get started." Virginia looked out at the deepening clouds. "If it isn't too wet tomorrow."

"West stopped by on Friday to see if we needed anything. They're pretty busy now, running that trout business besides the farm, but you might call and see if they could give you a hand."

At the mention of West's name, Randall eyed his mother.

"Maybe I can handle it myself," Virginia said. "I'll see how it goes."

"Don't try cutting on the highest part, that's all. Just leave it." Nathan got up the last bit of potato and gravy on the side of his fork, licked it clean. "Did I hear a rumor about short-cake?"

Randall helped clear the table and stood beside Virginia in the kitchen as she sliced the strawberries. She thought he was about to say something friendly.

"I don't want any cake," he announced. "I'm going to call Dad." He went into the small room off the kitchen, where there was an old black dial phone on the desk, and closed the door behind him. They had left their cell phones at home, because the hills surrounding the farm made reception unpredictable.

"We have phone cards," she assured Lydia. "So the calls won't be on your bill."

"That's fine, then." Lydia took two dessert plates and started back upstairs.

When the storm broke, Virginia had been asleep for an hour or so. She woke to the sound of thunder and saw a flash of lightning through the curtains. A moment later, she heard rain striking the metal roof. She was sleeping in Aunt Ida's room because her old bedroom, which Lydia was using for storage, reeked of mothballs. Uncle Herman's younger sister, Ida, was a teacher who lived in Pittsburgh, and she would stay with them for a few weeks every summer. Carrying a stout stick, she went for walks along the back roads and over the hills, picked bunches of wild-flowers to arrange in vases around the house, and read for hours on the front porch. "Ida thinks we're running a resort here," Nathan used to say. But all of them looked forward to her visits, the stories she told over supper, the songs she played on the piano in the evening. As she got older and started to lose her hearing, her singing grew increasingly off-key. Even so, it always felt a little too quiet after Ida left.

The thunder boomed again, louder and closer this time, and Cleo leaped onto the bed. Virginia couldn't help but think of Lydia sleeping beside her father. While they were eating supper, she had wondered about a soft pink bundle on the bed next to him, finally recognizing it as Lydia's folded nightgown.

"Fairly hostile," she'd whispered to Rob on the phone when he asked about Lydia. "But somewhat friendlier than my own son." Like Randall, Virginia had used the room off the kitchen to make her call, feeling furtive as she closed the door. The room had become her father's office, the heavy oak desk covered with record books and receipts, boxes of shotgun shells, pencil nubs. A wool jacket hung on a peg near the door and under it a pair of work boots with rims of dried mud around the soles. Against the walls, magazines were piled in ragged stacks: *The Dairyman's Companion, Poultry Farmer, National Geographic.* Probably thirty years' worth, she'd calculated, dialing the number at home.

Rob had sounded cheerful, telling her how a baked potato had exploded in the oven because he'd forgotten to prick it with a fork. She could hear music in the background, early Rolling Stones. Rob still had a turntable and a collection of record albums he treated with exquisite care, though he seldom played them. No doubt he enjoyed having the house to himself for a change. Near the end of their conversation, he told her Randall was nervous about the cows. "He said, 'They're not especially cooperative,' his exact words. Maybe you could help him out at first."

"I'm planning to." Virginia had already set the alarm for quarter to five.

"Good luck with everything, Ginny."

Good luck? Well, what could he do, two hundred miles away? She longed to be back there with him, dancing in the kitchen, eating charred potato.

Trying to relax so she could fall asleep again, Virginia pictured herself as a scarecrow filled with sand. As the sand poured slowly through her feet, her body sank by degrees, first her legs, then her torso, and finally her head. She concentrated on the sound of rain on the roof. How lovely it would be, she thought, if her mother were sleeping down the hall. If Aunt Ida were in the other twin bed, snoring softly as she used to do.

Chapter Five

———————

The noise was wild, joyful. On the hill below Virginia, Randall and Cody Moffat—West's youngest son—moved in parallel lines, beating the grass and whooping at the top of their lungs. Each of them carried a pair of wooden poles, which they cracked together loudly. They had set up a rhythm: stomp, stomp, *crack!* followed by a *swish* as they swept the knee-high grass. Over the sound of the engine, she heard their cries echo from the tree line at the top of the hill. *Whee-ah! Whup-whup!* Shifting carefully on the high tractor seat, she looked back in time to see a spotted fawn, not more than six feet in front of them, bolt from its nest and zigzag away on its skinny legs. She watched until it cleared the brook at the edge of the field and stood on the other side, panting, waiting for its mother to come and find it.

Yeeee-ah! the boys shouted, jabbing their poles in the air.

Virginia checked the angle of the cutter bar, straightened

the front wheels. The sun was hot on her shoulders, and a trickle of sweat was running down her back. Randall and Cody would be even hotter, because she had made them wear high rubber boots to protect them from snakes. Randall's hat hung from his neck by its cord, and he had taken his shirt off. He would have a sunburn before too long.

Their success in scaring the fawn out of the hayfield made them dance and spin. *Wo-wo-wo!* they called, their laughter ringing in the late-morning brightness. Virginia could hardly believe her ears.

The grass beating was Cody's idea. Virginia and Randall had been sitting on the porch after the morning milking, side by side in the wooden rocking chairs, watching the clouds trailing off to the east and listening to Lydia fry bacon inside, when they heard a rider coming down through the pasture.

"It's some kid." Randall had gotten up to look and stood on the step, shading his eyes with his hand.

The boy, who looked about eleven, stopped his horse at the edge of the porch. He lifted his straw cowboy hat in greeting and smiled down at them. His hair was the color of honey. "I heard you were here," he said.

"Hello," Virginia said. "You're out early."

"It's the best time." He stroked the horse's neck, to calm her. "Her name's Juniper, by the way."

"What's yours?" Randall asked.

"Cody Moffat."

When Lydia called them in for breakfast, Cody got down and tied his horse to the porch railing and followed. He sat at the table, watching as Randall helped himself to scrambled eggs and bacon.

"I only had toast this morning," Cody said. "I left before my mom got up."

Sighing, Lydia took another plate from the cupboard. She seemed on the verge of smiling, though, and Virginia wondered if Cody had come visiting before.

"What are we doing today?" Randall asked, stifling a yawn. "I wouldn't mind catching a little more sleep."

"I'll give you an hour," Virginia told him. "Then I'm going to put you to work in the garden with a hoe. Once it dries off a bit, I'll start cutting the near field."

"You know how to drive a tractor?" Cody asked.

"Sure," Virginia said. It was like riding a bicycle, she had assured Rob. Once you learned how, you never forgot.

"My dad won't let me drive ours yet." Cody was folding a piece of toast, making himself a bacon and egg sandwich. "He says my legs are too short."

"Really?" Randall glanced under the table. "They look normal to me."

Cody laughed, but his face quickly turned serious. "My brothers were driving by the time they were my age."

"I always liked haying," Virginia said. "All the Eastmans and Moffats would be over here, helping out, even the younger ones. Then we'd go on to one of their farms when we were done. It was quite a time."

"I could help you," Cody said.

"Once I get it baled, maybe you and Randall can load it on the truck for me." She doubted that either of them could lift the fifty-pound bales by himself. "There was one thing I hated, though. Sometimes animals got caught in the mowing—young rabbits and ground-nesting birds, even a fawn now and then. They'd be down in the grass, and the person up on the tractor couldn't see them."

"Why wouldn't they run away?" Randall rubbed his hands over his face, trying to wake himself up.

"Maybe they felt safe in their nests," Virginia said.

"Or else they froze," Cody added. Then he told them about a film he'd seen at school, how hunters in the African bush swept the grass with long sticks, shouting to scare the animals out so the other hunters could shoot them.

Reaching the stone wall at the edge of the field, Virginia raised the cutter bar and turned the tractor. The back wheels slid in the freshly cut grass, and she felt her leg tremble on the gas pedal. She took a deep breath, held it until the moment passed. When she began the next cut across the hill, she was pleased to see that the last swath was straighter than the one before.

To her relief, the tractor had started easily. After belching out a cloud of smoke, the motor had settled into its steady *putt, putt, putt.* Fred had already filled it with diesel fuel from the tank inside the tractor shed and topped off the oil, so Virginia had nothing to do but lurch away. The force of the clutch surprised her; the first time she let it out, her foot flew off the pedal and the engine died. Unlike the old tractor, the newer one had a lot of fancy levers and switches she was afraid to try. Chugging up the hill at last, she was reminded how it seemed much steeper riding on the tractor. When she eventually found the lever that lowered the cutter bar, the chatter of the metal teeth sent a shiver up her spine. Her father and Larry used to spend hours sharpening the triangular blades with a file, rubbing oil over the length of the bar to keep it clean.

Virginia had always liked looking down at the farm from that hill: the tall white house with its steeply pitched roof and narrow attic dormers, its two porches, the wide doors and weathered gray wood of the cow barn with its attached shed, the copper weathervane on top of the cupola. She watched the plump shapes of chickens scratching and pecking in the barnyard. From a distance, everything looked tidy, but up close she'd noticed that the porch needed painting and the shed roof was sagging. Her mother's flower beds were weedy, the grass around the house unmowed. The garden was only half planted; it needed weeding, too. Even before her father's accident, things had started to get away from them.

It would be good to have another person with a tractor, she considered. Alone, Virginia would have to do all the mowing, tedding, raking, and baling. *En plein air* for sure.

Cody stayed with them through lunch and into the afternoon, shaking his head when Lydia asked if his parents wouldn't be worried about him. He had left a note, he said. Virginia stopped mowing early because she had promised Randall a trip to town to buy some work pants and boots that fit. He had complained at breakfast about the odor of the barn in his clothes, the cow manure on his sneakers.

"I'll take you to LaClede's," she'd said, recalling the smell of new denim and boot leather and old Mr. LaClede with his greasy mustache.

"It hasn't been LaClede's for ten years," Lydia informed her. "It's Spurling's now."

"Fancy," Cody said.

Virginia saw what he meant when they got there. Along with the overalls and work boots, Spurling's stocked fishing gear, expensive hiking boots, even life vests and water shoes for canoers and kayakers. Randall bypassed the ordinary blue jeans and found the work clothes that came in colors like spruce and putty, the pants and shorts equipped with loops and extra pockets, the barn jackets with striped linings and corduroy collars. They were, Virginia had to admit, rather sharp looking, and so, instead of arguing with him, she picked out a few things for herself.

They eventually left the store with three bulging shopping bags. As Randall loaded them into the trunk of the car, he began to talk about what he wanted to plant in the garden—watermelon and pumpkins. Not the most practical choices, but Virginia didn't want to dampen his newfound enthusiasm. No doubt Lydia would set him straight.

Four or five miles out of town, the car's engine started to miss, and the temperature was climbing again. Remembering what the log truck driver had said, Virginia told Randall it was probably a bad plug; she was sure they could make it back to the farm. It would have been smarter to turn around and take the car to Mason's Garage, but it was already past four o'clock, and she didn't want to be late for the milking. A little farther on, the engine died.

She coasted to the shoulder of the road and turned the key in the ignition. Although it sounded as if it was about to start, nothing happened. She tried again.

"Pop it," Randall said. They both got out, and he lifted the hood. "That's weird. It's all wet under here."

"What do you think?" Virginia watched steam rising from the engine block.

"No clue," he said.

The road was deserted and no house in sight. The only sounds were the *whir* of insects in the fields on either side, the hiss of water on hot metal.

"Remember that yellow house about a mile back, beyond the curve?" Virginia asked him. "I think it belongs to one of the Hardings. I'm sure they'd let you use the phone."

Randall shifted uneasily, glancing down the road. "Who should I call?"

"Lydia, I guess."

Randall looked at her. "All right," he said and set off.

He hadn't gone far when Virginia saw a gray pickup in the distance, coming from the opposite direction, and called him back. When the truck reached them, the driver pulled over to their side, and when he got out, she knew it was West's oldest boy.

"What happened?" He was already rolling up the sleeves of his white shirt as he approached. The shirt was freshly laundered, his black pants neatly pressed.

"The engine died, all of a sudden."

When he leaned in under the hood, Virginia could see the marks of a comb in his damp hair. "It's your water pump," he said. "It's shot."

"Can I drive it like this for a little way? We have to get back to the farm."

"You can't drive it. You'll need to have Chick tow it to the garage." He looked at his watch. "I was on my way to work, but I'm a little early, so maybe I could run you home." Then, taking in the Maryland license plate, "Which farm do you mean?"

"The Rownd place. Nathan's my father."

"Oh, sure," he said, holding out his hand. "I'm West Moffat. Most people call me Weston, to keep me straight from my dad." He shook hands with Randall, too. "Cody was just telling us about you."

Randall closed the hood firmly—praying, his mother guessed, that Cody hadn't mentioned the sticks and the rubber boots. "Why don't we leave them until later?" he said when she asked him to get the shopping bags from the trunk.

The truck was fairly old, the vinyl of the dashboard cracked, the floor mats gritty. It smelled of motor oil and stale upholstery. Virginia wondered at first if it was the truck West used to drive. But no, it couldn't have been.

"Where do you work?" she asked as they set off.

"The Daily Catch, down in Fayette. That fish place?"

"I hear it's nice."

"The tips are good. Plus we get all the fried clams we can eat." He chuckled as he reached out to turn off the radio, which had suddenly blared to life. "People actually ask us if the clams come from the river."

Weston talked most of the way. He told them he was going to be a senior in the fall, that he was saving money for college, although he hoped to get a baseball scholarship. He asked Randall what sports he played, wanted to know how Nathan was getting along. At first glance, he looked exactly like West at that age, though the son was finer-boned, his shoulders narrow.

"You're wearing an earring," Virginia said.

"Yes." He touched the small gold ring in his right ear. "My dad loves it. You can imagine."

As they turned in to the driveway at the farm, Cleo bounded across the porch, barking. Lydia came out and hesitated on the top step, squinting until she recognized them, then went back inside.

Weston leaned out the truck window as they said good-bye. "Come down to the restaurant sometime," he said. "Try our freshwater clams."

"Is there really such a thing?" Randall asked as he drove away.

"I don't think so. Not in the Monongahela River, anyway."

In the milking parlor, Virginia washed the udders and teats with a warm antiseptic solution, and Randall followed, attaching the rubber teat cups. He treated the cows as if they were alien beings, keeping as much distance as possible. Normally dexterous, he fumbled with the cups. She could hear him cursing under his breath. When the first six cows had been hooked up to the milking claws, he switched on the machine, and they stood back, listening to the alternating *swish* and *sigh* as milk was drawn into the large glass floor pail. The cows were still skittish with them. Virginia had to lead each one into its pen with a hand on its shoulder, bribing it with a bit of hay.

"They actually like being milked," she told Randall. "Pretty soon they'll come trotting in like little darlings."

"We'll see," he said, rocking back on his heels.

In the holding area, the rest of the herd looked on curiously, rolling their mischievous Jersey eyes. When she was young, Virginia and her parents and Larry had milked sixty cows by hand, twice a day. Roy and Roger, the Jameson twins who lived down the road, helped out. Those boys had one bicycle between them and took turns riding on the handlebars. When it was snowy, Nathan went to get them in his truck. Caroline always made them stay for breakfast and heaped their plates with food. She saved Larry's outgrown clothes for them, too, and every winter she bought them warm hats and gloves. One afternoon Henny and Virginia were in town with Henny's father when they saw Caroline coming out of LaClede's with the twins.

"Prancer and Vixen," Henny had whispered. Roy was wearing a new red stocking cap, Roger a green one.

Flushed and happy, the twins had lifted their hands in the air so the girls could admire their matching mittens. Though they were only a year ahead of her at school, Virginia had lost track of Roy and Roger by the seventh grade, the year her parents got the first milking machine. One fall day when she was in high school, her mother went to the Jamesons' house with a box of Larry's clothes and returned after a few minutes.

"The house is empty," she told them sadly. "They've moved away."

Virginia's father always kept Jerseys, claiming they gave the best milk. She thought they were handsomer than other cows, with their fawn-colored coats and graceful heads. And, she assured Randall, compared to the larger Holsteins, which Henny's father kept, Jerseys were much friendlier. Nathan had reduced his herd to thirty-six and had the barn retrofitted with a new straight-six, walk-through milking parlor. They should have been able to do the milking in about an hour—ten minutes for each group of six cows. Randall, still rocking on his heels, looked dubious when she explained this.

With the old milking machine, they used to bring the cows into the regular bedding stalls and hook them up two at a time. Even then, Virginia felt as if they had lost something. Learning to milk by hand had been like learning to tell time—she had gained another piece of the world. She'd liked rising in the early morning dark, the dusty smells and muted sounds of the barn as the cows moved about—hooves striking the plank floor, the rustle of straw. She liked the way she got to know each cow, the way they set up a rhythm together, the squeeze and draw and release of the teat, warm milk splashing against the side of the metal pail. She liked the full, downy feel of the udder, bending forward on the three-legged stool with her forehead pressed against the cow's flank. She could almost fall asleep that way. But then the cow might suddenly lift her tail and let go with a stream of hot urine, making her sit up straight. The milking parlor, despite its homey name, was too much like a laboratory, all the surfaces hard and shiny.

Randall was careful not to stand directly behind the cows as he bent to release the teat cups. Even so, one of them kicked out sideways, and as he jumped away, he sprayed himself with milk.

"Shit!" Red-faced, he gave his mother a look meant to say it was all her fault.

"It happens," she told him, smiling.

Virginia swung aside the metal gate at the head of each pen, and the first six cows filed back out to the pasture, the high bones of their hips dipping from side to side. She brought in six more, bribing those as well.

When Virginia and Randall had finished rinsing out the milkers and hosing down the concrete, she took a clean pail and drew a gallon of milk from the spigot on the bulk tank for the house. The next morning, she told Randall, a truck from the dairy cooperative would empty the tank and take the milk to be processed.

"So it's not pasteurized when we drink it?"

"No," she said, closing up the doors at the back of the barn.

"And it still has all the fat in it."

"True. Jersey milk's about six percent butterfat, one of the highest."

"Are you trying to kill me, or what?" Walking ahead of Virginia, he stopped suddenly as he rounded the corner of the barn and waited for her to catch up.

A small blue car with a pom-pom on the antenna and a West Virginia license plate was parked in front of the house. A woman and a young teenage girl, both wearing cutoff jeans and halter tops, were standing beside it. Both had peroxide blond hair.

"Hi," Virginia said. "Are you lost?"

"In more ways than one." The woman had the gravelly voice of a smoker.

"We came to buy eggs," the girl said, lifting her eyebrows. "You have a sign out front. It says 'Eggs.' "

As she got closer, Virginia noticed that the girl had a tattoo above her right breast—a bird with outspread wings, a tiny heart in its beak. "Randall," she said. "Why don't you go tell Lydia someone wants eggs?"

"Tell her it's Jodie," the woman said. "She knows me."

"So you live around here?" Virginia handed the pail of milk to Randall, expecting him to take it into the house, but he didn't move.

"We're renting that little green house at the end of Riggins Road," Jodie said, looking Randall up and down. "You must be a handy fellow. Stop by sometime, and I'll put you to work."

"All right." He didn't take his eyes off the girl.

"We were living down in Beckley," Jodie went on. "Had a nice place in town, until my husband ran off with some slut from the Dairy Queen about six months ago."

"I'm sure they want to hear our life story," the girl said, pursing her lips. "He didn't run off with anyone, either. He went by himself."

"Irene knows everything. Just ask her." Jodie pulled a folded dollar bill from her pocket and held it out to Randall. "Any chance of getting those eggs?"

"I've got a fresh dozen for you," Lydia called, coming outside. As she handed the carton to Jodie, she plucked the bill from Randall's fingers. "It's a dollar and a quarter."

"I owe you, then." Jodie started toward the car. "Don't forget," she said to Randall, "come and visit sometime." She tooted the horn as they drove away.

"What happened to you, young man?" Lydia asked. "It looks like somebody threw up on the front of your pants."

Randall looked down where the splashed milk had dried, leaving sticky white splotches. Without answering, he gave the pail back to his mother and went into the house.

LYDIA

━━━◆◆◆━━━

I'm not one to take advantage of another person's misfortune. But I don't turn my back on a likely prospect when fate sets it down in front of me. The day Harriet Gleason called and invited me to dinner and mentioned in her whispery way that Art Simms would be there, I made an appointment to get my hair done. If I'd had the money, I would of bought a new dress, but I made do with the one I wore to my husband's funeral, adding a pink scarf to brighten it up.

Besides the reverend and Harriet, there would be four other people at the parsonage that evening—an odd number because she had invited Nathan Rownd, too. He'd been a widower not quite eight months, still raw in his grief, you might say. After Harriet's call, I thought a fair bit about Art, listing off his good points. He had an insurance office in Rownd's Point, nothing fancy but a steady business, and two grown children. His wife had left him after nearly thirty years for a pharmaceutical salesman. He was younger than I was, but he'd lost most of his hair, and he was stoop-shouldered from all those years at a desk. Harriet said we seemed about the same age.

I'd been on my own close to five years. By the time I walked up and rang the doorbell at the parsonage, I was prepared to think well of Art Simms and to welcome his attentions.

When the reverend asked who wanted a cocktail, Art said he didn't drink, he'd have a ginger ale please. Lord knows, that should of been another point in his favor. But when I asked for an old-fashioned and Nathan said he'd like the same, that touched off a little something between us.

"No one drinks these anymore," Nathan said, raising his glass. "I guess that's why they call them old-fashioneds."

"Then what did they call them in the first place?" Art asked, pleased with himself. "New-fashioneds?"

I laughed politely, catching Nathan's eye. He smiled at me over Art's shoulder, his eyes crinkling at the corners. Next to Nathan, Art looked somewhat sparse.

Later on, when I was helping Harriet in the kitchen, she said, "Now, I think maybe Art's feeling a bit neglected. He was looking forward to seeing you tonight." She paused in her cake slicing and dropped her voice even more. "Don't forget, it hasn't been a year yet since Nathan's wife passed away."

She said it as though I needed reminding about some point of good manners. I took her meaning, though. Nathan Rownd is not for you.

When Art Simms called a couple of days later and invited me to a movie, I said no thank you and wished him luck. That was the same day I cooked Moroccan chicken from a recipe I found in the newspaper. I arrived at Nathan's place as he was coming out of the barn with a pail of milk. He stopped and squinted in my direction, me standing there with my best casserole dish. Then he unbuttoned the pocket of his shirt and took his glasses out.

"Oh," he said. "It's you, Mrs. Will."

"It's Lydia, and I've made way too much chicken for one person," I said. "Plus, I thought you could use some cheering up."

"You're probably right about that," he said. "Come on in."

The week after, I took lamb stew, and he had a bottle of wine in the refrigerator. He didn't know that much about wine, he told me. Maybe the red wasn't supposed to be chilled. We can make up our own rules about wine, I said. When I left around nine o'clock, he held the car door for me and touched my shoulder as I got in. He said it had been a nice evening. Some people would say that wasn't much to go on, but I knew different.

Married to Bob Will all those years, I'd learned how to hold my head up in town and let the talk roll off my back. I'd been a good wife to him and faithful. I had nothing to be ashamed of, except picking the wrong man to marry. It wasn't like I could of known, either. At twenty-four, Bob Will was something to see—his black hair combed so slick and those snapping blue eyes, even the chip in his front tooth. I hadn't known him more than an hour before he was kissing me on the mouth, and I didn't mind.

Chapter Six

The jar of pickled eggs was gone, also the red Coca–Cola cooler. Bob Will was gone, too, of course. At one end of the counter, a metal rack held sticks of beef jerky, chewing gum, small packages of butterscotch drops and peppermints. Beside it sat a coffeemaker with a glass pot full of a brew resembling dark molasses, and next to that an open carton of half-and-half. The smell of coffee nearly overwhelmed the odor of grease and gasoline.

Virginia sat in the orange plastic chair in the small office, reading the previous week's *Messenger* and listening to country music through the open door of the garage. Above the sound of Chick's radio, she could hear the occasional *chink* of metal against metal. Lydia had given her a ride to the garage and dropped her off without waiting to see if the car was ready. Chick said it would be another hour.

She didn't mind. Randall had been groggy and resentful

when Virginia woke him at five that morning. He nearly started to cry when a cow stepped on his foot in the milking parlor. The milking and cleaning up had taken forever.

"When was the last time you had the oil changed?" Chick was standing in the doorway, grinning.

"I couldn't say."

"That's what I thought. Might as well do it now, while you're here." He took his cap off and wiped his forehead with his sleeve. "None of my business, but how's it going with your stepmother?"

"My what?"

"Lydia."

"I'm too old to have a stepmother," she told him. "Only kids have stepmothers. And unlucky girls in fairy tales."

Chick laughed softly. "I'll tell my dad you said so. He'd be here, too, but he had a doctor's appointment this morning." He went behind the counter and handed her a greasy ballpoint pen. "You might want to do the crossword in the paper. I started it, but I didn't get very far."

His head barely cleared the door when he went back into the garage. Virginia remembered when she was four, going with her mother to visit Chick's parents, Eva and Clyde, after he was born. Five weeks premature, he was no bigger than the doll Virginia had gotten for Christmas that year. Until he was seven or eight years old, he was so small and sickly that nobody was certain he would live. When his mother hadn't been able to conceive again, people said she was like a hen with one chick. They said it so often that the name stayed with him, even when he started to grow, even when he weighed nearly two hundred pounds and made all-state tackle his senior year of high school.

The summer he was twelve, Chick had a crush on sixteen-year-old Henny. Nearly every day he would ride his bicycle the eight miles from town out to the Eastman farm, pedal up the gravel driveway to their front porch, tap his foot on the bottom step, then turn around and ride back. If Henny happened to be outside, Chick would smile broadly and pedal even faster. He never spoke to her unless she came into his father's service station, when he would gulp some air and say, "Help you?"

"Henny," Virginia's brother once asked, "if you and Chick get married, what are you going to name your first kid? Egg?"

"Don't be silly," Henny replied, sticking her nose in the air. "We'd call him something classy, like Gizzard. Gizzard Beakforth Mason."

That was the summer Henny got involved with Drew Stevens. When Drew moved to town with his father, an engineer who worked on the river locks, people stared at him on the street. It wasn't just that newcomers were scarce in Tenney's Landing; it had more to do with his hair, a curly blond mass that reached his shoulders. He wore tie-dyed T-shirts and sandals. He smoked cigarettes in public, too, even though he was only sixteen. The first time Henny saw him, standing in front of the newspaper office, she and Virginia were riding by in Larry's car.

"Who's that little twerp?" Larry wondered.

"Pull over, and I'll ask him," Henny said.

As Larry and Virginia circled the block two or three times, Henny learned that Drew had moved with his father from Oswego, New York, on Lake Ontario, that his parents were divorced.

"I've never seen eyes that color," she told them, getting back in the car. "Sea green."

The next afternoon, when Chick came coasting down the Eastman driveway, he had to swerve to avoid a dented station wagon with New York plates.

Virginia heard the *ding* of someone driving up to the gas

pump and looked out to see a shiny black pickup with a fish decal on the door. "Get that, will you, Ginny?" Chick called, joking. "Oh, that's West," he said. "I guess he can take care of himself."

West noticed her as he was unscrewing the gas cap and went inside, still holding it. "Ginny. Weston said he gave you a ride yesterday."

"I was really happy to see him." She refolded the newspaper, glad to have something to do with her hands. "He seems like a great kid. Cody, too."

"I like them pretty well," West said, setting the gas cap down beside the cash register. "Buy you a cup of Chick's coffee?"

"Sure. Why not live dangerously?"

He stirred cream and sugar into two foam cups before adding the coffee. "Good luck," he said, handing her one and leaning against the counter. "How's your car?"

"Weston was right. It was the water pump. Fortunately, it started leaking and killed the engine before the whole thing froze up. Chick's almost finished with it." She took a tentative sip. "That's a handsome new truck you have."

"I got it a couple of months ago," he said, gazing out the window. "First time I ever bought a brand-new one."

"So you use it for the business?"

"Restaurant deliveries mostly—the Daily Catch and some others, too. Things are starting to take off." He added more cream to his coffee, stirred it for a long time. "Nathan told me you were coming up for the summer. How is everything?"

"My dad's worse than I expected. He sleeps a lot, and he needs help with everything, even getting out of bed. But Randall's learning to do the milking, and I started cutting hay yesterday."

"By yourself?"

"I think I can manage," she said, setting the coffee aside. "One day at a time."

"Call if you run into trouble, will you?" West glanced at the clock over the door, the clock with a pinup girl in the center that had been there as long as anyone could remember. "I have to get going, but I'll try to stop by soon."

Watching him at the gas pump, Virginia was struck again by the resemblance between West and his oldest boy. West had gained about twenty pounds since high school, and his hair, though flecked with gray, still caught the light. Clean-shaven, dressed in jeans and a khaki shirt, he seemed younger and more at ease than he had at her father's wedding. When he went into the garage to pay Chick, she was reminded of the way she used to stand at the hall window when he dropped her off after a date, the little fear that she would never see him again. Unfolding the newspaper, she tried to focus on the crossword puzzle.

"You're ready to go," Chick announced half an hour later.

Writing a check, Virginia noticed the gas cap still on the counter and held it up.

"Oh, well," Chick said. "He'll be back."

When she reached the cutoff for the Eastman farm, Virginia decided to make a detour. She could visit with Henny for half an hour and still get back to the farm in time for lunch.

Turning up the driveway, she heard tractors in the field beyond the barn and then saw Henny's parents. Roland was driving the big red Farmall with the tedder, Liza following on the smaller John Deere with the rake. They would be ready to start baling by afternoon. It occurred to Virginia that the decent thing to do would be to come back with Randall after supper and help them load bales. But she really wanted to finish cutting her own field and get the tedding done before dark.

Henny was at the kitchen table, shelling peas. "I heard you were back," she said, running her thumbnail along the spine of a pod, splitting it open. She nudged the peas into a large brown bowl and dropped the empty pod into a bucket on the floor.

Virginia took a seat across from her and reached for a handful of unshelled peas from the pile in the middle of the table. "We got in Sunday afternoon."

"And your car broke down already."

"The big news travels fast." Choosing a large pod and splitting it carefully to keep it hinged on one side, Virginia placed it on her nose, as they used to do when they were very young.

"That's nothing," Henny said, laughing. "I can even tell you how much you spent at Spurling's yesterday."

"You're kidding."

"I am not. My mother's friend Selma Mitchell called last night. She was in the store buying socks for her husband when you checked out, and she heard the clerk say, 'That comes to three hundred and forty-two dollars.' Selma said she nearly fainted."

"Huh. I didn't notice anyone else in the store."

"Selma's not that big," Henny replied. "And will you please take that off?"

"Big mouth, though." Virginia tossed the pod in the direction of the bucket.

"My dad calls Selma the Voice of the Valley."

"I don't even know who she is."

"Sure you do. She's the one who married Theresa's uncle Jerry after his first wife drowned. It was in all the papers, about fifteen years ago. The drowning."

"I'm out of touch, I guess."

Listening to the steady rumble of machinery in the hayfield, Virginia pictured the Eastmans in their wide-brimmed straw hats, working in the sun. A little older than her father, they would be exhausted by the end of the day, and she didn't know if Henny was able to cook a meal for them. There were so many things she didn't know about her friend's life. She often wondered what would become of Henny when her parents died. Both of her brothers had moved away years ago, to Cleveland and Dallas. Virginia hated the thought of Henny in her wheelchair, alone in that house built for a family of twelve.

"How's your dad?" Henny asked.

"A little better." Virginia opened another pod, added the peas to the bowl between them. "Rob says we should get him out of bed and walk him around, so Randall and I gave him a tour of the upstairs hallway last night. Then he sat up for a while, teaching Randall how to play five-card stud."

"That will come in handy, I'm sure." Henny watched Virginia's hands. "How's it going with Lydia?"

"I think she's already sorry she asked us to come."

"It's got to be strange for her, living in your mother's house. Besides," Henny added, expertly flipping a pea across the table so that it fell into the front of Virginia's shirt, "she knows you can't stand her."

"I wouldn't say that, exactly." Virginia asked if Henny knew anything about Jodie and Irene. "They're renting that house where the Jameson twins used to live. They stopped to buy eggs yesterday, and Randall was practically drooling on the girl. She has a tattoo, right here," she said, fishing the pea out of her shirt.

"They came by one time and asked about somebody we'd never heard of, which was fairly strange. All I know is the mother's on welfare, and the girl hasn't gone to school since they moved here. When Ted Kraft went to see them—he's the new principal—the mother said she was home-schooling." Henny rapped her knuckles on the table. "School of hard knocks, most likely."

"That would be my guess," Virginia said, getting up to go. "Listen, call me if your folks finish baling this afternoon. Randall and I can bring my dad's truck over after supper and give them a hand."

On the way back to the farm, she couldn't shake the image of Henny at the table, shelling peas, or of Chick Mason—a scrawny kid on a bicycle, making his daily pilgrimage to her house. When word got around that Drew had left town after the accident, Chick, barely eighteen, showed up at the hospital and asked Henny to marry him. She was still in traction, her face purple with bruises, her mouth wired shut.

"Get out of here," she'd hissed at him through the grid of silver wires.

If she had said yes, Chick would have moved her into the yellow house across the street from the garage. He would have carried her from room to room in his big arms, rubbed her feet with his grease-stained fingers to warm them. In the end, Chick had married an energetic woman named Bonnie, who planted tomatoes and hollyhocks in the yard, who walked across the street every morning with cinnamon rolls for Chick and his father. They had three daughters, the oldest one about Randall's age. Virginia reminded herself to be happy for the way Chick's life had turned out.

Braking suddenly, Virginia watched the little blue car burst out of her father's driveway and take off in a swirl of dust. She wasn't sure, but she thought Randall was in the backseat. She raced up the porch steps, calling his name.

"You just missed him," Lydia said. "He's gone swimming with Jodie and Irene." She was at the sink, washing dishes.

"You let him go off without asking me?"

"He said you wouldn't mind." Lydia rinsed three plates and placed them in the drying rack.

"I mind very much. Who are those people, anyway? Do you even know where they're going?"

"That swimming hole near their house. Nathan said he used to take you and Larry over there." Lydia twisted around with a fistful of soapy silverware. "How could we ask you if you weren't here?"

"I was waiting for my car," Virginia reminded her. "Why didn't you call the garage?"

"Randall did call." Lydia turned back to the sink. "Chick said you left more than an hour ago."

"Oh, for crying out loud." Virginia went upstairs to have a word with her father.

Pausing in the doorway, she saw that he had fallen asleep with a book in his hands. Walking softly to the bed, she slipped it from his fingers. It was not, as she expected, one of his mystery novels but a volume of Frost's collected poems. On the flyleaf was an inscription: "Happy 60th Birthday, dear Nathan, with love from Caro." Virginia carried it to the window, but as she turned the pages, her eyes blurred with tears. Listening to the small brown body of a wasp ticking against the screen, she pulled the shades down and left the room.

"I'm sorry about getting upset," Virginia said, back in the kitchen, making herself a sandwich. "But from now on, don't let Randall go anywhere unless he checks with me first. If I'm not here, he can wait."

"I didn't think it mattered," Lydia said. "It looks like he does pretty much what he pleases."

"It does matter. And if Randall were doing what he pleases . . ." Virginia let her voice trail off. They wouldn't be there milking the cows and cutting the hay and putting up with Lydia. She took her sandwich and a jar of water to the tractor shed, sat up on the warm seat to eat her solitary lunch. Lydia's remark bothered her. Randall was definitely not at his best.

After checking the oil, she filled the gas tank and chugged up the hill toward the partially cut field of alfalfa, which looked enormous. Drowsing in the shade, lazily flicking their tails, the cows turned their heads to watch as she went by.

Overhead, the sky was a chalky blue with thin clouds that looked like curdled milk. Virginia once knew a saying about such a sky, but she couldn't remember it. Like other farmers, her father would study the sky and the water in the brook, the leaves on the trees, and predict the weather. More often than not, he got it right. In Laurel Springs, the weather didn't matter that much; it was only something to talk about.

Before long, Lydia came outside—wearing pants, which was unusual—and walked up to the barn. A few minutes later, Virginia saw her in the garden, hoeing weeds. She couldn't help but think Lydia was making a show of doing Randall's work while he was off playing. The night they arrived, right after supper, Lydia had announced the division of labor.

"The way I see it," she'd said, "you and Randall are responsible for all the outside work and the barn work. The house and the cooking, those are mine. Except for the chickens—I take care of them, too. And I take care of Nathan, of course."

Nathan had looked surprised, but he'd said, "Yes. Yes, you do."

Watching Lydia's clumsy attempts with the hoe, the way she stooped to pull the weeds with her hands, it occurred to Virginia that her life with Bob Will would not have been easy—living in the cramped apartment above the Wiggins

Grocery, never knowing when he'd go off drinking. Sometimes he would disappear for two or three days at a time, then Clyde Mason might find him sleeping in one of the cars outside the garage. People said Clyde was a saint for letting Bob Will keep his job. He didn't do that much, either, except pump gas and make change. He was supposed to clean the station, but he tended to let that slide. Women used to come slamming out of the restroom, complaining that there were no paper towels, no soap. "It's filthy in there!" they would exclaim, and then Clyde would send Chick in with a mop and bucket and fresh supplies.

When Virginia was a girl, she'd felt sorry for Bob Will, figuring Lydia would drive anyone to drink. A soft-spoken man with a gentle sense of humor, he gave the impression that life had treated him unfairly. Virginia and Henny often stood around the office, talking to him and drinking their Cokes, while their fathers pumped their own gas. In those days, the fathers were never in a hurry. They would meet each other at Mason's Garage or LaClede's Store, drift into talk about the prices of milk and beef, somebody's new hay baler, and an afternoon would float along until some child finally whined, "Please, can we go now?" or a wife called out from the steps of Wiggins Grocery, "Come and help me carry these sacks."

One time Bob Will told the girls a story about crossing the river on horseback. Not the Monongahela River, but the West Branch of the Susquehanna, in the middle part of the state, where he grew up. It was late winter, he said, and his father had sent him to the doctor to get medicine for his grandfather. On the way back, it started snowing hard, a real blizzard. He knew it would be dark before he could reach the bridge, so he decided to cross over on the ice. He didn't know it, but the ice had already started to break up because of some mild weather the week before, and suddenly he found himself and his horse on a piece that floated free.

"It wasn't much bigger than that door over there," he said, nodding at the entrance to the garage. "And I could feel the horse just start shaking underneath me. I got down slow and hung the saddlebag with the medicine over my shoulder, in case we had to swim for it. The snow was driving in my face, so I was nearly blind. We kept floating, bumping up against great big chunks of ice, me talking to the horse the whole time. Over the noise of the storm, I could hear the ice creaking—like the rigging in one of those old sailing ships. Finally, we snagged up on something solid, and I started walking the horse, sticking my foot out to feel ahead every step, thinking we might go under any minute. We went on like that for what seemed like hours. And I was praying, too, I don't mind telling you."

At last, he said, he felt his boot strike muddy ground, and they scrambled up the riverbank. They had drifted pretty far downstream, so it took him another hour to find his way home. "I'm about frozen by the time I get there, glad to be alive, and I back myself up to the fireplace to tell the story. My old man doesn't even let me finish. He says, 'Well, you damn fool, take the bridge next time. If you'd a lost that horse, your hide wouldn't be worth a nickel.' " Bob Will chuckled, wiped his mouth with the back of his hand as if he'd just downed a shot of whiskey. "Yep," he said. "My old man was tender that way."

When Bob Will stopped talking, the garage was quiet. Clyde and Chick, both bent over the open hood of a car, had stopped what they were doing to listen. Chick, supposedly learning his way around an engine, had been watching Henny the whole time.

Later, riding home with Virginia, Henny said, "I bet that story wasn't true. I bet he read it somewhere."

"That's crazy," Virginia replied. "People don't go around making up stuff like that."

"That's what you think," Henny said.

Virginia had made good progress on the field and Lydia had gone back in the house to start supper when Jodie's car finally returned. Randall, wearing his swimming trunks, got out of the front seat and held the back door for Cleo, who jumped to the ground and shook herself. Randall seemed happy, letting the dog lean against him and patting her side as Jodie backed the car around and tooted her good-bye. When he looked up the hill toward the tractor, Virginia pretended not to see him. If she waved, he might take it as a sign of approval.

Randall was subdued during the milking, his hair still damp and matted. He tried hard to do everything right, and when Virginia asked him how the afternoon had gone, he said only "It was fun."

Eating supper, Randall gradually became more animated, telling Nathan how he and Irene had put up a rope swing and dared Jodie to try it. "She might have a pierced belly button," he said, "but she was still too chicken."

"Who has a pierced belly button?" Lydia asked.

"Jodie," he said, darting a glance at Virginia. "It's weird, I guess, for somebody's mother."

"Does she also have a tattoo?" Virginia asked.

"Just a little one," he said, touching the top of his left thigh. "Right here."

As the two of them drove back to the Eastman place in her father's big blue farm truck, Virginia tried to sound casual. "In case you don't know," she told him, "we have the same rules here as we do at home. If you want to go somewhere, you need to ask me first."

"Give me a break," Randall said. "What was I supposed to do, tell them I had to wait until my mommy got home?"

"I'm sure you could have invented a more manly explanation."

"You're so funny." Randall licked his thumb and rubbed at a cut on the back of his hand.

When they arrived, Virginia was surprised to find West and his three younger boys there, gathering the bales into bunches and then loading them onto a truck nearly identical to the one she was driving. In the distance, she saw Henny's father, still baling at the far end of the field.

"Hey," West said. "The cavalry's here." He and Cody were in the back of the truck, stacking the bales as the others threw them on. After introducing Sam and Hunter, West jumped down and suggested that Randall and Cody work together.

Randall tucked the leather gloves his mother had given him into his back pocket and accepted Cody's hand up into the high truck bed. None of West's boys was wearing gloves. Even with hers on, Virginia could feel the taut baling twine cut into her fingers as she lifted the first bale. She staggered a little, remembering to clench her stomach muscles.

"Ginny," West said. "Drive the truck for us and let the guys load it."

"I'm all right," she assured him. "I need to get the hang of this again."

Sam and Hunter, shirtless, were very tan with farm-boy muscles. They were nimble, too, picking up and tossing the heavy bales as if they were feather pillows. Virginia recognized them as the two she had seen mowing the church lawn. They exchanged a look when Cody asked Randall if he wanted to go riding sometime.

"I don't know," Randall said.

"Don't do it," Sam said, shaking his head with mock seriousness.

"Yeah," Hunter chimed in. "Our mom was hoping for a girl she could go riding with, but she got old Cody instead. So she decided to buy him a horse and make the best of it."

"Ignore them," Cody said. "They're jealous."

Virginia smiled. Growing up, the boys she knew wouldn't be caught dead on a horse. They either hitchhiked or rode bicycles until they were old enough to get a driver's license, and then they wanted a secondhand pickup. Unlike his brothers, Cody was slight, with his mother's blue eyes. As they moved down the field, Virginia remembered Henny telling her about Cody being in the hospital a few years ago. Pneumonia, she thought it was, or maybe something worse.

Soon her shirt was soaked with sweat and her forearms covered with scratches. Her shoulders ached. Even so, she began to feel lighthearted, watching the truck fill up, breathing the sweet, dry scent of freshly made hay. The sky was losing its color as evening came, the hills above them looming darker. Virginia imagined they could go on and on and never finish.

It was nearly dark when they did. Sam and Hunter sprawled in the grass in front of the house, groaning, scraps of hay clinging to their hair. Cody came out of the house with two bottles of Liza Eastman's homemade root beer and gave one to Randall.

"Where's ours?" Sam said.

Henny's father appeared with a cooler and began passing

drinks around. "A hundred and fifty bales," he said, handing a Rolling Rock to West. "Not a bad day's work."

Virginia took one, too, and held the cool green bottle against her cheek.

"I thought you were an Iron City man, Roland," West said, sitting near Virginia on the porch steps.

"I go back and forth," Henny's father said. "In point of fact, I don't drink that much these days."

"Same here." West tilted his head back and took a long swallow.

"Where's Henny?" Virginia asked Liza when she brought out two bowls of salted popcorn.

"I think she's gone to bed."

"Henny, get out here," West called. "Or I'm coming in after you."

"All right already." Henny's voice was muffled. "Give me two seconds."

"I wish Weston could be here," he said, watching Sam and Hunter pulling their shirts on.

"Is he working tonight?" Virginia asked.

"He is. For some reason, I hate to think about him waiting tables, even if he is making good money." He took another long pull on his beer. "He doesn't have any thoughts of getting into farming, that's for sure."

"Can't say I blame him," Liza said.

Virginia heard the screen door creaking open and got up to hold it as Henny wheeled through. With his beer in one hand, West scooped Henny into his arms and did a little twirl.

"What do you think you're doing?"

"Stop complaining. Join the party." He twirled once more and set her down on the step.

Out of her chair, Henny looked small and unprotected.

She straightened the blanket over her legs and asked for a root beer.

"Henny Hennis," West said, lightly rubbing her back. "The one and only."

As Virginia sat down again on her other side, the boys looked up all at once. "Shooting star," Cody said. "Make a wish."

Virginia leaned against Henny for a minute, thinking back to the Easter night twenty-three years before, the night Drew smashed his car into a concrete bridge. Virginia had been home from college, visiting her family. When Sissy called with the news, sometime after midnight, she was the one who got up to answer the phone. She threw on her clothes and drove alone in her father's pickup to the hospital in Fayette. Sissy and Jere were there already, and Henny's parents and brothers, sitting on the vinyl couches outside the emergency room.

"They're still working on Henny," Sissy told her.

"Working on her," Virginia said. "My God."

She could remember looking out the window at the nearly deserted parking lot. The ambulance that had brought Henny and Drew was parked near the emergency entrance. Inside it, she saw two men in tan jackets drinking coffee, their faces a ghostly green, illuminated by a small blinking light on the dashboard. She had turned away by the time West drove in, so she didn't see him until he was standing in front of her. They hadn't been in the same room since their high school graduation.

He didn't say anything, but when he opened his arms, she stepped into them. He held her close, and she let her head rest on his shoulder. He smelled like cold air, as if he'd come in from a long time outdoors. Clasping her hands behind West's back, Virginia felt the hard nub of her new engagement ring. Rob was at her parents' house, sleeping in Aunt Ida's room.

Anxious to get to the hospital, she hadn't thought to wake him, or anyone else.

Down below, the boys were lying on their backs, eating popcorn, talking in low voices. Virginia heard one of West's boys asking which was the Dog Star and Randall explaining how to find it. Henny's parents were side by side on the porch swing, nearly asleep. The fireflies had come out. They were up high, in the trees—hundreds of tiny, hopeful flickers.

Chapter Seven

———

Wakened by the sound of a car door slamming, Virginia turned on her side and squinted at the clock on the bookcase: 11:26. She lay on her back again, listening to Rob climbing the steps, crossing the porch, opening the kitchen door. All day, she had been excited about seeing him, and now it was so late. They had expected him in time for supper, but he'd called from the hospital to say he wouldn't be able to leave until 7:00.

She heard him bump against the table and then Randall's footsteps in the hallway. "Dad?" he called softly from the top of the stairs.

When she got to the kitchen, Rob and Randall were standing together in the circle of light from the small lamp on the sideboard. Rob glanced up as Virginia stepped through the doorway and gave her an appraising look. It was the way he might look at an old friend who had been through some trouble, calculating its effect. There was a slight chill in the moment.

"You made good time, didn't you?" Virginia moved ahead, into his embrace. His shirt was cool from the air-conditioning in the car.

He kissed her hair, brushed it behind her ears. "I thought you might wait up for me."

"City guy," Randall said. "Don't you know anything about farmers' hours?"

"Different from doctors' hours?" Rob smiled at them. "This country life must agree with you. Both of you look healthy as horses."

"That's exactly what we're going for," Randall said.

Virginia offered to make hot chocolate, but Randall declined, yawning and moving off toward the stairs. "I'm done in, too," Rob said. "I had four surgeries today, and the last one was a bitch."

Upstairs, Virginia and Rob pushed the twin beds together and fumbled through the sheets until they found each other. She asked him to rub her back and shivered as he lifted her nightgown. He hovered over her, kissing his way up her spine, pausing when he reached the top.

"The nape of the neck," he said, running his thumb along the downy hollow, "must be the sweetest spot on the human body." He kissed her there. "It gets to me every time. Even the nastiest, gnarliest patient—if I see the back of his neck as he's going under, I always feel sorry for everything that's about to happen to him." Lying down beside her, he rubbed the space between Virginia's shoulder blades with the tips of his fingers until she felt the muscles relaxing.

When the alarm started beeping at 4:45, Rob stirred and opened his eyes, but Virginia knew he didn't see her. She lunged for the clock, which she kept on the far side of the room, and shut it off. Dressed in her barn clothes—stiff and pungent, in need of washing—she leaned across the bed and pulled the sheet up over Rob's chest.

She and Randall were hooking the last six cows to the machine when Rob and her father came into the milking parlor together. Walking with a cane, Nathan moved stiffly. His face still bore the marks of his slide down the hill. Rob looked groggy, his eyes puffy from sleep. "You two . . . ," she began.

"Don't look so hot," Randall said, laughing. He came to life under his father's gaze, quickly and expertly fitting the rubber cups in place, patting the cows on the rump. Switching on the machine, he watched the flow of milk into the floor pail.

That was the first time her father had walked as far as the barn, and Virginia knew he'd done it to prove something to Rob. She had once overheard him telling her mother that Rob was too concerned about keeping his hands clean. "A strapping fellow like that," he'd said after a day of loading hay, "and he's a bit dainty, afraid of getting a callus."

Always Rob's champion, her mother had replied, "Well, of course he is. He needs those hands."

"And what about mine?" Nathan had asked her.

Now he was making an effort to hold himself upright and compliment Randall on his progress with the milking. He had also shaved that morning—or allowed Lydia to shave him. There was a dot of dried blood on his chin.

Randall was not only touching the cows but talking to them, giving them names like Dixie and Curly Top and Little Jeanie. He explained to Rob how the vacuum pump worked, the way it pulsed on and off to mimic the action of human hands. He talked about the superiority of milk from grass-fed cows. Overnight, he had become an expert on dairy farming. Virginia suspected he'd been thumbing through her father's magazines when he shut himself into the office to make his many phone calls.

On the way back to the house, Rob let Randall walk ahead with Nathan. "He's really taking to this, isn't he?" he asked Virginia. "I didn't think you'd have such an easy time of it."

"Right," she said. "Piece of cake."

At breakfast, Lydia fussed over Rob, asking how he wanted his eggs cooked, whether he liked his toast light or dark. Virginia was secretly pleased by the flicker of irritation on her father's face as he tried to cut his bacon with the side of his fork. Normally, Lydia gave him her undivided attention, cut everything into bite-size pieces before she put his plate on the table.

"Nathan, you have two tractors," Rob said as Lydia poured his coffee.

"That New Holland tractor belongs to West Moffat," Nathan told him.

"He's helping us with the haying," Randall said. "We loaded bales at their place on Wednesday, and he brought his tractor over here yesterday to do the raking."

"I thought he quit farming." Rob buttered his toast methodically, making sure he reached the edges. "Isn't he doing something with fish?"

"Trout," Randall said. "They raise them in ponds."

"They still have the dairy operation, too," Nathan said, giving up on the bacon, pushing his plate away. "That fellow puts in a long day."

"Cody said they had to diversify," Randall explained.

"That's diverse, all right," Rob said. "Next thing you know, he'll start raising bats."

"I need to move along," Virginia said. "I told West I'd have the middle field baled by this afternoon. He said they'd come around three to help us load."

"Don't you ever take a day off?" Rob asked her.

"Tomorrow," she said. "Once we finish milking, we can goof off all day. Until five, anyway."

"Maybe you could show me how to drive one of those tractors," Rob suggested halfheartedly.

Virginia told him that West had finished raking the field, leaving it ready for her to bale. Her father had a project in mind for Rob and Randall—building a new three-sided shelter in the pigs' pen. He had bought the wood and the aluminum roofing but hadn't gotten to it before his accident.

"They're decent pigs," Randall told his father. "Two brown Hampshires named Bubble and Squeak."

Lydia walked out with Virginia, on her way to the chicken house to collect eggs. "Your husband is a nice man," she said, in a tone that left Virginia puzzled.

"Yes," she agreed. "He is."

Out in the field, with the steady *thump* of the hay baler behind her, Virginia wondered what Lydia had meant. Maybe her father had said something. Virginia knew it bothered him that Rob had never taken much of an interest in the farm. Rob could not, for instance, have begun to appreciate the rows of raked hay West had left for her. From a distance, they looked as neat as braided cornrows on a young girl's head. They fed easily into the baler, producing uniform, compact bales. The afternoon before, crisscrossing the field with the tedder, West behind her with the rake, she'd been reminded of how West's father had once made the best hay in the county.

Back when West and Virginia broke up, late in the fall of their senior year, she'd believed that her parents, her father especially, would be sorry, so she had tried to hide it from them. They would have noticed that she took the bus to school instead of riding with West, that weekends came and went with no sign of him, but they didn't mention it, either. Then the week before Christmas, she heard West drive up to the front of the house one afternoon. She went outside and climbed into his truck.

"I brought you a present," he said. The inside of the cab was warm, the windshield wipers flapping against the steady fall of wet snowflakes.

"I can't accept it," she told him, touching the window, leaving behind a fingerprint on the damp surface of the glass.

"Yes, you can." He took a box wrapped in gold foil from his jacket pocket. "This is a nicer way of saying good-bye. It's a memory."

Inside the package was a delicate silver chain with a silver heart. Virginia held it in her palm, aware of the beating of her own heart. "You mean a memento?"

"Maybe."

She unhooked the clasp and slipped the chain around her neck, tucking the small heart under the collar of her sweater. "Thank you," she said. "But you know this doesn't change anything."

West leaned across the seat and kissed her cheek. "I do know," he said.

When she went back into the house, her parents were waiting together, as if they expected some news. "We broke up," she said. "For good." She felt the locket settle into the hollow of her collarbone as West pulled away.

Her father looked at her for a long minute before he left the room, but her mother put her arm around Virginia's shoulder. "I know this is hard for you," she said in a way that made Virginia feel she'd done the right thing. Virginia could see their reflection in the window above the sink, blurred by the twilight and the blowing snow. Her mother was slightly taller, her hair like a halo in the humid kitchen.

Virginia had worn the locket until she and Rob got engaged, and then she put it away in the cigar box in the closet of her old bedroom. The night West gave it to her, she'd snapped it open and found their initials engraved inside: VR & WM. And below, 1963, the year they were born—two months apart, at the hospital in Fayette.

As she turned the tractor on the far side of the field, Virginia was thinking about that necklace, tarnished now, lying in the box with her school pictures, when she caught a glimpse of Rob and Randall, carrying boards out of the barn. Earlier, outside the tractor shed, where Rob had helped her unhitch the tedder and hook on the baler, he'd suggested the two of them go out somewhere for dinner.

"A Saturday night date," he said. "I even brought a dress for you."

"Are you serious?"

"I figured you wouldn't have one with you, in your farmer's wardrobe. I brought shoes, too, those strappy ones I like."

"You're unbelievable."

She had tried to sound enthusiastic, but after haying, nothing was more appealing than a cold beer and a shower, dropping into bed as soon as it got dark.

From the field where she was working, the house and barn were indistinct shapes through the trees growing along the brook. When she noticed a flash of blue, Virginia guessed it was Jodie's car. Jodie had gotten into the habit of dropping Irene off and leaving her there for hours.

The first time, Irene had seemed embarrassed, not quite sure what to do with herself. She had hovered near Randall, watching him scrape paint from the porch railings. "What are you doing, anyway?" she asked him.

"Getting this old stuff off so I can repaint," he explained.

"Maybe you'd like to help him," Virginia suggested. "I could find another scraper for you."

Irene watched for a few minutes. "I don't think so. I'll sit here on the steps and keep him company."

As Virginia was gassing up the tractor, she heard Irene say, "Randy, I bet you have a lot of girlfriends back in Maryland, don't you?"

"Tons," Virginia called out. "I have to drive him to school in an armored car."

"What's that mean?" Irene asked.

"It's my mother's idea of a joke," Randall said, making the paint chips fly.

By lunchtime that day, Irene seemed right at home, slathering mayonnaise and mustard on the bread as she helped Lydia make sandwiches. She made a show of filling glasses with ice, carrying a pitcher of cold tea to the table, as if everything she did were extremely important and difficult.

"Randy, do you like pickles?" She giggled, reaching into the jar and holding up a misshapen dill spear.

Lydia told her to sit down and be sensible.

Later that day, Virginia agreed to take them for a swim. As they drove up to the old Jameson place so Irene could change into her bathing suit, Virginia glimpsed a man inside the house. Wearing a cap and smoking a cigarette, leaning against the wall near the door, he moved out of sight when he heard the car. There was no other car in the driveway.

"It doesn't look like your mother's at home," Virginia said. "And somebody's in the house. Why don't we come back later?"

"No, it's okay," Irene said. "That's her friend. She probably went to the store or something."

When Virginia asked if Irene wanted her to go in, too, Irene laughed and shook her head.

The house, which had looked so sturdy when the Jamesons lived there, seemed to be sagging at every corner. Moss was growing on the shingles at the edge of the roof. The man stepped outside, exhaling a cloud of smoke as he held the door for Irene. He nodded in the direction of the car, tossed his cigarette butt into the weeds, and went back in.

"He was here the other day, too," Randall said. "Jodie called him Lee."

"Her boyfriend?"

"Don't know." Randall lowered his voice. "He's a little weird. He hardly ever says anything."

Noticing a new sound, a kind of whirring mixed in with the regular clamor of the hay baler, Virginia stopped the tractor and got down. The last few bales had broken apart and lay scattered. When she walked back to look at them, she discovered there was no twine holding them together. There should have been plenty, because she'd installed a new roll herself. It had taken nearly two hours, with the John Deere manual open beside her. She peered in under the cover of the baler and saw that somehow the twine had come out of the guides and snarled itself into a knot. She would have to walk down to the house and ask her father's advice.

Virginia heard Jodie's voice before she saw her. In the ell of the barn, Jodie and Irene were sitting on top of the fence, watching Rob and Randall removing rotten boards with a crowbar. Jodie's hair was a new color, a sort of dark orange. Their jewelry glittered in the sun.

"I was just telling Randy, I see now where he gets his good looks," Jodie said when she saw Virginia. "No offense to you, of course."

"None taken." Virginia noticed thumb-size bruises on Jodie's thighs. Mother and daughter were dressed in their matching cut-offs, the moons of their knees tilted toward Rob.

"What's up?" he asked, crossing his eyes at Virginia, a sign that he wanted her to take those two off his hands.

"I'm having a problem with the baler. I was going to ask my dad about it." Virginia shrugged back at him.

In the far corner of the pen, half-grown Bubble and Squeak stood together, watching the humans, their pink noses sniffing the air. They were sweet, but Virginia had learned never to get attached to the pigs, who would be butchered the day before Thanksgiving.

She found her father propped up on the living room couch, reading a week-old newspaper, Cleo on the floor beside him. "I heard you shut the tractor off," he said.

"I've got six or seven broken bales out there. Something's gone wrong with the twine. It's all tangled up."

"I had that problem last summer, too," Nathan said, hoisting himself upright. "But I thought I'd fixed it."

"What should I do?"

"Drive me out in the truck, and I'll take a look at it."

"Are you sure?"

"Hell yes. I'm going to turn into some kind of fungus, laying around the house all the time."

"Lying, Dad."

"That, too," he said.

Virginia found a pair of shears and a hand rake and helped her father into the cab. Cleo jumped in and sat next to him. Virginia drove slowly, watching the cows scatter as they approached the ford in the brook. Her father braced himself with his right hand against the dashboard.

"I would like to know what that woman has on her mind," he said.

"Lydia?"

"No. That mouthy one with the eye makeup and the over-excited girl."

"Ah, Jodie. Right now, I believe she has Rob on her mind."

"Well, you want to keep an eye on that situation. With Randall and the girl, I mean." He looked away. "She spends too much time over here."

"Don't worry, Dad. I'm all over it."

"Are you?"

He whistled when he lifted the cover of the baler. "You've got a real mess in here. Give me those shears."

"Let me," Virginia insisted. "You tell me what to do."

Within half an hour she had cut away the tangle and rethreaded the twine. "Keep your fingers crossed," she said. "I'll drive you back to the house before I rake up those broken ones."

"I don't feel like going back to the house. Drive me up a little higher. I'd like to sit out here in the truck for a while."

By seven o'clock, Virginia and Rob were on the highway to Fayette, where they had a reservation at the Washington Inn. Rob's car was more luxurious than hers, and it was a pleasure to relax in the cushy seat. She had showered away her tiredness, shaved her legs for the first time in two weeks, put on the dress he'd brought for her. It was black silk with a deep V neckline, a bit fancy for where they were going. Virginia thought it made her shoulders look too bony, but her friend Jan had insisted she buy it.

Rob reached across the small space between them and took her hand, kissed her knuckles, which were scratched and bruised. "Why don't we run away together?" he said.

"We are running away together."

"Oh, good."

He slid a disc into the CD player. It was one she hadn't heard before, jazz piano. The road curved into the distance ahead, the river on their left—deep green with ink black shadows along the shore. On the right, a long stretch of field was newly cut, a red tractor at one end. From the porch of the farmhouse, a child waved as the sleek silver car went by.

The dining room of the Washington Inn was dimly lit, somewhat musty. There were a few other diners—mostly older couples, picking at their baked chicken and talking quietly. They ordered steamed mussels and veal scallopini and an expensive bottle of wine. The mussels were overcooked and the veal slightly tough, but the wine started to work its magic, helping them through the awkwardness that came with having spent so much time apart.

"I'm surprised we didn't get carded," Rob said. "The rest of these birds have us beat by at least thirty years. Our waiter must be a hundred and two."

"Careful. They'll hear you."

"I doubt it. I'll bet they're all deaf as doorknobs."

"I'm sure the Daily Catch is a more happening place, but I thought we'd be overdressed for clams and French fries. That's where West's son works, his oldest."

"How many sons does he have, exactly?"

"Four."

Rob concentrated on his dinner, cutting neat squares of veal, pushing mushroom slices onto the back of his fork with his knife. He ate in the European way—left-handed. Virginia used to think it was an affectation until it occurred to her that he'd learned it from Maria, the Italian woman he'd dated before they met. From time to time, just watching him eat could make her jealous.

"Randall had a good time working with you today," she said. "He's been missing you."

"He's getting to be quite the guy." Rob poured each of them a half glass of wine, emptying the bottle.

"Sometimes I wonder how it would have been if we'd had another. Do you ever think about that?"

"Never. Why?"

"Oh, I don't know." The way he was looking at her made her wish she could take the question back. "Maybe it's seeing him with Cody lately . . . I wonder if being an only child isn't a little lonely."

"Are you thinking of Randall or yourself?" Rob picked up his knife and fork again and took a last bite.

Virginia had told him, before they married, that she hoped to have many children. They had eventually agreed on two and then waited to have the first until Rob finished his medical training. And somewhere in the midst of Rob getting his practice under way and Virginia starting a new teaching job and their buying the house, he had proposed a vasectomy. She remembered the evening he sat in their one comfortable chair with an ice bag on his lap, sipping Scotch and joking with a doctor friend who'd stopped by to see how he was doing. It had happened too fast.

When the waiter approached their table to take away the plates, Rob asked for two coffees and a crème caramel. They were the last ones left in the dining room.

"Anyway," Virginia said. "My dad's concerned about Randall. He's afraid Irene will lead him astray."

"I wouldn't be surprised if she made a good effort."

"My dad thinks I should talk to Jodie."

"And say what?"

"Something about keeping Irene at home more. Honestly, I feel sorry for that girl. I don't think she has any friends."

"She's not your responsibility, you know."

"True, but still . . ." Virginia realigned the salt and pepper shakers, straightened the packets of sugar in their crystal dish. Rob was always advising her not to get too involved with her students, the troubled ones who needed a sympathetic ear. She had tried explaining to him that an art class was a place where deep feelings might rise to the surface. He would make her laugh then, insisting that a swirl of black paint was not necessarily a cry for help.

"Randall will be fine," Rob said, slicing the crème caramel into identical halves. "We had the sex talk two years ago, so he's informed." He held up a hand, anticipating her response. "We also discussed the importance of respecting young women, the emotional hazards of getting involved too young, all that."

"Two years ago, it was only theoretical," Virginia said.

They hadn't quite finished eating when they heard someone vacuuming the hall outside the dining room. "No hurry," the waiter assured them, sliding their check onto the table.

Driving back to the farm, they began making up a story in which Jodie was an escapee from the witness protection program and Lee a federal agent trying to rein her in.

"I think this needs to be a musical," Virginia said. "I see Irene in tap shoes and a swirly red dress."

"She's not Jodie's daughter at all, but an orphan exploited by the FBI," Rob added. "In fact, there is a whole orphanage of singing, dancing kids who get farmed out to live with witnesses in hiding, to make them seem like normal people with families."

"But the orphans get sick of it and revolt. They want to be adopted by actual normal people, or at least live together in the orphanage, where they're free to dance up and down the stairs at the drop of a hat."

"Irene is their ringleader," Rob said. "I see a big production number in that red dress—"

He was interrupted by a deer leaping from the bank beside the road. The headlights caught it, suspended in midair above the car. For one terrifying instant, Virginia thought it was going to crash through the windshield, but they heard its hooves strike the hood and saw the flash of white tail as it landed on the other side. Rob slowed the car, and she turned to see that the deer had fallen on its knees. As she watched, it rose and shook itself, then disappeared into the trees. Later, in the light from the porch, they could see where its feet had left an impression—the sharp points of the hooves stamped into the metal of the hood.

The next morning, as Virginia was getting out of bed to turn off the alarm clock, Rob caught her ankle and pulled her back under the covers. "Don't go," he whispered.

She lay still for a moment, listening to the insistent beeping of the clock, worried that it would wake her father and Lydia. Her head hurt from too much wine and too little sleep. "I know," she said, sitting up. "You come with me. We can let Randall have a morning off."

"Is that your best offer?" he asked, sliding a hand across her thigh.

"I'm afraid so." She crossed the room and punched the alarm button.

"I don't think these cows like me," Rob complained, as he tried to help her. Wearing her father's barn jacket, which was too short in the sleeves, and her father's boots, a size too small, Rob leaned hard against one of the Jerseys, trying to keep her from pushing her way into the milking parlor. "It's not your turn yet," he insisted, pushing back.

"Don't fight with them," Virginia said over her shoulder, as she began washing the teats of the first six. "You have to sweet-talk those girls. Ask her nicely to step back so you can close the gate."

"Sure," he said. When he relaxed, the cow slipped beneath his arm and, instinctively, he grabbed her in a headlock, digging in his heels.

"Dad, what are you doing?" Randall walked through from the front of the barn, surprising them. "Dixie," he said, "behave yourself." Rob stepped aside, and Randall gave the cow a friendly swat and turned her with one hand on her neck. When she was back in the holding area, he swung the wooden gate into place and latched it.

"She's the worst," Randall said.

"We wanted to let you sleep." Virginia stepped aside so he could hook up the milking claws. "How come you're up so early?"

"Good question." He watched his father brushing himself off. "Did you guys have fun last night?"

"Yes, we did," Rob said. "What about you?"

"Cody came over with his clarinet, and we played some tunes together. He's actually not that bad."

"Did he come on his horse?" Rob asked.

"Sam drove him," Randall said. "He stayed and pretended he was playing drums on the kitchen table. Kind of a pain."

"That must have been a treat for your grandfather and Lydia," Rob said. "You and your band."

"They didn't care. They were in the living room, watching TV." Randall walked over to check the flow rate. "Unchaperoned."

Chapter Eight

———————————

By the time Virginia arrived with Cody and Irene, Randall had nearly reached the bottom of the narrow path that snaked down the hill toward Richard's Falls. Rob, with Henny in his arms, was just behind him.

"We're here," Cody called as Virginia unloaded the picnic gear from her car. Cody had arrived at the farm while Rob was still cooking Sunday breakfast, and they were figuring out the logistics of getting everyone into Rob's car when Randall said he "might have mentioned" the picnic to Irene.

Sitting on her stoop, Irene had brightened momentarily when Virginia and Cody arrived to pick her up. "Where's Randy?" she asked, wrinkling her nose as she got into the backseat with Cleo.

"We'll meet him there," Virginia said. Jodie's car was gone, and the house looked dark and quiet. "Isn't your mother around?"

"She and Lee went to some party," Irene said finally. "They're not back yet."

"You mean you were here alone last night?"

"Yeah." She gave Cody a lopsided smile when he turned in the seat to look at her. "No big thing."

"You could have called us," Virginia said. "If you were worried."

"Oh, I don't mind it. Besides, we don't have a phone, remember?"

Watching Rob and Randall disappear around the final bend, Irene said, "That looked like the wheelchair lady. What's she doing out here?" She tossed a towel over her shoulder and started down the path, leaving Virginia and Cody to carry everything else. He had persuaded Virginia to stop at Spurling's Store and buy him a diving mask, even though she assured him there was nothing in the water except rusted beer cans.

Irene and Randall were already wading into the shallow pool beneath the falls when they got there. Down below, standing beside the larger, deeper pool, Rob was arguing with Henny about whether or not she would go in.

"I'd sink like a ton of bricks," she was saying.

"Not if I hold you up," he insisted. "You'll see."

Finally, he set Henny down on the lip of stone, where she could dangle her feet in the water. In the oversize shorts that must have belonged to her mother, Henny's legs were scrawny and pale, the knobs of her knees waxy. The seam of a scar ran the length of one shin.

Distracted by shrieking from above, Rob said, "I think some parental oversight might be in order."

"You two go ahead." Cody pulled on his mask and slid into the water. "I'll stay here and find a treasure for Henny."

As Virginia and Rob approached, Irene was ordering Randall to crouch down so she could sit on his shoulders. "Watch this," she called to them, curling her legs under his arms and crossing her ankles behind his back. "Okay, you can stand up now," she said, lifting her arms above her head.

Randall straightened slowly, thrusting one leg forward to balance himself. His arms and back had already grown stronger from the farmwork, but in his baggy surfer trunks, his legs looked no bigger than Henny's.

"I can't believe he got her up," Virginia whispered. "He's stronger than I thought."

"He's highly motivated."

They could see Randall's arms tremble as he tried to help Irene into a standing position. When her feet slipped, she clutched his head to steady herself.

"Great," Rob said. "Now she's going to give him a compression fracture." He waded in and grasped Irene firmly by the waist.

"We weren't finished," she complained as he lifted her down.

"Let's not do that again," he said. "It's a good way to kill someone's back."

"Oh yeah, he's a doctor." Grinning at Randall and then at Rob, adjusting the top of her bathing suit, she walked into the falls and stood with her back to them, hunching her shoulders as the water poured down.

Randall joined her, moving closer as she took a step away from him.

Below, Cody was bringing something to the surface and handing it to Henny. She held it on her open palm, studying it. He dove again, the pink soles of his feet visible for a moment. With one kick, he aimed a spray of water at Henny, who leaned away, laughing.

"Henny didn't want to come," Rob said. "When we got to her house, she said she'd changed her mind. Randall had to persuade her."

"We used to spend a lot of time here when we were kids." Virginia saw Randall and Irene climbing the rocks toward the top of the falls. "It's slippery up there," she shouted to them. "Be careful."

"Why haven't we come here before?" Rob asked. "It's kind of nice."

"I haven't been here for ages myself."

The last time, she told Rob, she and West had left a school dance to meet Drew and Henny. By then, the beginning of their senior year, they didn't really see Henny outside of school. She and Drew spent most of their time together drinking and driving. And having sex. "It's something he's good at," Henny told her once. Virginia felt sorry for the way Drew cut her off from everyone. And she envied her friend a little. How thrilling not to give a damn what anybody thought of you.

"They'd been here for a while, drinking rum and Coke," Virginia went on. She remembered the practiced way Drew poured half the can of cola on the ground, then added rum from the bottle. It was too sweet, and the alcohol burned her throat, but she drank it anyway. The lavender dress and matching shoes that had seemed so perfect at the dance began to embarrass her, so she took the shoes off and tossed them into the darkness, then slipped her panty hose off, too. She sat at the edge of the pool, splashing the water with her toes, sipping steadily from the can. She could hear West and Henny and Drew talking nearby, and West telling her to go easy, but she wasn't able to answer. After a while, lying on her back, looking up at the sky, she was aware of the wilting gardenia corsage still pinned to her dress, the hard, cool stone beneath her. She tilted her head back and saw West standing on one side of her in his blue blazer and corduroys, Drew on the other, wearing a flannel shirt and jeans.

"It's a nice night," Drew said, smiling down at her. "I think I'll go in." As she watched, he unbuttoned his shirt. Then he stepped out of his jeans. In the hazy moonlight, his body glowed. Virginia let her eyes rest on the smooth muscles of his stomach, the curve of his penis, the dark blond hairs curling against his pale flesh. "What about you?" he asked, flexing his hands.

All she could do was look.

"Let's go, Ginny." West took her hands and pulled her to her feet.

"Wait," she said, dizzy as they started away. "What about Henny?"

Stepping out of the shadows to stand beside Drew, Henny gave an almost imperceptible shake of her head.

They had gone a few miles in the truck when Virginia noticed that her feet were cold. She had left the lavender shoes behind, the shoes her mother had bought with her egg money.

When they got to her house, West said, "Good night, Ginny." He didn't walk her to the door, and he didn't kiss her. The next time she saw him, he acted as if it had never happened.

"After all this time," she said to Rob, "it's still mysterious to me."

"What is? That Drew was trying to come between you and Henny?"

"I understood that much." She was watching Randall and Irene on the rocks high above the falls. "I was convinced I'd done something wrong, but I couldn't figure out what."

Rob got to his feet, held his hand out to Virginia, and led her into the water.

The cold stung her toes. She had never told Rob the story of how she and West broke up a few weeks later.

"You'll get used to it in a minute," Rob said, rubbing her arms with his two hands, as they stood in the knee-deep pool. "That son of a bitch wasn't even hurt when he crashed his car, was he?"

"Drew broke his wrist. The last time I saw him, he was walking out of the hospital with his father, while Henny was still in surgery. He went to visit her once, three or four days later." Not long after that, he sent Henny a letter with a Michigan postmark, no return address. Henny wouldn't let her read it.

"And she never went out with anyone else?"

"Not before or since. She was offended when Chick Mason asked her to marry him. Twice. Once at the hospital and once after she got home."

"Well, Chick was lucky."

"I suppose."

Virginia and Rob moved under the falls, letting the cold water pour over their heads. When they came out, gulping air, Randall and Irene were still on the rocks above.

"Those two are having a real heart-to-heart," Rob said.

"Maybe she's telling him how her mother went off to a party and left her alone all night."

"Oh, those troubled girls," Rob said. "They do get a fellow mixed up inside."

"The voice of experience."

"I've told you before, you were a godsend."

Cody burst out of the water as they reached Henny, tugging his mask off and holding up an oval stone the size of a robin's egg. He had made a circle of similar stones on the ledge beside her. Some were tan, some light gray with darker veins, some flecked with mica. "Feel how smooth these are," he said. "Aren't they pretty?"

His hair was slicked back and his cheeks flushed, his features clean and precise. Virginia was wishing she had brought her sketchbook and pencils along, but maybe that would have embarrassed him.

"Good, they're coming." Cody nodded at Randall and Irene, who were making their way down the rocks. "Now we can eat."

Intrigued by the stones Cody had found, Randall had to try out the diving mask first. Irene sank down next to Henny, sighing deeply. She was fifteen, a year older than Randall. Absently fingering the little stones, she tossed one back in the water. When she picked up another, Henny clamped her hand on Irene's wrist.

"Cut it out," Henny said. "Those are mine."

"They're only dumb rocks," Irene said, pulling her arm away.

"Cody gave them to me, and I want them."

"Fine." Irene wandered off, pretending to be interested in a plant with a spiky yellow flower growing near the water's edge. Cleo followed, wagging her tail, and Irene told the dog to go away.

Irene was uncharacteristically quiet as they ate their picnic of fried chicken and potato salad and sliced watermelon. She seemed bored by Randall and Cody's talk of playing music, their idea of getting a jazz combo together to practice during the summer. The only time she perked up was when Cody mentioned Agatha Mason, who played the piano.

"Who's that?" Irene asked, setting her plate aside, licking her fingers.

"Chick's daughter," Cody told her. "The oldest one."

As they were packing up to leave, Virginia heard Irene tell Randall he should ride in their car. "Put the dog up front and sit in the back with me," she said.

Nearing Irene's house, Virginia saw five or six cars and a couple of motorcycles filling the driveway. Music was booming through the open windows and doors.

"Looks like you have company," Randall remarked.

"Guess so." Irene opened the car door before Virginia had come to a full stop. "See you. Thanks for everything."

"I'll come in with you," Virginia said. "I want to say hello to your mom."

"You don't need to."

"Be right back," Virginia told Randall. "Wait here."

Wherever Jodie had been the night before, she had brought the party home with her. Virginia and Irene walked into a din of music and voices, a haze of smoke. Most of the twenty or so people crowded into the small space were sitting on the floor or leaning against the walls. At one end of the couch, a woman was sound asleep, an empty tequila bottle and a crumpled bag of chips on the coffee table nearby. Virginia spotted Jodie in the kitchen, sitting on the counter, Lee beside her, waving a cigarette as he talked.

"Come on," she said, taking Irene by the arm.

As they crossed the room, a man with long sideburns and a goatee stuck his foot out to stop them. "Who's your friend?" he asked, staring at Irene's tattoo.

The woman next to him laughed and swatted his leg.

"Well, Virginia, you're the last person I expected to see here," Jodie called out. "Come on over and get yourself a drink."

"We can't stay," Virginia said, making a sudden decision. "We came by to get Irene's things. The kids want to get up early to go fishing tomorrow, and I thought it would be easier if Irene spent the night at the farm."

"Fishing?" Lee reached out and tapped Irene under the chin. "I can't see this girl sticking a worm on a hook."

"I'm sure Randy will do it for her." Jodie winked at her daughter.

"I'll bring her back tomorrow afternoon."

"Okay by me," Jodie said. "Have fun."

Virginia was going outside to wait for Irene when she realized that Lee had followed her. "After you," he said, holding the screen door.

In the bright sun, he looked older. Leaning against the metal railing of the stoop, setting his drink down, he seemed exhausted.

"You don't know who I am," he said.

Virginia looked at him more closely. "What do you mean?"

"I used a live here." He jerked his head toward the house. "Leroy Jameson."

"Roy?" Maybe there was something familiar about his eyes; she wasn't sure.

"I switched to Lee. What I wanted a say was, I heard about your mother dying. I felt real bad about it."

"She always wondered what happened to you."

"She'd be the only one, I expect."

Virginia wasn't sure why she was so surprised that he'd turned up again. It didn't seem right for some reason. "How's your brother? Roger."

"You look like your mother," Lee said. He reached for his drink, stirred it with his finger. "Roger got killed back in 1991. Kuwait, two days before the cease-fire."

"He was in the Marines?"

"Army. He joined up after high school."

"I'm so sorry to hear that." Virginia had a vague memory of Roger crying in their kitchen one morning, telling her mother he'd lost the new mittens she'd bought him. Her father found them later that day, frozen in the snow behind the barn, where Roy had hidden them.

"That makes us a couple a sorry people."

She wanted to ask him where they'd gone when they moved away, whether Roger had a wife and children, but just then Randall got out of the car.

"What's going on?" he asked, watching Lee.

"Irene is coming home with us for tonight. So we can get an early start tomorrow."

"Okay." Randall was taking in the scene through the living room window.

"Another thing," Lee said as he started inside. "I know you're not going fishing."

When Irene came out at last, she was carrying a pink backpack covered with flower decals and a dingy white teddy bear with a purple ribbon around its neck. "Randy, meet Snowball," she said, touching the bear's nose to his.

———

Back at the farm, Rob was outside, the trunk of his car open. He gave Virginia a curious look as Randall led Irene into the farmhouse, carrying her pack. "Is it my imagination, or is she here for a sleepover?"

"You should have seen all the lowlifes packed into their house—drinking, smoking dope."

"Sounds like our old med school parties."

"Exactly. You wouldn't want one of your kids there."

Rob closed the trunk with a metallic click. "She's not our kid."

"What would you have done?"

"Look," he said, putting his hands on her shoulders. "I'm sure Irene is used to this. And I don't mean to be harsh, but unless she's actually being mistreated, there's nothing you can do."

"I can give her one night away."

"Oh, please." He let his hands drop. "What about that student of yours, the Bisconi boy? What was his name?"

"Eddie." She had found him sleeping in a cardboard box one

Saturday morning while she was walking the dog behind the school. When Cleo stopped to sniff, Virginia saw Eddie's eyes through the flaps he'd tried to close from the inside. He came out, blinking in the brightness of the November day, hugging himself with his thin arms. His father had kicked him out of the house the day before, for having a smart mouth, he told her.

"Yes, Eddie," Rob said. "The boy who took forty-five-minute showers. Who stole my sweater."

"I gave it to him. It was too small for you." Eddie Bisconi had stayed with them for nearly two weeks before his mother made peace between him and his father. It had been pleasant having him around. He walked Cleo in the mornings, shot baskets with Randall, took his shoes off by the back door. One evening Virginia had found Eddie and Rob on the couch, feet propped on the coffee table, the light of the television playing over their sleeping faces.

"I thought we'd never get rid of him."

"You liked him. You helped him with his algebra homework."

"Trust me, Irene and Jodie's situation is different. That's a black hole waiting for you to fall in."

While Virginia and Randall did the milking, Rob moved one of the twin beds back to the other side of the room and made it up for Irene. He left after dinner, hugging his wife and son together on the porch. "I'll be back in a week," he said. "Don't do anything crazy, either one of you."

RANDALL

—————◆————————

My friend Glenn Oakes is lucky. He has six brothers and sisters, and he's right in the middle. His parents love all seven kids, you can tell, but they don't focus on any except the oldest and the youngest. I like to spend the night at his house. We can stay up past midnight if we want and eat anything we find in the refrigerator.

I call Glenn to wish him happy birthday, and he's on his new cell, out in the tent they set up in the backyard. Not a party tent, a real one. The boys sleep in it most of the summer. He has a job now, at Mister Softee, so you can imagine all the shit he gets from his brothers. That's the thing about Glenn, though. He doesn't care.

A couple of his brothers must be right there, because he's all, like, "So, Farmer Joe, how's it going with the women up there?"

I think he means my mom and Lydia. The women.

From my granddad's office, I see my mom and dad standing out by the car, all serious. I know they're talking about Irene.

Glenn goes, "The chicks. Come on, man, what's up?" He doesn't sound like himself.

I just laugh.

Then he says, "I hate to break it to you. But I saw Bethany at the mall yesterday, with Bon Jovi."

Bethany is the girl I slow-danced with at our graduation party. We made out some, right before her father came to pick her up. Bon Jovi is Jason Sturm, this sort of punk tenth-grader with blue hair. "Maybe she ran into him there," I say.

"Right. He had his arm around her." Glenn does this little snort. "She had her hand in his back pocket. Palming his skinny butt."

I don't say anything.

"You need to know, man." I hear someone in the background. "That's right," Glenn says after a minute. "Don't be saving yourself."

That night, I wake up and find Irene sitting on my bed. It feels like she's been there for a while, looking at me. I'm wearing my old basketball shorts with the Laurel Springs Middle School decal peeling off one leg. The sheet has slipped down, and I smell my own sweat.

"I can't sleep," she says.

She's closed the door. "You have to get out of here," I say, sitting up. I can practically hear my mom and my granddad and Lydia breathing out in the hall. The last thing my dad told me before heading back to Maryland was don't do anything crazy.

"I only want to talk for a while." Irene has on some kind of nightgown that isn't exactly see-through, but I see her tattoo and the dark rings of her nipples. I make myself look away.

"If my mom knew you were in here, she'd go ballistic." That isn't true. Even when my mom is really pissed, she'll just say something that makes you feel like a lower life-form. Which is worse than yelling, the way Glenn's mom does.

"Oh, Randy." Irene shuts her eyes and lets her head fall back. She's the only person who calls me Randy.

I want to reach out and touch the smooth skin of her throat, but I get out of bed and open the door. "Go," I whisper. "Seriously."

She gives me this kind of slap on the stomach on her way out and says she hates me, too loud.

I go back to bed. Now I can't sleep, either, wondering what we would have done if I'd let her stay. I also wonder how Bethany and Jason got together. I'd be embarrassed if I was walking around with some girl and she stuck her hand on my ass. I go and open one of the windows all the way and take some deep breaths and look at the stars, which, I have to admit, are pretty wild out here in the middle of nowhere. It smells like freshly mown hay. My mom has been mowing just about every day since we got here.

She brought Irene back to the farm because everyone at Jodie's place was drunk. Always wanting to save things. My mom even gets sad when a dish breaks. She'll glue it back together, and then it just falls apart again in the dishwasher and she says, "Oh, well." Caro told me my mom once brought home a baby porcupine she found in the woods, trying to nurse on its dead mother. She fed it milk from a bottle and let it sleep in a box in her room. The porcupine liked to sit

on my mom's shoulder and nuzzle her neck and suck her ear-
lobe. Caro said its quills were so fine, they felt like soft fur
when you stroked its back. After my mom put the porcupine
to bed for the night, Caro had to use tweezers to pull the little quills from her neck and ears.

Chapter Nine

———————————

The next morning, Virginia got up a few minutes early and shut off the alarm before it could wake Irene. The white bear had fallen to the floor, and one of Irene's hands hung over the side of the bed, as if she were unconsciously reaching for it. She could be anyone's child, Virginia thought, pausing to look at her. Irene stirred then, drawing her hand beneath the pillow. Hearing rain beginning to fall on the roof, Virginia dressed quickly and went to wake Randall.

By the time they finished milking, it was raining hard. They stood in the open doorway of the barn, watching the water sluicing off the eaves of the house, flattening the grass below. All at once she and Randall made a break for it, splashing through the puddles in the dooryard, laughing as they ran up onto the porch. Her father, leaning on his cane, opened the door for them.

"I was listening to the weather forecast," he said. "Drying

conditions will be fair to poor today. In case you hadn't figured that out already."

"Sounds like an all-day rain to me," Lydia remarked, turning down the volume on the small black radio that sat on the kitchen counter. "I don't know where it's likely to be fair."

Virginia was partly glad for the reprieve; it meant she wouldn't have to get on the tractor and start mowing after breakfast. But she was sorry to lose more time. She'd hoped to be finished with the first cutting by the Fourth of July, only six days away. Otherwise, there wouldn't be much growing time before she had to start the second cutting in mid-August. As she watched Randall drying his hair with paper towels, Virginia remembered that she had promised to take the kids fishing. Now that was out, too—not that she expected them to care, but she would have to think of something to occupy them until she took Irene home. She wanted to wait long enough for the partygoers to clear out.

"Are you going to let that girl sleep all day?" Lydia asked, bringing a platter of bacon and eggs to the table.

"Might as well," Nathan said, giving Virginia a look. "What else can we do with her?"

"You could teach her to play poker, Granddad." Randall heaped his plate with eggs, reached across the table for toast. "I bet she'd be good at it."

"Maybe I'll show the two of you how to play blackjack. Unless your mother disapproves."

"I'm a big fan of blackjack," Virginia told him. "That and five-card stud. I think all children should be taught to gamble."

Irene came downstairs, her hair still damp from the shower, after the rest of them had finished breakfast. She seemed uncharacteristically self-conscious as they turned to look at her, but only for a moment.

"We saved you some eggs," Virginia said. "I can heat them up, if you like."

"No, thanks. I'll just have coffee." She got herself a cup and poured her own.

"That's a good way to stunt your growth," Nathan remarked, trying to sound jovial.

"I don't care." Irene grimaced as Randall drained his glass of milk. "I quit drinking milk when I was ten. It makes me sick," she said, stirring three teaspoons of sugar into her cup.

Randall began washing the dishes, and Lydia went out with her egg basket, one of Nathan's jackets draped over her head. Left at the table with Irene, Virginia and her father talked about the rainy summer, the quality of the hay. The girl ignored them, primly sipping her coffee, watching Randall at the sink.

"Randy," she said. "Put a slice of bread in the toaster, if you don't mind."

When the phone rang a few minutes later, Randall picked it up. "Cody," he mouthed after a minute, shaking his head. "He's coming over," he told them, replacing the receiver. "His mom is going to drop him off on her way to Fayette. She has to deliver cards or something."

"That gives me an idea," Nathan said. "You boys can clean up the barn."

"Just as long as you don't play any music." Irene licked a crumb from her upper lip.

"Most girls like my saxophone," Randall replied. "They think it's . . . kind of cool."

"Whatever." Irene refilled her cup and stood looking out the window while Randall finished the dishes.

Sexy. It occurred to Virginia that Randall had started to say the girls thought his playing the saxophone was sexy. It gave her a glimpse into her son's future—the years of proving himself that lay ahead.

Irene was still at the window when Cody arrived, carrying his clarinet case. "Who's that?" she demanded as he came through the door.

"My mother?"

"No, the guy."

"That's my brother Hunter. She's taking him to his dentist appointment."

"He's cute," she said, handing Randall her empty cup.

By mid-morning the kitchen was hot and steamy, moisture beaded up on the insides of the windows, the rain settled in for the day. Lydia had asked Virginia and Irene to help her can the bushel of green beans she'd picked in the garden the evening before. It had been years since Virginia had done any canning, but the routine soon felt familiar. She and Irene washed the beans and snapped the ends off, sorted them by size and shape, then Lydia blanched them in boiling water. Twenty sterilized quart jars were lined up across the kitchen counter, gleaming in the light reflected from the bulb over the sink.

Because the cows were staying in the barn that day, Nathan had taken Randall and Cody to muck out the stalls and put down fresh straw. With the boys gone, Irene chattered away about her old school in Beckley and her best friend, a girl named Shelby. It saved Virginia from having to make conversation with Lydia, helped divert her attention from the peculiar sensation of being in her mother's kitchen with two strangers.

"Shelby, she's like the funniest person you could ever meet,"

Irene said. She went on to tell a story about a day the previous summer when her father took her and Shelby to a carnival, where he won her bear Snowball by knocking down iron pins with a baseball. "So Shelby goes, 'I can do better than that. I'm going to get that big purple dog up on the top row.' She spent about three dollars, but she couldn't knock the pins down, and my dad was teasing her. Then she saw this big biker guy with tattoos and a leather vest walking with his girlfriend. She called him over and said, 'I want you to win me that purple dog. Here's a dollar for three chances.' So the guy wound up, and when the ball hit the pins they just about exploded. The guy working there, he goes, 'Don't throw any more! Take the freakin' dog!' "

"The freakin' dog," Lydia repeated with a cluck of disapproval.

While she talked, Irene was lining beans up in front of her, dividing them into piles according to size. When she finished the carnival story, she didn't laugh. She kept snapping beans, adding them to the little piles. "Zack, that's what Shelby named the dog," she said, more quietly. "That was a boy in our class she liked. My dad gave her a hard time, said he was going to tell Zack next time he saw him. He didn't, though. He didn't even know who Zack was."

"You're doing a nice job there," Lydia said, picking up handfuls of beans and dropping them into the wire blanching basket that she lowered into the steaming pot. "You're a hard worker, aren't you?"

"Sometimes," Irene replied. "When I feel like it."

Virginia began to pack hot beans into the jars, standing them upright. Using a metal cup, she filled the jars with the blanching water, leaving a little space at the top. She was thinking of one August when Aunt Ida was at the farm while they canned tomatoes. On a particularly hot, humid morning, Ida, who always wore a long cotton skirt, plunked down in a chair, mopping her face with a handkerchief.

"I must say, this is a ridiculous business," she declared, hiking her skirt up to her knees.

Nine years old that summer, Virginia was surprised at the sturdiness of her great-aunt's legs. Ida had on cotton ankle socks and her usual walking shoes, brown leather lace-ups that reminded Virginia of her own Buster Browns. With her rosy cheeks and her hair askew, she seemed like a large, happy child.

"It's far too much work," Ida continued. "Wouldn't it be more sensible to buy tomatoes at the store? They come in cans, you know."

Caroline had stopped what she was doing and turned to Ida in mock astonishment. "You're kidding," she said.

"I know, I know." Ida heaved herself to her feet, heading for the porch to cool off. "You think they don't taste as good. And they don't, either. But still."

On the last day of Ida's visits, Virginia and her mother would pack a box with freshly canned beans and tomatoes, pickles and beets, blackberry jam. Ida always placed it carefully on the passenger seat of her old Ford sedan before starting the drive back to Pittsburgh and a new school year.

Dragging a chair over to the cupboard on the far side of the kitchen, Lydia climbed up and reached for a large pot on the top shelf. When she brought it to the stove, Virginia saw that it was her mother's pressure canner, the twelve-quart one with the dial gauge on the lid. She wouldn't have known where to find it.

"I'm going out for a minute," she said, stepping onto the porch.

It was only slightly cooler outside. White wisps of fog floated across the hilltops, wrapping themselves around the trees like gauzy scarves. Huddled together in their shelter, Bubble and Squeak were watching her, their noses pink in the watery light. With their squinty eyes and their up-curled lips, they appeared to be laughing at something.

Virginia had made up her mind to have a talk with Jodie, and she was dreading it. She tried to imagine what her mother would do. Although they had often teased Caroline about the way she fussed over the Jameson twins, she never minded. If Caroline felt any hesitation about visiting their house with her boxes of hand-me-down clothes, the chocolate cakes she baked for their birthday, it didn't show. She waded in with the conviction that they needed her. But Roy and Roger—Lee and Roger—were sweet boys, mostly, and their parents seemed grateful for the help.

After lunch, Virginia left Cody in the kitchen, waiting for his mother, and set off for Irene's house. Sitting in the backseat with Randall, Irene explained the dangers of botulism and the precautions taken to avoid it.

"Who would think a jar of beans could kill you?" she said, holding the quart Lydia had given her up to the light. "One single bean, even. You could die because you didn't process them long enough at the right temperature and pressure."

"Killer beans," Randall said. "There's way too much stuff that can kill you, if you think about it."

Jodie's car was the only one in the driveway when they arrived. The rain had let up, and Virginia suggested that Randall and Irene go for a walk to give her a few minutes with Jodie.

Getting out of the car, Irene paused. "My mom's probably in a bad mood today. She always is when she has a hangover."

"That's all right," Virginia assured her. "It's no big deal."

She tried to convince herself of that as she tapped on the

screen door. The house was quiet. She saw a vacuum cleaner in the middle of the living room, smelled the stale after-scent of liquor and marijuana. She knocked again, louder, and finally heard footsteps in the hall. Jodie came to the door in a bathrobe, the crease marks of a pillow on one cheek.

"Oh," she said. "It's you. Where's Irene?"

"Taking a walk with Randall. Down the road."

"Come in, I guess."

Jodie pulled a pack of cigarettes from her pocket and sat on the coffee table as she lit one. "Sorry about the mess. I started cleaning up, but to tell you the truth, I feel like a piece of dog shit." Taking a long drag, she turned away to blow out a stream of smoke.

"You might think this is none of my business . . ." Virginia decided against brushing away the crumbs on the couch before taking a seat.

"But you're here to tell me what a bad mother I am." Jodie drew on her cigarette again, got up and walked into the kitchen. "You want a cup of coffee or something?"

"I just had some. Thanks."

Returning with a glass of water, Jodie stubbed out her cigarette in an already overflowing ashtray. "Well?" She sat down again, facing Virginia.

Virginia wondered if Lee was in the bedroom, listening to them. "The thing is," she said, "I was surprised that you left Irene alone here the other night."

"She's fifteen. What's the big deal?"

"There's no phone. It's kind of isolated." Virginia wiped her sweaty palms on her jeans, hoping Jodie wouldn't notice.

"Did she say something to you?" Jodie looked at her suspiciously.

"No, but I could tell it made her uncomfortable."

"If she wasn't happy about something, she'd let me know." Jodie laughed abruptly. "She doesn't hold back, trust me."

"That party we walked in on yesterday . . ." Virginia paused, noticing a pyramid of empty beer cans in one corner. "I think it could be confusing for a girl her age to see her mother in a situation like that."

"Really?" Jodie reached for the cigarette pack again. "You probably don't think I should smoke, either."

"That's your business."

"And Irene isn't?" Jodie asked with a sour smile, studying the unlit cigarette in her hand.

"She looks up to you," Virginia said. She wanted to add something about the kind of example Jodie set, but she knew how prissy that would sound. And then she came out with something worse. "That guy with the goatee? He was leering at her. He had his eyes clamped on her chest."

"That 'guy with the goatee' has been a friend of mine for ten years." Jodie's head snapped up. "Frank might not be the citizen of the year, but he would never touch a hair on her head." She set the cigarette aside. "Here's the deal. I'm not some hypocrite who wants my kid to think I'm perfect. If you're afraid my daughter is going to contaminate your precious boy, don't worry about it. We won't be stopping by your place anymore. And I'd be just as glad not to see you around here, either." Getting to her feet and tightening the belt of her bathrobe, she walked back down the hall.

Virginia sat there a little longer, considering how badly she had done. Her uncle Herman used to have similar kinds of talks all the time, she reflected, with much better results. And he was no diplomat. She pushed herself off the couch and went outside.

Stepping into the wet grass, she heard a rumble of thunder

in the distance. Randall and Irene were standing in the road, not more than fifty yards beyond the house, holding hands. As far as Virginia knew, Randall had never had a girlfriend before. Noticing his mother, he dropped Irene's hand, and they started walking toward the house.

"Your mother *was* in a bad mood," Virginia said, touched by the girl's tearstained face. "And I probably made it worse."

"It's okay," Irene said with a loud sniff, wiping her nose with the back of her hand. "My mother's been weird since my father left—all the parties and stuff."

"Well, she's pretty angry with me, but I hope she'll get over it." Virginia would be sorry, she realized, not to see Irene again. She and Randall stood beside the car as Irene went into the house, carrying her backpack and Snowball and her quart of beans.

"Why were you talking to Jodie?" Randall seemed agitated as they drove away.

"I'm concerned, that's why. Maybe Jodie's friends aren't the best role models for a fifteen-year-old girl." Virginia glanced over at him. He was frowning, gingerly touching the three or four coarse hairs that had recently sprouted on his chin.

"Role models," he said. "You sound like the school guidance counselor."

"If you don't mind my asking, what was Irene crying about?"

"She's kind of emotional. You know how girls are." He looked out the window, thinking it over. After several minutes he said, "She has this idea that things would be better if her dad came back. She believes her mother knows where he is but won't tell her."

When they returned, the farmhouse was quiet, too. Cody was gone. Lydia had already washed the canning equipment and put it away. The sink handles and faucet gleamed, even in the dull light. Virginia looked into the living room. Her father, covered with an afghan Lydia had made for him, had fallen asleep on the couch. Lydia was dozing in a chair nearby.

The rain came back with sudden force, striking the windows at the far end of the room, running down the glass in crooked rivulets. How was it possible, Virginia wondered, that Lydia Will was sleeping in her mother's chair? She turned away, nearly colliding with Randall.

"They look cozy," he said. "I think I'll go sack out, too."

———

Virginia's room felt dark and stale. Sliding the curtains back and raising the windows partway, she saw that one of the small cupboards under the eaves had been left open. Nosy Irene, she guessed, not even bothering to cover her tracks. As she bent to close the door, she spotted a stack of ledger books and lifted one out.

More of her father's farm logs, she assumed. Over the years, he had kept a meticulous record of crops planted, yields per acre, gallons of milk produced by each cow, milk prices, birth dates and weights of calves, pounds of meat from each pig butchered. The logs were a concise history of the farm since he took it over from his father. Each day, Nathan wrote down the morning temperature, as well as the high, noted general weather conditions. If something unusual happened, such as the appearance of an albino skunk near the henhouse, he might mention it. From time to time, Virginia looked through the logs in his office downstairs, amused that his records contained virtually no reference to the farm's human inhabitants. Aside from an occasional "G and family here this weekend" or "Card from L yesterday," it was as if the farm magically ran itself.

This book was dark green, not black like the other logs. When she opened the cover, Virginia found her mother's hand-writing inside—the round, even letters that looked as if they came out of an old Palmer penmanship book. "Smoke Rise Farm," Caroline had written at the top of the first page, and under that, "Rownd's Point, Pennsylvania."

Virginia took the book over to the bed and sat down, tracing the letters with her fingers. Smoke Rise Farm. She loved the name. They hardly ever used it, though. Everyone called it Second Farm, because the original family place, where Jonathan Rownd had settled in 1767, went to his oldest son. The younger son, Thomas—Virginia's great-great-great-great-grandfather—built his house and started cultivating the fields on a hilly piece of land farther from the river.

"Look there," Virginia's mother had said to her on a summer morning when she was seven, pointing into the distance below.

They were at the top of the farm's highest hill, picking blackberries. Looking down, Virginia saw a cloud of mist billowing in the valley. She watched as it moved in, blocking the road from view. It broke apart as it drifted across the field where her father was cutting hay, muffling the sound of his tractor, and rose up the hill in long white fingers. She reached out, trying to catch hold of the swirling vapor, but felt only dampness on her hands.

"It looks like smoke," she said.

"Doesn't it?" her mother agreed. "It comes off the river. That's why they named this Smoke Rise Farm."

By the time they had filled their buckets and were walking

down the hill again, the sun had burned the mist away. As they reached the house, Winn Moffat, West's father, was driving up on his big New Holland tractor. West was riding behind him, standing on the hitching bar. Winn called hello and went on to the barn to hook on the hay rake, but West jumped off.

"What are you going to do with those berries?" he asked them.

"We're making pies," Virginia said.

"Good." He took a handful and tasted one. "I'll help you."

"You can if you want," Caroline said. "But won't your father be missing you?"

"He doesn't care," West told her. "All I do is ride on the back."

Virginia remembered West's flour-smudged face as he struggled with the rolling pin. "It's too hard," he complained, as the ball of dough refused to flatten out. "You try it, Ginny. I bet you can't do it, either." He had soon gone out to the field to join the haying crew.

Turning the page of her mother's book, Virginia found a date at the top: June 1, 1958. That was about two months before Larry was born, when Caroline and Nathan were living on the farm with Nathan's parents. Under the date was a sketch of lilacs done in colored pencil, the green leaves drawn precisely, the flowers tiny smudges of purple. "This unborn baby is making me do crazy things," her mother had written. "The sight of lilacs covered with morning dew was irresistible. I picked off a few of the flowers and decided to taste them, thinking they looked so deliciously purple. They are not delicious at all, rather bitter. I'll leave them to the bees and the butterflies."

Flipping through the rest of the book, Virginia saw that many of its pages were decorated with sketches. She slid it under her pillow and settled in for a nap. Strange, she was thinking as she drifted off, that she had never known about her mother's journals.

She woke with a start, unsure of how much time had passed. From the kitchen she heard the sounds of voices and running water. It seemed very late, but as she turned to face the windows, Virginia saw that it was still daylight. The rain was falling gently now, the sky suffused with streaks of brightness. When she closed her eyes again, there was Irene standing in the road near her house. Then she heard Randall on the stairs, calling her name, and knew she had to get up.

Chapter Ten

O n the sidewalks of Tenney's Landing, spectators stood three deep, shielding their eyes with their hands. Rolling slowly down Main Street, their big, clean wheels whooshing on the warm asphalt, the fire engines gleamed in the late morning sun. Leading the Fourth of July parade, West's uncle Hal Moffat, chief of the volunteer fire company, drove the ladder truck, his signature cigar tucked into the corner of his mouth. He smiled when he recognized Virginia, touching the brim of his cap in a two-finger salute. As the truck went by, she could hear the horns and drums of the high school marching band in the far distance, bringing up the rear.

"Who's that guy?" Rob asked. He had arrived at the farm the night before, and they had come early to get a place in front of the Good Food Market.

"The chief," Virginia said vaguely.

Between the ladder truck and the tanker truck, children

rode bicycles decorated with flags and crepe paper, waving and squeezing the rubber bulbs of the horns on their handlebars. Behind the trucks came the equestrians, dressed in formal riding wear, their horses' coats burnished, manes and tails braided with ribbons. The horses pranced along with arched necks, their hooves clicking smartly on the pavement, Reverend Gleason out in front on his big bay gelding. As Virginia watched him, thinking how her uncle Herman, who loved the Fourth of July parade, wouldn't have been caught dead riding in it, a horse moved out of formation, brushing her shoulder. She looked up to see Theresa, wearing a long black skirt and a ruffled white blouse, riding sidesaddle on her roan mare. Coolly, she flicked the horse with her riding crop and guided it back into position.

"That was West's wife," Rob said.

"Theresa."

"Do you think she did that on purpose?"

"Of course not."

"Cody looks like her, doesn't he? Those blue eyes."

"I guess he does." Virginia pretended to be absorbed in the floats, homemade concoctions pulled by tractors or pickups, until her bumping heart calmed down.

Spotting Randall on the other side of the street, walking with Hunter and Sam, she elbowed Rob. "There go the hippest dudes in town," she said. West's boys had invited Randall to join their team for the annual baseball game. Now the three of them were wearing matching caps and shirts with the team name stenciled across the back.

Rob gave a low whistle. "What are they again? The Rodents?"

"The Woodchucks."

"Oh, right." He waved, and Randall, nodding in their direction, continued on his way.

He was looking for Irene, Virginia guessed. True to her word, Jodie had not come by the farm all week. "Maybe you should go to their house and apologize," Randall suggested one afternoon as his mother drove him to the high school for a practice.

"Why?"

"Because what you said was sort of . . . butting in."

"What I said was perfectly reasonable. You even agreed with me."

———

The evening after her talk with Jodie, while her father and Lydia were working on a jigsaw puzzle in the dining room, Randall had sat in the living room, flipping through the television channels as she tried to read. Finally, he turned to her and asked, "What did you say, anyway, that ticked her off?"

Virginia repeated their conversation, almost word for word. She had gone over it so many times in her head that she had it memorized.

"Are you leaving something out?" he asked, suspicious, fingering the hairs on his chin.

"No, Detective MacLeod, I am not."

"Well, it doesn't seem that bad," he said, letting his hand fall. "Irene told me her mother is kind of a bitch sometimes." Blushing at the word, he kept his eyes on his mother.

"I think Jodie means well. She's a little immature, maybe."

"And she's like, what . . . forty?" His hand went back to his chin.

"Don't worry. We'll probably see them before long." Virginia opened her book again. "By the way, if those hairs on your chin are bothering you, why don't you shave them off?"

"Dad said I should wait."

"For what?"

Randall blushed again, crimson to the tips of his ears. "He says once you start shaving, you have to keep it up."

"At your age, we're probably talking once a week. I don't like to disagree with your father, but I'd say it's your chin and your decision. If you change your mind, he left a can of shaving cream and some of those plastic razors in the medicine cabinet upstairs."

"Really? It's all right with you?" Randall jumped up, rubbing his palm against the soft, nearly invisible fuzz on his cheek, as if shaving were suddenly urgent.

Virginia had wanted to go to him and take his smooth boy's face between her hands one last time. "Don't rush, or you'll cut yourself."

Hearing laughter in the crowd, she looked away from Randall to see her favorite part of the parade, the lawn chair ladies. Disguised in baggy housedresses, wigs, and gaudy sunglasses, a group of twelve women marched ahead of the band, doing a sort of dance routine with folding aluminum chairs. They opened and closed the chairs in time to the music, holding them first above their heads and then out to the side, as if they were pom-poms. When they were in their mid-fifties, her mother and Sissy had been among the first of the lawn chair ladies, a relatively new addition to the parade. Virginia scanned the faces but didn't recognize anyone until a woman wearing a bouffant blond wig paused in front of her. It was her cousin Carrie. Virginia raised her hand in greeting, feeling guilty that she hadn't yet gone to visit. Sissy had written when Carrie's baby was born, soon after Nathan's wedding.

A ripple of applause followed the lawn chair ladies down the street, and then a cheer went up as the marching band brought the parade to an end. People on the sidewalk began milling around. Most of them would go down to the park for the fire company's chicken barbecue and the baseball game. Some of the men would pitch horseshoes in the evening, while their wives set up tables to sell the boxed picnic suppers that benefited the First Presbyterian Church Ladies' Aid Society. Those with cows to milk would have to go home for a while and return later for the strawberry shortcake and fireworks.

"There they are," Rob said, taking Virginia by the arm and crossing the street. He had found her father and Lydia at one of the small tables in front of Paula's Café.

Virginia stopped on the way to say hello to her aunt Hillary, who was cradling Carrie's sleeping baby. She lifted the brim of his hat so Virginia could get a better look at him. Already he looked like a miniature Gerald, but Virginia didn't say so.

"Did they ever decide on a name for him?" she asked.

"Starling, if you can believe it. That was Carrie's bright idea."

"Hello, Starling," Virginia said, touching one of his feet. He sighed and drew a hand across his cheek.

"The problem is everything sounds a little strange with Dibbs," Hillary said, pulling the hat over the baby's eyes again.

"Listen," Virginia said, "I hate to rush off, but I have to go get Henny. Are you coming to the barbecue?"

"I don't know. Dan is hiding out in the newspaper office, but I suppose Carrie will expect me to show up. Anyway, come and see us sometime. I know Dan would love it."

"I will," Virginia promised. "I'm just about finished with the first cutting."

Dan was her mother's younger brother. He and Hillary had gone out of town the weekend Nathan got married. They had sent a gift, though, a small mantel clock in a rosewood case. It was a pretty clock, yet Virginia suspected it was meant to hint at how little time had gone by since her mother's death.

"It's a pleasure to get out for a change," Nathan said, rising from the small metal chair with some difficulty. His left arm was still in a sling, his ribs still sore and tender.

Virginia reached for him, awkwardly placing one hand under his good arm and the other on his back to give him a boost. "Dad, why don't you ride with me while I pick up Henny?"

"I'd like to, Ginny, but I'm too stiff. I need to walk a bit." He straightened up and shook his legs one at a time. "I'm getting to be quite the fossil."

"You are not," Lydia said, putting an arm around his waist and guiding him away in the direction of the park.

"Are you okay to get Henny by yourself?" Rob asked.

"Sure. I was hoping I might have a chance to spend a few minutes with my dad is all. It seems like he's either asleep or Lydia's right there, hovering over him."

"Well." Rob kissed her on the forehead. "See you soon."

Virginia wasn't certain Henny would come. They had argued the night before, when Virginia called to ask if she was planning to be at the parade.

"No," Henny had said emphatically. "My parents have to go in early so my dad can cook chicken with the firemen, and my mom needs to do who-knows-what with the Ladies' Aid. I'd be sitting on the sidewalk at least two hours, waiting for the parade to start. Or else making sandwiches with the church ladies. And I don't know which would be worse."

"We'll come by and pick you up, then."

"I said I don't want to go."

"But the parade is so much fun."

"For you, maybe." There was a silence, then Henny said, "I

don't like being hemmed in by a crowd. So don't do me any favors."

Although she'd seemed to enjoy the day at Richard's Falls, Henny had been out of sorts ever since. Virginia probably should have known better than to take her there.

Years ago, shortly after the doctors diagnosed her spinal cord injury, Henny had defended Drew when Virginia called him a coward for leaving town.

"It's better this way," Henny had insisted. "For both of us. He's the one person who understands me."

The remark still stung. Virginia tried to put it out of her mind as she negotiated Rob's car through the post-parade stragglers in the street. The big "Closed for the Rest of Day" sign on the door of Chick's service station cheered her up a little. Chick was the town's baseball umpire.

Henny had finally agreed to come into town for the barbecue and the game when Virginia told her Randall would be playing shortstop. "It would mean a lot to him if you were there," she said.

"Are you aware," Henny replied, "that you use your son to get your way?"

"I was about to say that he'll be heartbroken if you don't come."

"You really are shameless." And then, after another pause, "All right, then."

One of the reasons Virginia had wanted her father to come along was so she could ask him about Caroline's journals. Reading them in bed at night, she could picture her mother writing and sketching at the desk by the window in Aunt Ida's room, claiming a little space for herself. Virginia hoped to take them home with her at the end of the summer, to keep them from Lydia's prying eyes.

She was reading them in order, getting to know the young woman who had grown up in town—the daughter of a dentist—as she learned to be a farm wife. There was a touching mix of wonder and frustration in the way Caroline described daily life. Of her mother-in-law, Hattie Rownd, she had written: "H is a *harumpher.* She does not criticize, exactly, but I know when I have done something wrong. She will look at me sideways, and then I hear *harumph,* a sort of throat clearing. In a minute she will get around to explaining. We do not wash the eggs with soap and water to get the chicken droppings off, as she found me doing yesterday. *Harumph, harumph.* We sandpaper them. I do not like to sandpaper eggs, it sets my teeth on edge. And washing works perfectly well." Above this entry, her mother had sketched a chicken with its breast feathers puffed out and a dark, appraising eye.

When the Eastman house came into view, Virginia saw Henny waiting outside—a good sign. She pulled the car up to the left side of the porch, where Henny's father had built the wheelchair ramp.

"So, you decided to join us," she said, getting out and opening the passenger door.

"I said I would."

"You're obviously in a festive mood." Virginia held tight to the handles of Henny's wheelchair as she guided it down the ramp.

"Pardon me if I don't get all jazzed up about the Fourth of July."

"You and Uncle Dan. He's planning to spend the day in his office."

"Smart."

With the chair in place beside the open car door, Virginia set the brakes against the wheels and dropped the arm so

Henny could slide onto the car seat. It was a maneuver she had seen many times, yet she always felt her breath catch at the moment when Henny braced herself with her left hand and reached with her right to sweep her legs in. The sight of her friend's neatly laced black sneakers, side by side on the floor of the car, nearly made her weep.

"Any excitement at the parade?" Henny asked as they pulled out of the driveway.

"Let's see. Theresa tried to run me down with her horse, but other than that, no."

"Are you serious?"

"The horse only brushed me. It must have been spooked by something."

"Theresa's extreme displeasure when she saw you."

"You told me once Theresa doesn't like me. Is that true? I mean, did she ever say anything?"

"Not really." Henny pulled down the visor and checked her hair in the mirror. "I'll tell you something, though. That night you were at our place loading hay? The next morning, my dad said, 'I see there's still some unfinished business between Ginny and West.'" She closed the mirror cover with a click.

Embarrassed, Virginia concentrated on the road. She felt as if she had been caught doing something foolish, the same feeling she used to get when Mr. Fisher, their ninth-grade math teacher, intercepted the notes she and West passed to each other in class. Virginia hated the way he would take them to his desk and unfold the squares of paper, squinting through the thick lenses of his glasses. She was having strange dreams that year, the kind that left her shaken in the morning, and she used to write them down and give them to West. His notes were about things that happened in his family, like the time he fainted when he was helping his father castrate one of their bull calves.

Mr. Fisher would scan them with a little smile before refolding them and sliding them into his jacket pocket. At least he never read them out loud.

When Virginia and Henny got to Riverside Park, there was a long line snaking across the grass toward the firemen's barbecue. Wheeling Henny into the shade of the tent, where people were finding seats at the wooden tables, Virginia saw that Rob had already been through the line and had their dinners waiting. She placed Henny at the end of their table, next to Nathan.

"Nice to see you," he said, patting Henny's arm. "How are you getting along?"

She looked him over, shaking her head. "You really took a tumble, didn't you?"

"Where's Randall?" Virginia asked Rob, taking a seat beside him.

"He's skulking around with the rest of the Woodchucks. He said something about eating at the team table."

"Henny," Lydia said in a rather severe tone. "Do you need help with that chicken?"

Henny looked up, her plastic knife and fork poised above the drumstick. "Don't worry. If I keep sawing at it, something's bound to come loose." She glanced at Virginia and quickly turned back to her plate.

The menu for the firemen's barbecue was the same, year after year: half a chicken, stewed corn, tossed salad, a wedge of corn bread with a pat of butter on top, iced tea so strong it left a film on your teeth. The men would start up the fire in the barbecue pit early in the morning and cook hundreds of chicken halves on greasy, blackened wire racks, dousing them with a vinegary sauce that crisped the skin. The sauce recipe was a secret among the firemen, as was their recipe for stewed corn. Caroline had tried to make the corn at home, when

Nathan was a volunteer fireman, but she could never get it quite right.

"Hey," Weston Moffat said, dropping onto the bench beside Virginia, out of breath. "How's your car?"

"Fine," she replied, swallowing a mouthful of corn bread, catching a whiff of his clean, soapy scent. "Chick put in a new water pump."

"Great." He reached across her plate to shake hands with Rob. "Should be a close game this year. Randall's a good player."

"You pitching again?" Nathan asked him.

"My brother Sam. I couldn't get to many practices because of my job." He stood again, snagging a bite of chicken from Henny's plate. "I'll be in the outfield," he said, moving on.

"When you go for pie," Virginia's father told her, "get me a slice of cherry. And make sure it's Sissy's."

"None for me," Lydia said, dabbing at her lips with a paper napkin.

Virginia and Rob cleared the table and found a metal drum stuffed with broken plastic forks, soggy paper plates, and chicken bones. Iridescent green flies cruised nimbly up and down the bones, picking up sweet and salt on their tongues and feet. Virginia saw Theresa among the other firemen's wives, cutting pies and setting the slices out on small paper plates. She had changed out of her riding costume and was wearing a short pleated skirt and a clingy knit top. She noticed them coming and looked down, running a knife cleanly through a crest of meringue.

"That's a beautiful horse you have," Rob said, standing in front of her.

Theresa finished her cut. "Thanks," she said, wiping her hands on a kitchen towel, not quite meeting his gaze. "She has a mind of her own sometimes."

Rob leaned toward her. "Which pie would you recommend?"

"They're all good," Theresa said. "We have apple, cherry, lemon meringue, chocolate cream. And peach." She paused, studying a button on Rob's shirt. "I made the peach."

"That's the one I want, then." His eyes followed her as she moved down the table and returned with a wedge of pie, syrupy peach slices sliding out from under the golden crust. "Looks delicious," he told her.

"I hope you like it," she said, flustered.

A few feet away, West was standing in the smoke from the barbecue, a bottle of beer in one hand, a long-handled fork in the other, talking with Henny's father and Jere. Virginia found a plastic tray and chose three more pieces of pie. As she headed back to their table, she heard Sissy call her name and turned to see her sitting with Henny's mother.

"You weren't with the lawn chair ladies today," Virginia said.

"No. It isn't much fun without your mother." Sissy poked at the salad on her plate. "Time to let the younger ones take over, anyway."

"I see you got Henny to come out," Mrs. Eastman said. "Good for you."

"I'm glad she's here," Sissy said. "Your father, too."

"Come and join us."

"No, I don't think I will." Sissy looked over at their table, her gaze settling on Lydia.

Rob caught up with Virginia as she was leaving them.

"Don't tell me you were flirting with Theresa all this time," she said.

"Maybe." He took the tray of pie. "Just a little."

Back at the table, Jodie and Lee had appeared out of nowhere and were sitting next to Lydia. Sipping from a blue plastic cup with "Go Mountaineers" printed in gold letters, Lee was watching Virginia, amused. She was certain Jodie had told him about their talk, her meddling. Jodie continued her conversation with Lydia, as if Virginia weren't there.

"Get out of town!" Jodie exclaimed suddenly, leaning back to look under the table. "Let's see them."

Lydia stood and lifted one of her feet onto the bench. "There," she said proudly. "Size six. And that's a girls' size six. I have to buy my shoes in the children's department."

"Aren't you something?" Jodie said. "I knew you had small feet, but I had no idea."

Lydia lifted her chin at Virginia as she sat down again. Not daring to look at Henny, Virginia was relieved when her friend said, "I need to get some air, Ginny. Can you come with me?"

Pushing Henny ahead of her, Virginia jogged down the path leading to the town swimming pool and stopped under the awning of the deserted refreshment stand. The pool was something new; it had been built six or seven years before. It wouldn't open until two, when the barbecue was officially over. Inside the chain-link fence, everything was still. Only the pool's surface rippled, the jets at the bottom continuously pumping in recycled water, while water at the top slipped over the lip around the edge. Refracted sunlight made a shifting hexagonal pattern against the sides, spiderwebs of light undulating across the aquamarine tiles. A strong smell of chlorine came off the water.

"Lord," Henny said. "Lydia's tiny feet. How can you stand it?"

"It's one of her favorite subjects." Virginia sat on the bench near the shuttered window through which teenagers in red, white, and blue T-shirts would soon be passing ice cream bars and sodas. "The first time we came to visit—it must have been Easter—Randall found a pair of her shoes on the porch and asked if some child had left them. 'Those are mine,' Lydia informed him. 'I've always had dainty feet.' That was the word she used."

"I wonder what your father—" Henny stopped when she saw Randall and Hunter walking toward the baseball field, Irene between them, wearing a pink tank top. "Uh-oh," she said. "Possible love triangle."

"Don't laugh," Virginia said. When she called out to Randall, asking him if he'd eaten, he stopped in his tracks and struck a muscleman pose.

"For sure," he said. "We are Woodchucks, ravenous beasts."

Irene looked up at Hunter, and the two of them smiled.

"What's with Randall?" Henny asked after a minute.

"This is the first time he's seen Irene in a week."

"Ah. Remember when a week was forever?"

Later, in the car—after the Woodchucks had lost 4 to 3 to the team from Lynchtown, after the fireworks—Virginia turned to ask Randall a question. Looking out the window, he didn't notice her. He had made a spectacular catch that afternoon, when the Lynchtown first baseman hit a line drive sailing past Sam Moffat. Randall dove for it, and Rob was already on his feet when they heard the *whump* of that hard-hit ball in Randall's glove.

Rob rested a hand on her knee, and she laced her fingers through his, reminding herself that she had done nothing wrong.

A few nights before, she and West had stood alone in the hay barn, high on the hill at his farm, listening to the voices of the children as they walked down to the house. They had finished stacking more than two hundred bales, and both of them were tired, their shirts stained with sweat, bits of chaff clinging to their arms and necks. Hay dust still floated from the loft, shreds of dried alfalfa swirling in the warm air. Virginia could see the sky through the second-story windows, turning from dusky blue to deep purple. In the fields nearby, crickets were chirping. They stood near each other, silent, as the sounds of their children grew fainter.

West took a step closer, plucking a strand of hay from her hair, his palm grazing her cheek. "It's been a long day."

"Yes." She felt her blood rushing. She could have covered his hand with hers, could have stepped forward to meet him. She hesitated, and the moment passed.

They went outside and slid the barn doors shut, started toward the farmhouse. To their left, the faces of the three fishponds darkened in the falling light. She pictured the trout suspended near the bottom, all pointing in the same direction, tails wavering. Fed by cold springs, the ponds descended the hill, one flowing into another. Virginia and West and Henny used to swim in them when they were young, in the evenings after haying, thrilled by the icy threads of the current winding around their ankles.

"The fireflies are gone," Virginia remarked.

"I know. Three weeks ago, this field was full of them."

Near the house, she stumbled slightly, and when West reached out to steady her, she saw Theresa inside the dark house, moving away from a back window. A light went on. One of West's boys called to his mother from the porch.

Chapter Eleven

Pretending to read a CPR poster on the wall, Virginia studied her father out of the corner of her eye. Nathan was sitting in the chair beside her, thumbing through a back issue of *People* magazine. He had some color that morning, and his hair was freshly washed, combed back over his ears. A month short of seventy, he was a fine-looking man, still trim with a firm jaw, although his reading glasses magnified the lines around his eyes. Years of squinting into the sun.

To Virginia's surprise, Lydia had asked her to drive Nathan to his doctor's appointment at the clinic in Tenney's Landing. A dozen years before, when old Doc Brooks finally retired, the state had bought the small brick building that had been his office and started sending doctors just finished with their residencies. They stayed for two years, fulfilling a service requirement, and then moved on. Although they were mostly eager and pleasant, it wasn't the same. After patients saw one of the "little doctors," as they called them, they would often go visit Doc Brooks with some small gift—tomatoes from the garden, a pair of hand-knit socks—and ask his opinion about the diagnosis. Sometimes two or three of his former patients would be at his house at the same time. As often as not, they would have a shot of whiskey and decide they felt fine.

The waiting room had been painted recently and smelled of new carpet. In one corner, an open cabinet held neatly stacked children's books and an assortment of stuffed animals. A vase of pink gladioli sat on the counter where patients checked in. No one else was waiting. The only sound was the *tap tap* of the receptionist at her keyboard behind the sliding glass window. Doc Brooks's office had been a noisy place, children sneezing and whining as the appointments backed up, farmers with mangled fingers impatiently watching the clock as blood seeped into their homemade bandages. Then Doc Brooks would come out in his white coat to call the next patient in, and they would all forgive him. Young women had crushes on him because of the tragedy. His son, Stevie, had died at the age of five, shot by another child.

"Why is it," Nathan asked, turning to show Virginia the magazine, "that women nowadays try to look like prostitutes?" He pointed to a group of young actresses posing at a Hollywood event in skimpy dresses that barely covered their breasts and thighs. "Every page. Look."

"You need to get out more," she said, smiling at him. At Randall's graduation, Rob had commented on the fourteen-year-old girls, transformed by eye shadow and mascara, three-inch heels and slinky skirts. They suddenly looked twenty-five.

"Irene, now. She has the tiniest clothes I've ever seen." Nathan tossed the magazine onto the table. "Is this what your women's lib business was all about?"

"Sometimes I wonder myself."

When the inner door opened, a nurse dressed in white pants and a maternity top told Nathan to come in. Virginia stood to help him out of his chair and said she'd like to speak with Dr. Wallace when they were finished.

"She doesn't trust me," he said, nodding at his daughter.

Something about her father's bearing as he went through the door, some hesitation in his movements, made him seem lost. Virginia had noticed it more than once in the previous weeks. It saddened her to think of the unexpected turns in his life.

She remembered how pleased he'd been when Larry decided to study agriculture and animal husbandry at Penn State. The two of them had started making plans for the farm, talking into the night during Larry's school vacations. They discussed new crops and soil enrichment and the rare breeds of livestock they wanted to raise. American Cream draft horses. Pineywoods cattle. Gloucestershire Old Spot pigs. Narragansett turkeys. Her father liked saying the names out loud. He read about them, clipped the articles, and sent them to Larry at school.

They would have to start slowly, they agreed, when Larry graduated. The new ideas were expensive. When Larry and Marilyn got married, they moved into the farmhouse with Nathan and Caroline, to save money. Virginia was a senior in college by then, spending most of her free time with Rob in Cincinnati. When she thought about the farm, it seemed very far away.

That morning in the waiting room, she began to sense the depth of her father's loneliness. On the phone, after her mother died, he would tell her about visits from Sissy and Jere, the Eastmans and Moffats, the casseroles and pies they brought him. Virginia never let her mind dwell on the reality of his workdays, the nights wandering about the house, the small confusions about things like how to run the washing machine. For the first time, she imagined her father sitting on the porch steps after supper, alone, watching the moon rise. Her parents used to make a point of watching out for the full moon, thrilled by the way it appeared above the tree line on the easternmost hill, as delighted each time as if they had never seen it before.

"There it is," Nathan would say. "Booming up over the hill."

"Yes," Caroline would reply, leaning her head against his shoulder. "Back again."

Virginia had recently read something in her mother's diary about her father. "Until today," Caroline wrote,

I hadn't understood how N feels about the baby. He has been happy, excited—all of that—from the beginning. But N seems afraid of him, too. This afternoon, when I thought Larry should be waking up, I went to him and found his crib empty. Panic. I called Nathan's name. No answer. I looked in every room. His folks were shopping in town, and the house was empty. When I ran outside, there was N, up above the barn, walking along the brook. He had Larry in his arms, bundled up in his hunting jacket. Even from a distance, I could see that N was talking to him. He stopped at the big sycamore, where we have seen the barred owl five or six evenings now, and pointed up. They went all the way to the top of the hill, N stopping every few feet. When they got back, N looked sheepish. "Showing him the farm," he said. "Guess I should have told you." Larry sat in the crook of his arm, wrapped in the red-and-black-checked wool, cheeks rosy from the chill, perfectly content. Normally, at that time of day, he is crying to be fed. "How does he like it?" I asked. "Fine," Nathan said. "He likes it fine."

The outer door opened with a swish, and Elizabeth Tenney walked into the waiting room. Virginia looked up expectantly, but Elizabeth gave her only a vague smile as she went to check in. Virginia had always been a little in awe of her. Though it was quite warm that day, Elizabeth looked cool, her legs tan and smooth in open-toed sandals, her gray hair falling below her ears in soft curls.

"Elizabeth Tenney has a certain air of mystery about her," Henny had remarked once, when she and Virginia were in their mid-twenties. They had gone to the post office to mail a package to Larry, shortly after he moved to South Dakota. Henny was waiting for Virginia in her wheelchair by the big front window when she saw Elizabeth stride past with an armload of books.

They were thrilled when Kate Batchelder, the postmaster, told them Elizabeth Tenney got mail from Colombia. "Pretty regular, too," Kate said. "A letter every six weeks or so." She lowered her voice, leaning over the counter. "She never answers them, though."

"How do you know?" Henny asked. "Maybe she mails her letters from another post office."

"I know this," Kate said. "That woman went to South America—by herself—two years ago, and she hasn't been the same ever since."

"Oh, Virginia Rownd," Elizabeth said, turning away from the receptionist. "I'm sorry I didn't recognize you at first, but my eyesight isn't what it used to be." She sat down next to Virginia, laughing lightly. "What do they say? 'Old age is not for sissies'?"

"I'm sure you don't know the first thing about old age," Virginia told her.

"That's sweet of you, but I'm here because of my bursitis," she said, rubbing her shoulder. "It's giving me fits."

"My dad's in with the doctor now. You probably heard about his accident."

"I've been meaning to stop by and see him. Gordon and I just got back from Cleveland," she said, her face lighting up. "We went to visit our first grandchild, Sarah's baby girl."

"No wonder you're glowing."

"But please, tell me how your father's doing."

"He's recovering, slowly. He hardly seems like himself."

"His pride must be wounded, too, you know." She touched Virginia's hand, as if she were about to say something more, but the sound of voices made her pause.

Nathan came through the inner door, standing taller when he saw Elizabeth. He crossed the room and bent to kiss her on the cheek. "The little doctor said to go on back, Ginny. I'll sit right here and enjoy Elizabeth's company."

Virginia's shoes squeaked loudly on the freshly scrubbed linoleum of the hallway. Passing one of the two examining rooms, she noticed the pregnant nurse tearing the crumpled paper cover off the table and replacing it with a clean one.

When she saw Deanna Wallace at the desk in her office, Virginia was shocked by how young she seemed. Although she must have been in her late twenties, she looked about Randall's age. Gesturing toward the empty chair, the doctor held up a finger to let Virginia know she was nearly finished typing. Focused on the small screen, she gave an impression of absolute confidence and physical perfection. She was not so much pretty as immaculate, with her boyish haircut and slender shoulders.

"Sorry," Dr. Wallace said after a couple of minutes, giving Virginia her full attention. "I like to enter my notes as soon as I've seen a patient, so I don't forget anything."

Two more details were surprising. One was the green of her eyes, an intense, almost glassy green. Contacts, Virginia decided.

So, a little astigmatism, perhaps. The other was an engagement ring. It was hard to imagine such a self-contained person being in love, the clean edges of her life blurring into someone else's.

"I'm worried about my father," Virginia said, her voice scratchy and uncertain, as if she hadn't spoken in a long time.

"Tell me."

"He seems sort of . . . detached." She heard Elizabeth in the hall, talking with the nurse. "He's always been so vigorous and determined, but he has no energy these days."

"Your father does need to exercise," Dr. Wallace said briskly. "He needs to take his arm out of the sling at least three times a day. I gave him a sheet that describes range of motion exercises." She looked at Virginia with those green eyes, unblinking. "He should walk, too. Nothing strenuous at first. Maybe start with half a mile. The activity will improve his mood. We're also stepping down his pain medication. Same drug, but I gave him a new prescription for a lower dose. It should make a difference." Ever so noticeably glancing at her watch, she asked Virginia if she had any questions.

"How long have you been here in town?"

"Since January." Dr. Wallace punched a button on her laptop and folded the screen down. "I like working with these old farmers. A dying breed, aren't they?"

Nathan was scowling at the sheet of exercises when Virginia went out. "Well?" he asked, folding the paper with one hand and jamming it into his trouser pocket.

"You need to get up and move around, Dad. That's what Rob said, too, remember?"

"I suppose," he said.

It was too early in the day for a visit to Doc Brooks and his whiskey bottle. Instead, Virginia suggested they drop off her father's prescription and go out to Bright's Dairy for an ice cream.

"Before lunch?"

"We won't tell anyone."

Twenty minutes later they were sitting at a picnic table in the shade, Nathan taking small bites of his double-decker raspberry cone. "Maple walnut," he said as Virginia tasted hers. "That's what your mother always ordered."

"I found her journals in Aunt Ida's room," Virginia said suddenly. "I suppose you know about them."

"I remember her working on them. But I've never looked into them, if that's what you mean."

"Weren't you curious?"

"She ought to have a little something of her own, that was my thinking."

"I've been reading them."

"I expect she hoped you would, one day." Nathan turned away, closing the subject, and nodded toward the dairy. "Those must be some of the Bright grandchildren," he said.

Inside the dairy, two teenagers wearing white shirts and hairnets stood at a counter, packing ice cream into round quart containers. When Virginia was growing up, Bright's was famous for its hot fudge sauce. "Made on the Premise," their sign had announced, and no one bothered to correct it.

"People don't go for Sunday drives anymore, do they?" Virginia was thinking about how Henny's parents would invite her along on the afternoon rambles that always ended with a stop at Bright's.

"I doubt it. I would say meandering is out of fashion."

Being aimless had been the whole point. Even when Henny's father had a destination in mind—a burned-down barn or the site of a car crash—that was only a small part of the afternoon. The main thing was simply driving the back roads, waiting to see what came along. If they drove by the house of a friend, they might stop and visit for a while. They might drink a glass of lemonade in the front yard or wander out to the garden to admire a pumpkin. The friend might show them a postcard from some relative gone traveling. On the way to Bright's, they might have to stop the car to let a flock of wild turkeys cross the road. Once they had a flat tire, and everyone got out, offering advice while Mr. Eastman dug the jack and lug wrench out of the trunk.

Henny's father made sure to get Virginia home in time for the evening milking. She would sit on the metal stool, drowsy from the momentum of the car, her stomach full of ice cream and hot fudge, breathing in the salty, grassy scent of cows. Soon she would be in the house, helping her mother set out Sunday supper, then facing the math homework she always put off. But there was still that last lazy piece of the day, the sound of milk squirting into the metal buckets, the friendly chatter of her father and Larry and the Jameson boys.

"Dad," Virginia said, savoring the news she was about to deliver. "Did you recognize Jodie's boyfriend the other day, when you met him at the barbecue?"

"That skinny fellow who didn't say two words?"

"He's an old friend of ours." She paused for effect. "Leroy Jameson."

"Roy?" Nathan looked skeptical. "You're kidding."

"He told me so himself. He goes by Lee now."

"Lee Jameson," he said slowly, turning the idea over in his mind. "Well, whatever happened to them? Did he say?"

"No. He only told me who he was because he'd heard about Caro. He wanted me to know he was sorry."

"Wouldn't your mother be surprised to see him today?"

"Here's the sad part. Roger's dead. He was killed—in the army, Lee said, in Desert Storm."

"Oh, now." Nathan crumpled his paper napkin, squeezed it into a ball. "Caro always had a soft spot for Roger. She'd deny she had a favorite, but I know it's true."

Glancing at the empty sky, Virginia took a deep breath. "You must miss her sometimes."

"Of course I do." Nathan looked at her intently, then got up and went to the car.

He kept his eyes on the road as she drove, ignoring her feeble attempt to make a joke about Dr. Wallace. After a few miles she said, "I'm sorry if I upset you, Dad. I didn't mean to."

"Pull off over there." He pointed to a side road. "I have something to tell you."

Slowing the car, Virginia knew she didn't want to hear it. She guessed the doctor had given him some bad news. "What?" she asked, shutting off the ignition.

He cleared his throat and studied the balled-up napkin he was still holding. "We haven't decided anything yet, but Lydia and I are talking about selling the farm."

It took a moment to sink in. "You can't mean that." She stared at the dry skin of his palm, the tiny white scars of barbed-wire cuts. "Dad?"

"It's harder and harder for me to keep up. You can see that."

"You're only thinking this way because you're hurt. Once you feel better . . ."

"Farming is a young man's job."

"But you could hire someone to help you after I leave. I'm sure we can find somebody."

"I have to consider the future, Ginny." He turned to face her. "Lydia and I don't have a nickel set aside for our old age. Everything we have is tied up in that place."

"It's her idea, isn't it?"

"No." He closed his hand again, looked away. "It's mine."

Virginia recalled Henny's remark—so cockeyed at the time—about Lydia's relatives taking over the farm. "I don't believe you," she said.

"Don't be rude, Ginny," her father said quietly.

A car was coming along the main road, the driver looking inquisitively in their direction. Virginia waved, and it went on by.

"Rude?" She rested her forehead against the steering wheel. "Caro gave forty years of her life to keep it going, and now you decide to walk away?" She heard him shift on the seat, listened to the sound of his breathing in the cramped space, an old man's anxious breathing.

"If your mother were still with me, we'd be facing the same decision."

"I doubt that."

He dismissed the remark with an impatient flick of his hand. "Start the car, then. Let's go."

Driving back, they didn't speak. Virginia watched the familiar landscape streaming past, dry and dusty in the heat of midday. The trunk of the massive oak at the edge of Hoveys' cornfield was scabby, the leaves an unhealthy, diluted green. It looked as if a good wind might send it crashing into the road.

As they turned up the driveway, Nathan said, "Bernie Bishop is coming out tomorrow afternoon, to look the place over."

"So you've already made up your mind."

Cody's horse was cropping grass near the house, her bridle hanging loose. Cody and Randall had dragged a bicycle into the open doorway of the barn and were brushing cobwebs from its faded blue frame. Virginia recognized Larry's old Schwinn Roadster, with its arching crossbar and wide seat.

"No, we haven't," Nathan said. "And no need to say anything to Randall just yet."

Pulling up close to the steps to let him out, Virginia realized that they had forgotten to pick up his prescription. She told him she would go back for it, grateful for the excuse to escape Lydia and the happy faces of the two boys.

In the rearview mirror, she saw her father holding on to the porch railing, watching her drive away.

She went the long way, intending to drive past Bernie Bishop's house. She had known him at school, a nice kid with curly hair and a funny, pinched laugh, and four older brothers whose clothes got passed down to him. Bernie's shirts and jeans were always soft and faded, which made him seem that way, too. The only new thing he got to wear was the jacket his grand-mother gave him every Christmas. Year after year, they were nearly identical—some shade of blue with a collar that was sup-posed to look like fur. Henny once said that his grandparents, who lived near Pittsburgh, must own a jacket factory.

After high school, where Bernie made a name for himself as a guard on the basketball team, he went to work for a real estate agent in Archerville. A few years later, when he rented space above the newspaper office in the Landing and started on his own, people gave Bernie their business because they were afraid he'd fail otherwise. Then they began to notice his good wool suits, the black Lincoln Town Car he bought used and polished every weekend. By the time he was thirty, he had the balls—so Chick Mason said—to marry twenty-year-old Gwen Short, the reigning Miss Washington County.

Bernie's house was a monstrosity, a fake plantation mansion with boxy columns and a plaster fountain in the center of a wide lawn. Virginia stopped at the end of his driveway, letting the car idle for a few minutes. The lawn was freshly cut and raked, the curtains drawn against the afternoon sun. When she finally knocked on the front door, the stillness persuaded her no one was at home. Noticing a gap in the curtain to the right of the door, she bent down to peer inside.

At the same instant, an upstairs window was raised, and a gruff, boyish voice called down, "Can I help you?"

Above her, leaning out over the sill, Virginia saw the image of Bernie at ten—the elfish hair and brown eyes. Only this boy was stocky and rosy-cheeked, bold. "You must be Bernie's son," she said.

He looked from Virginia to her car and back again, yawning peevishly. She guessed that she had wakened him from a nap.

"I'm an old friend of your father's," she said.

He blinked at her, rubbing the back of his neck. "I'm not supposed to talk to strangers or let anyone in," he said at last. "My dad's working, and my mom took my sister shopping." He smiled then, revealing a fretwork of blue metal braces. "I hate shopping with them."

"Maybe I'll come back another time." Virginia stood there uncertainly.

"Oh, crap," he said, looking down the driveway. "Here's my dad now." He shut the window with a slam.

Bernie pulled his big car up beside Virginia's, squinting as he got out and took off his sunglasses. "Hey, it's Ginny Rownd. Nathan told me you were here."

"Bernie." Once they were face-to-face, she wasn't sure what to do. "I need to talk to you," she said.

"Are you okay?"

She shook her head.

"Come inside," he said. "I'll get you some water."

The living room was chilly. Virginia sat in one of the matching wingback chairs, aware of the faint hum of air-conditioning. Bernie was speaking to his son in the hallway, asking him to wait upstairs until he'd finished talking with Mrs. Rownd.

"MacLeod," she said, when he handed her the glass of water. "It's Mrs. MacLeod."

"That's right." Bernie had taken his jacket off, and he loosened his tie as he sat on the couch. "So, Mrs. MacLeod, what can I do for you?"

"Don't sell my father's farm."

"Don't?" He gave her a quizzical look. "But he asked me to come out and do an appraisal."

"He doesn't mean it."

"He sounded serious when we talked on the phone." Bernie leaned forward, so that their knees were nearly touching. "We could get a good price for that farm, Ginny. What do you call it, Second Farm? It's a beautiful place."

"Yes, it is." If he didn't know the real name was Smoke Rise, she wasn't going to tell him. "Two or three years from now, he'll be sorry."

"Most people Nathan's age have retired already," Bernie said gently. "I think he and his wife might be ready to take it easy for a change."

Virginia sat back in her chair, to put some distance between them. She liked Bernie, she reminded herself. "Listen," she said, "whatever's behind this—his accident, financial worries—selling our farm is not the answer."

"I know how you feel," Bernie said. "The old homeplace. It's hard to let go. But it's happening all over."

"You have no idea how I feel," Virginia said, cutting through the goodwill between them. She was thinking of the house where Bernie grew up, a skinny house on a back street of the Landing with cardboard taped inside the broken windowpanes. Watching his cheeks flush as he stood and walked to the center of the room, she guessed that he was, too.

"I don't want to fight with you, Ginny," he said, tracing the design in the rug with the toe of one polished shoe. "I'm sure this is a rough time for you, with everything that's happened lately." He darted a glance in her direction. "But I'll be at the farm tomorrow, like your father and I agreed on. If you think he's making a mistake, that's something for the two of you to work out."

"I want you to back off." She made an effort to keep her voice steady. "There's no reason for you to get involved, Bernie."

"Who would you prefer?" he asked her. "Some stranger?"

"What I prefer," she began with a sweeping gesture that sent her water glass flying. She made a grab for it, but the glass bounced onto the couch, and she could only watch as the water soaked into the heavy fabric.

"I'll get a rag," Bernie said, rushing out of the room.

Virginia stood beside him as he mopped at the wet spot. "We need to use a blow-dryer," she told him. "Otherwise, it's going to leave a ring."

The boy—Bernie introduced him as Benjamin—followed his father downstairs when he came back with a Hello Kitty dryer and watched solemnly as Virginia waved it back and forth over the damp cushion. "I won't tell my mom," he assured her when she shut it off.

"Okay, look," Bernie said later, as he walked Virginia outside. "There are a few ways we can go. If your father's willing to subdivide, we could sell off a couple of good-size parcels and keep the land with the buildings intact." He opened the car door for her. "We'd make a nice bundle of money for your father, and then you and your rich doctor husband could buy what's left. You'd still have the house and barn and good pastureland, if you ever wanted to get some horses, use it as a vacation home."

"A vacation home? Do you have any idea how repulsive that sounds?"

"Sorry," he said. "Real estate talk. It would be the same house, of course."

Maybe, Virginia thought, it wasn't a terrible idea, but as she got closer to town, the prospect of carving up the farm made her sick at heart all over again. Good-size parcels, Bernie had said. With vacation homes.

When she saw West's truck parked by the gas pump at Mason's Garage, Virginia slowed and pulled in. From the office, she heard the sound of voices and laughter coming from the mechanics' bay. Chick and Clyde and West, standing beneath a car on the lift, still chuckling over their joke, seemed embarrassed for a minute.

"Ginny," West said.

"What is it?" Clyde asked. "Car acting up again?"

Chick cocked his head at her, his smile fading.

Struck by the almost identical expressions on those three faces, she felt foolish for rushing in. They were men who would have done anything for her, she knew, but clearly she couldn't burden them with her problems.

Chapter Twelve

―――――••••――――――

Nathan was standing on the porch steps, wearing the canvas sun hat Caroline had bought for him years ago. Preferring his faded John Deere cap, he had rarely worn the hat, claiming it made him look like a tourist. Waiting for Lydia, he was about to go on his first official walk, as recommended by Dr. Wallace. At the end of the driveway, he and Lydia would turn left and go as far as the plank bridge, where the brook that flowed down the hill ran beneath the road—a distance of about a quarter mile.

"As soon as the dew burns off, I'm going to start cutting Ida's field." Virginia was inside the screen door, impatient, fidgeting with the flimsy hook latch.

"I wasn't sure you could handle it," Nathan said, looking over the mown fields above the house. "But you're doing a fine job."

She and her father hadn't found much to say to each other since their conversation the day before. Hearing Lydia on the stairs, Virginia stepped outside and held the door for her. As they set off, her father seemed unsteady, trying to strike a balance between his cane on one side and Lydia on the other.

"What do you think?" Randall asked, pushing Larry's bicycle out of the barn. He and Cody had polished away the rust spots and oiled the chain, pumped up the tires.

Virginia watched as he turned it over and rested it on the seat and handlebars. His interest in the bicycle would have pleased her more if she hadn't understood what was behind it. Since she was no longer welcome at Jodie's house, Randall needed a way to get there. "It looks good, kiddo."

"Kiddo yourself." Randall spun the back wheel and listened to the steady *click, click, click*. She hadn't called him that in years.

Out on the tractor by eight-thirty, the sun already hot on her shoulders, Virginia settled into the routine of mowing. Crossing the wide field, the old Ridgeway place coming into view, she felt the day tilting toward two o'clock, when Bernie Bishop would arrive. And after that, everything would be different. She'd heard that people from as far away as Philadelphia and Washington were buying up choice farm properties to use for second homes. Smoke Rise, with its open fields and its views of the river and the distant mountains, would go quickly.

Approaching the barbed-wire fence that marked the far boundary, she saw the deserted Ridgeway house surrounded by a dense growth of weeds. Its lower windows had been shot out by high school boys with their deer rifles. Here was a two-hundred-acre farm standing idle. Virginia wondered why Bernie hadn't pounced on it. Most likely, it was still owned by

Taylor Ridgeway's daughters, women in their sixties who had moved on to other lives long before.

It was shocking how quickly the house had deteriorated since Taylor's death. What had it been—six years, maybe seven? From her seat on the tractor, Virginia could see that shingles had fallen from the roof. The bricks of the two chimneys seemed to be disintegrating. The rooms would be inhabited by squirrels and mice who shredded the wallpaper and the curtains to make their nests.

Virginia thought of Oona, Taylor's wife, crocheting curtains for the dining room, the steady looping of the thread over her silver needle. Oona had worked on the curtains through one fall and winter, finally hanging them in the spring. She had invited Caroline and Virginia over for tea the day she put them up.

"Not a proper English tea," Oona had remarked in her crisp accent, fussing over the arrangement of scones on a plate, pouring from the plump brown pot she had brought with her when she came over to marry Taylor. "You can't buy what you need here." She and her husband had met after the Second World War, when Taylor was stationed at an army base near her parents' home.

Even as a child tasting tea for the first time, Virginia had felt Oona's homesickness. When she described the village near London where she had grown up, Virginia understood that she was missing the lanes where she used to ride her bicycle, the talk of neighbors when they met at the shops in the morning. Oona had gone back to England once—alone, because they could afford only her ticket—to celebrate her sister's seventieth birthday. She had not returned. She died in her sister's house the morning after the party, of a heart attack that knocked her to the floor as she stood brushing her hair. Oona's family arranged a funeral at the small stone church where she had been baptized, and she was buried next to her parents in the churchyard beside it. Taylor stayed at home. Every spring for the next twelve years, he washed and ironed the lace curtains, as Oona had done, and hung them again, as if he were expecting her back any day.

There was a picture Virginia wanted to find, of herself at age two or three sitting on one of Taylor's big workhorses. It used to hang in an oval frame over the sideboard in the kitchen, before Lydia took it down. Virginia couldn't really remember the day it was taken. Her mother had told her a traveling photographer came up to the Ridgeway farm one afternoon and asked if he could take a picture of Dane and Dolly, Taylor's team of Belgians. Then he wanted to get a shot of Virginia on Dane's back. In the picture, Virginia is wearing a flowered dress and holding a fistful of the horse's mane. Dane's back is so wide, her legs stick straight out, and she points her bare toes at the camera, like a ballerina. She looks pleased with herself—a little girl on top of the world.

Those horses were his single extravagance, Oona used to say, proud of all the ribbons they won at the county fair. Taylor had brought them to the farm as yearlings and trained them to pull the farm equipment he'd inherited—the plow and the mowing machine and the hay rake—as well as a wagon. Over the years, he used his tractor more and more, but every summer he hitched Dane and Dolly to the mowing machine and made a few passes across his field to mark the start of haying season.

"Ceremonial, like the queen," Virginia remembered Oona saying. She loved to watch them running free, their manes and tails flying, their heavy hooves thudding so that she could feel the ground vibrate. It amazed her that creatures that large could be so graceful.

Larry and her father used to talk of raising a rare breed of draft horse called American Cream, Virginia remembered. She had never seen one, but her father had once shown her an article on heritage breeds with a photograph of two colts born on a farm in Iowa. A light cream color with pink noses, the colts kicked up their heels in a pasture.

"They're gorgeous, Dad," she'd said. "You should get a pair."

"One of these days." He'd closed the magazine. "I do like the look of them."

Flattered by her interest, her father had told her what he knew about American Creams. The breed had been developed in Iowa, beginning with a cream-colored mare named Old Granny, sometime in the early 1900s. An odd name, Virginia considered, given that the mare had produced so many offspring with her distinctive cream color and white markings. American Creams were slightly smaller than other draft horses, she recalled, with gentle dispositions that made them easy to handle.

One of these days.

Easing the tractor to a stop, Virginia took in the long slope of Ida's field, her heart thumping. She set the gearshift in neutral and jumped down. In the center of the field, the leaves of the sycamore under which her great-aunt's ashes were buried seemed to wave at her in the light breeze.

"Ida," she called. "Ida, what an idea!" She was on the verge of racing down the hill to embrace the vast trunk, as if it were Aunt Ida herself, when the idling tractor gave a snort and went silent. "And what an idiot I am."

On her way to the tractor shed for a can of gasoline, she decided the best thing would be to surprise her father. She just needed a little time to figure everything out.

Dressed in his old basketball shorts, with a bandanna tied around his forehead, Randall had started painting the porch railings. He had moved the kitchen radio to the windowsill in her father's office and tuned it to an oldies station—Rob's influence. Cleo, nearly deaf, slept under the open window.

Randall motioned to her with the paintbrush. "I have a message for you," he said over the music. "Dad called. He's going out to dinner with Jan and Steve tonight, for their anniversary. He won't be home until later."

"Oh, no. I completely forgot." The two couples had gotten into the habit of celebrating their anniversaries together, and Virginia was dismayed that she hadn't thought even to send a card. Maybe she could still order flowers.

Inside, Lydia was vacuuming the upstairs hallway, dragging the old Hoover across the bare wood floor. Virginia found her father in his office, standing in front of the desk, on which he had stacked his farm journals. He seemed perplexed.

"Sorry about the noise," she said, turning down the radio.

"Don't be. It's good having a young person around." He gestured helplessly at the clutter. "I'm not sure what to do with all this stuff. Lydia asked me to tidy up in here."

"We can probably hide most of it in the closet, but I need to ask you something first."

"Trouble with the tractor?"

She shook her head. "Let's go out front."

"Funny, isn't it?" Nathan remarked as they stood together, admiring the lawn Randall and Cody had mowed the day before. "All the years I've lived in this house, and I forget we have a front porch. It's nice out here."

"I need you to promise me something," Virginia said. "Can you wait until Labor Day before you sign a contract with Bernie? You should take the time to think this through."

"I've thought about it every day since I got out of the hospital."

"Dad, your family has worked this farm for more than two hundred years. All I'm asking is that you wait a few more weeks before you let it go."

The vacuum cleaner stopped. They heard it clank down the hall and then start up again in one of the bedrooms.

"I don't know," her father said. "I'd have to speak with Lydia first."

Virginia stepped down and stood on the grass. "Why can't this be between the two of us?" she asked, turning to look up at him. "She doesn't care about this place."

"I'm surprised that you do." Her father was watching her curiously. "You haven't had much time for it yourself."

"Out in Ida's field, I was thinking about her sycamore and how no one but us would know it was hers, or even who she was. And they wouldn't know about Taylor and Oona." She looked away.

"Don't be so sad, Ginny." Her father held his good arm out to her and hugged her around the shoulder when she went back to him. Patting her awkwardly on the back, he promised not to make a decision before Labor Day.

"You might take a break from your painting and go for a swim this afternoon," Lydia suggested to Randall as they ate lunch.

"Maybe I will," he said, surprised. "I can try out the bicycle."

"Just put the cans and brushes in the shed before you go."

"Okay." Randall raised his eyebrows questioningly at his mother.

Lydia had already changed into one of her good dresses. She had put fresh towels in the downstairs bathroom, Virginia noticed. Getting everything ready for Bernie. Yes, Virginia decided, she would definitely go to town for the afternoon.

"Oh, too bad," her uncle Dan said when Virginia walked into his office. "You missed Carrie by about ten minutes. She was here with the baby, finishing up this week's calendar." He stood and motioned her to his chair. "How's everything at the farm?"

"Great." She nodded. "Everything's fine."

Within a few minutes, he had set her up at his computer and gone off to a meeting. When the pictures of the horses started coming up on the screen, Virginia knew they were the answer. "You beauties," she whispered, reaching out to touch them.

Reading through one website after another, Virginia discovered two bloodlines that seemed promising. It looked as if she could find a yearling colt from one and a filly from the other, both on farms in Iowa. Picking up the phone to find out if they were still available, she paused and put it down again. She had no idea what questions to ask. Maybe the two horses she favored weren't the best. She printed out several pages and stuffed them into a manila envelope before her uncle returned.

Virginia wished Taylor were still around to advise her. She didn't know of anyone who kept draft horses anymore—except for the horse loggers upstate, and they used the bigger breeds, like Percherons. West's father, Winn Moffat, used to tell them stories about farming with horses, she remembered. He always referred to them as the "shire horses," and she had assumed that "shire" was another word for "big."

Winn had been at the nursing home in Fayette for a couple of years now. Some days he recognized his visitors, sometimes not. If you caught him on a good day, her father said, he could tell you the history of the county, chapter and verse, right up to the day his brain clouded over. The doctors couldn't say what had happened to Winn. It came on too suddenly to be Alzheimer's, they thought. One morning he woke up and didn't know where he was, didn't recognize his wife. There he was, seventy-four years old, in his tough old farmer's body with a mind that wandered about and occasionally shut down altogether.

Checking the clock in the newsroom, Virginia saw that she didn't have time to visit Winn that afternoon. She didn't want to go home, either, because Bernie would still be there—creeping around in his shiny shoes, making notes on his clipboard.

On the way to Henny's, she stopped to admire the Hoveys' cornfield, the waist-high plants a deep, healthy green. For weeks now, Virginia had been driving past her father's corn with barely a glance. With all the rain they'd had, it was probably fine, but she ought to make a few passes down the rows with the harrow to keep the weeds under control. A low-flying crow caught her eye, and she followed its silent flight beyond the field, where the dark line of trees rose suddenly, the oaks and softwoods trailing up the gentle rise of hills, growing thicker as they ascended. She watched until the crow disappeared, remembering the day twenty-seven years before when West had taken her up there along the brook.

They were both seventeen, seniors in high school, when West had asked Virginia to come along one morning while he checked his traplines. She had said yes without a thought. In those days, the time she spent with West was the best time, no matter what they were doing. Besides, it was an honor to be asked. Most boys wouldn't have wanted their girlfriends along.

It was just past dawn on a gray November morning when they set off in his father's pickup. When he stopped in town to buy five dollars' worth of gas at Mason's Garage, West brought Virginia a paper cup of coffee and a cinnamon-sugar donut from inside the dingy station. Bob Will, hardly more than a dark smudge behind the cash register, waved with a flip of his hand as they pulled away.

A light snow began to fall. West turned the heater up, but he kept the radio low so he could explain what they were going to do. First, they would walk along Hovey Brook, up to the pond where he was trapping muskrats. For water animals like muskrat and beaver, he told her, he used Conibear traps that held the whole body. For the others, he used leghold traps.

He picked up the leather holster on the seat between them. "This is the twenty-two-caliber pistol my father gave me last year," he said, a shimmer of pride in his voice. "If everything works right, the muskrat will drown, but sometimes you have to shoot them. You want one clean shot in the head, so you don't spoil the fur." He set the holster down again. "With the leghold, you always have to shoot the animal."

Something twisted in Virginia's stomach. Wrapping the remainder of her donut in the little waxed paper square, she placed it beside the gun and rolled the window down partway to let the cold air blow over her face. It would be all right, she told herself—exciting, even, something to tell Henny about later. She finished her coffee, watching the snow falling on bare branches.

West parked on a dirt track at the edge of the Hoveys' field. Reaching behind the seat, he brought out two red-and-black-checked hunting hats. He watched as Virginia put hers on and pulled down the earflaps. "Suits you," he said, leaning over to give her a brief, coffee-flavored kiss.

She slid out the passenger side and waited while West took two burlap bags out of the back, rolled them up, and handed them to her. Then he slung the holster over his shoulder, and they started off along the brook. A crust of ice had begun to form at the edges of the water, where it touched the bank, and around the larger stones in the channel. The only sounds were the steady splash of the brook and the cawing of a pair of crows as they flew over the deserted cornfield.

Where the ground started to rise and the bank got steeper, West knelt down and motioned her closer. "Right here," he said. "Muskrat tracks."

Virginia knelt beside him and saw in the partially frozen mud what looked like the imprints of many tiny hands. The tracks seemed purposeful, an alternating pattern of large indentations partially covering smaller ones, running along the edge of the bank.

"These bigger ones are the back feet," West said, taking a glove off and rubbing his fingers over the shallow impressions. "They have five toes on the front and back both, but the front feet are a lot smaller. See the little thumb mark here? Look, you can see the nails, too."

"The tracks go down to the water and disappear."

"There's a burrow under the bank. They've been up here feeding." West stood and adjusted the holster. "These guys have a lodge above the pond. It's like a beaver lodge, only not as big. Come on, I'll show you."

Her eyes on the leather strap across his shoulder, Virginia followed. The lucky ones drowned, he'd said.

Before they reached the pond, West dropped to his knees again. "Oh, man, I can't believe this," he said, leaning out over the water.

"What?" Virginia took hold of his jacket to keep him from falling in.

"Look." He pulled up a square steel trap, dripping water. "It's sprung, and the bait's gone." Sitting back on his heels, he turned the trap over in his hands. "I don't get it."

The next four traps were empty, too, all of them sprung. "This never happened before," West said.

All at once the crows set up a ruckus. There were six or seven of them by then, wheeling over the field below, screeching and cawing as if they knew all about it. Virginia watched them circle twice before she said it might have been raccoons raiding the traps.

"Not likely." West stood there, squinting at the crows.

"What about these?" Virginia pointed to the tracks criss-crossing the ground in front of her. No other animal walked like that, she knew. Around the farm, raccoons stole at every opportunity, then ambled away, leaving their side-by-side prints in the dust of the grain room, the hind feet and front feet alternating sides. The pattern of it reminded her of the charts the gym teacher used at school when she was trying to teach them how to dance.

West scuffed at the tracks with the toe of his boot. "Crap," he said, then turned and headed back toward the truck. By the time Virginia caught up with him, he had the motor running.

"What are you going to do?" She stuffed the burlap sacks into the narrow space behind the seat.

"Check my other traps." He jammed the balky gearshift into reverse and gunned the engine, making the truck fishtail in the wet snow.

About half a mile down the road, he pulled off again. Virginia was hoping he would lose interest in his traps and remember the previous Saturday night, when they had parked not far from there, when he had leaned into her, unzipping her heavy jacket. The next morning, in church, all she could think about was the way his fingers had trailed down her back and then brushed across her breasts, pausing at the line between fabric and skin. It came to her that he had been waiting for a sign, some subtle shift or whispered word. By the time she rose with the congregation to sing the last hymn, Virginia was giddy with the knowledge that she and West would cross that boundary together.

His thoughts were elsewhere. He snatched the gun off the

seat and began to stalk off into the trees, finally stopping after several yards to wait for her. "I'm glad you're here," he said. "But I'm pissed about those traps. And I forgot to bring any bait."

"What do you use?"

"Little stinky fish. Sometimes carrots." He put his arm around her, and they walked on together. The snow came harder, sticking to their hats and boots.

As they neared a small clearing, Virginia heard a low growl like the sound of a barn cat with a freshly caught mouse. A warning to back off. Then she saw the fox, one of its hind legs caught in a trap staked down between two birches at the clearing's edge. It was a small red fox, probably not more than a year old, and as they got closer, it flattened its ears and snarled, its back tensing as if it were about to run. The fox looked steadily at West. As he moved toward it, drawing the pistol out of the holster, its eyes darkened with fear.

"You're not going to shoot it, are you?" Virginia asked.

"I have to."

When he raised the pistol and took aim, Virginia lunged at him, clamping her hand over his wrist. "Just let it go."

With his free hand, West reached across his outstretched arm to push her away. "If you don't want to see this, go on back to the truck."

Virginia didn't move. She hardly flinched at the sound of the shot. She could see the bullet break open the skull, the fine spray of blood and fur. The small body went slack instantly. She watched as West went over to release the trap.

Replacing the pistol in its holster, West lifted the fox by its back legs. "Let's go," he said, not looking at Virginia. He started down the hill, holding the animal high enough that it wouldn't drag along the ground. The dainty black feet swung from side to side with the motion of his steps.

Virginia wanted to reach out and stroke the tail—the rich auburn fur tipped with silver hairs—that now hung limply down its back. She could smell the blood that dripped from the head wound, leaving a trail of red drops in the snow. At first, she thought the wet warmth on her face was blood somehow, and then she realized she was crying.

She wondered how long it had been in the trap. The winter before, from her bedroom window, she had seen a sleeping fox curled on a flat rock in the sun, its tail wrapped around its body. It had wakened leisurely and stretched, drunk from the brook before trotting back up the hill. This fox probably had a den nearby, lined with moss and soft pine needles, empty now.

"I didn't know you were trapping foxes," she said to West's back, embarrassed by the shakiness of her voice.

"Well, what did you think?" When they reached the truck, he asked her to spread the burlap sacks in the back. He placed the fox's body on top of them, running his ungloved hand over the thick pelt, and told Virginia he would take her home.

"I'd rather walk," she said, turning away.

"Ginny, it's nine or ten miles, at least. Come on."

Before she reached the road, West stopped her with his hands on her shoulders. "I'm sorry you're upset," he said. "But really, what did you think?" He tried to embrace her, but she flung away from him. Eventually, he persuaded her to get into the truck.

"It doesn't matter that much to you, does it?" she asked after a few miles, taking off the hunting hat and using it to wipe her face. "Killing things."

"No. It bothers me, some." West watched the windshield wipers make two clean arcs across the glass. "Overall, trapping is good for the animals. It weeds out the weak and sick ones."

"That's bullshit." Virginia took a long, unsteady breath. "You have a handkerchief or something?"

"Try the glove compartment. There might be something in there." He risked a glance in her direction. "Mother Nature does a lot worse. You know how many animals die in a bad winter?"

Virginia blew her nose on an oily rag. "So you're Mother Nature's little helper."

"Now you're being stupid." West took his hat off, too, and tossed it at the windshield. When it fell at Virginia's feet, she kicked it away.

"Great," she said as they drove into her dooryard. Her father and brother waved from the tractor shed, where they were putting new plugs in the John Deere.

"Ginny, I'm sorry," West said, holding her arm when she tried to pull away. "I shouldn't have asked you to come."

"I can't talk now. I have to go."

He released her. "I'll call you later, okay?"

"No. Don't call."

Virginia was out of the truck and running up the porch steps, through the front door and up the stairs to her room, ignoring her mother's voice. When she drew the curtain aside, she saw West standing beside the pickup with Larry and her father, admiring the fox. West was talking excitedly, raking his fingers through his dark hair.

She could hear the slick metallic sound of her mother sharpening knives in the kitchen, and she slid to the floor, her back against the wall. In a few days, they would butcher their pigs. It sickened her, all of it. Chickens with severed heads running around the barnyard, blood spurting from their necks. The blood of baby rabbits caught in their nests in the hayfield, slashed by the mowing blades. The pigs with their throats cut, hanging by their back legs over the metal tubs, their blood dripping for hours. How did the earth soak up so much blood?

Even though she no longer believed in it, she closed her eyes and prayed. She was thinking of Greenfield, the college in Ohio she and her mother had visited in the spring, the campus with its narrow walkways and white clapboard buildings on the outskirts of a genteel town. Both of them had liked the school, and as the deadline approached, her mother was urging her to apply. Virginia had been working on the application essay for a while, but only in a halfhearted way. Every time she started to write, she felt torn between wanting to go and wanting to stay close to Henny and West. "Please, God," she whispered as she listened to West's truck pulling away. "Let me get in."

HENNY

Ginny burst into the kitchen and found me with Bonnie Mason, going over the monthly receipts for the
garage. "Oh," she said. "I didn't know you had company."

We both looked at her. Bonnie's car was parked right in
front of the house.

She wanted to tell me something, Ginny said, something
important. She was clutching a big manila envelope against her
chest.

Bonnie offered to come back later.

"You don't need to leave," Ginny said. "As long as you
promise not to tell a soul. Both of you."

Out of habit, I pressed my right hand against Ginny's and
said, "Swear."

Embarrassed, Bonnie reached out, too. "All right," she said.
"I swear." Then she folded her arms and tucked her hands out
of sight.

Ginny sat across from us and set the envelope down and opened and closed the clasp three or four times. "It's my father," she said finally. "He's talking about selling his farm. He's got Bernie over there right now."

I couldn't believe it. Nathan Rownd would never put his farm up for sale.

Bonnie asked if he was sick. She wondered if his spill from the tractor had done more damage than they knew at first.

"His doctor says he should be healed up by the fall." Ginny glanced toward the window. We could hear my parents out in the garden, where they were hoeing the rows, side-dressing the tomatoes and beans.

For once I couldn't think of a word to say. I asked her if she wanted a glass of iced tea.

"Why is it," Ginny said, "that when someone's in trouble people offer them a drink? I went over to Bernie's yesterday, and he gave me a glass of water. I ended up spilling most of it on Gwen's couch."

"Uh-oh." Bonnie smiled in spite of herself.

"What do you have there?" I nodded at the envelope.

Ginny opened it shyly, spreading several pages in front of us. "These are American Creams."

"Aren't they sweet?" Bonnie said. "These little ones."

"Handsome," I said.

"Yes." Ginny nodded at the upside-down pictures. We waited for her to say something more.

"A pair of young horses would be a wonderful 4-H project for your boy, Randall," Bonnie ventured. "He made a big impression on our three girls, you know. They couldn't stop talking about him after the baseball game." She paused, her cheeks coloring. "If he were living here, I mean, about the 4-H."

I put a hand on Bonnie's arm. "What are you thinking, Ginny?"

"My dad wanted to get a pair of these draft horses, years ago. You might remember when he and Larry had this idea about breeding heritage livestock to sell, maybe cutting back on the dairy operation."

"I do remember some talk about that." At the time, my father had said it sounded like they wanted to turn their farm into a sideshow.

"I've decided to surprise him with a pair of American Creams for his birthday," Ginny said, turning one of the pictures around.

"But how will he keep them?" Bonnie asked. "If he sells his place?"

"That's the point," Ginny said. "What he needs is something to get his blood stirring again, something to make him stop feeling like a tired old dairy farmer."

I went to the door with her when she left. Once she finished haying Ida's field, she told me, she was going to make the trip to Iowa and find the horses.

There was something I wanted to tell her, too, but this didn't seem like the right time. If I hadn't been so full of my own news, I might have argued with her, advised her to think it through. Instead, I wished her good luck. I watched until her car turned in to the road at the end of our lane before going back inside. I knew, and possibly Ginny didn't, that her father had financed his milking parlor and paid for his new tractor with a mortgage on the farm. Like the rest of us, he was getting by from one year to the next by paying off interest. But Nathan was a shrewd farmer, a hard worker. He always made it through.

Later, I sat out on the porch with my parents as the evening settled in. Our first cutting was finished. The fields were fragrant with new growth, alive with the stir of insects. We watched the scrim of clouds in the east pick up the sun's last rays reflected off the river, a rose and silver glow along their underbellies. In the pasture beyond the barn, one of our heifers called out. A car's headlights came wavering up the road, and I smiled, thinking it might be Marcus, but it went on by.

Chapter Thirteen

———————◆———————

Virginia sat on the couch in the dark, waiting for Rob's
call. She was calculating the cost of buying the horses
and bringing them to the farm, planning how she would
explain it all. Rob was generous, but they didn't have as much
as people assumed, even with her teaching salary. There was
malpractice insurance, saving for Randall's college, their retirement account. She did have her Old Age Fund, as they called
it, the money Aunt Ida had left her.

She let herself lean against the padded arm of the couch and
pulled her father's afghan over her shoulders. She hoped Rob
would call soon.

There were muffled footsteps approaching, and then West
touched her arm and said something in her ear, the way he had
at her father's wedding. As she strained to understand him, she
felt his breath warm on her neck. She woke suddenly, with the
sense that the phone had been ringing. She heard nothing but

the sounds of the house settling for the night, the ticking of the metal roof as it cooled.

Sitting up, Virginia pulled the little chain on the lamp, closing her eyes against the brightness. She had once dreamed that the principal of her school—a stout, balding man with a bushy mustache—had kissed her on the mouth. It was a passionate kiss, the two of them standing in the shadowy alcove where the faculty mailboxes were. He had placed one hand on the small of her back and drawn her close. The next time she saw him, she noticed his lips and wondered if kissing him would really be that thrilling. Not likely, she decided.

At least it made sense that she would be dreaming of West. The memory rose again sharply. It still troubled her that a person as fine as West might act that way. When she had asked her father's opinion, back then, he'd said it struck him as a cruel practice, killing wild things for money.

"Still," he'd said. "All our ancestors were trappers as well as farmers. You know that. West's grandfather taught it to him. It was a bond they had."

West might have given it up, if she had asked him. Late at night, studying in her dorm room that first year away, she sometimes imagined what it would be like if he came to get her. She stopped asking Henny about him, because there was always the mention of some girl. She had the impression West was running wild that year—drinking too much, driving too fast. Once, she heard, he got his eye cut in a bar fight. The boys at her school were awfully sedate by comparison.

Virginia picked up the journal she had been reading before she dozed off. Running her fingers over the grain of the cover, she opened it and found her place: August 21, 1960. Larry would have been two years old.

"A difficult day," her mother had written.

Everyone on edge because of the drought, and Larry with new teeth coming in—feverish and fussy. No rain since the thunderstorm on July 30, and every day since the temperature has hit 90. The cows lie under the trees, panting like dogs, or else they crowd into what's left of the brook and get right down in the mud. At milking time, ambling to the barn in their coats of mud, they look like clay statues come to life. N says it helps keep the flies off them. The heat is hard on the chickens too. I found a dead one this morning, one of the big white meat birds. N and his father burned it, in case it had a virus, but Hattie said it was probably heatstroke. H very sharp with me when I started to run a little water to bathe Larry. She said to rub him down with alcohol. I decided to visit my mother instead. Drove off in N's truck and didn't even say where I was going. Nice to be home. Larry got a shampoo and a real bath, then fell asleep on the couch. I sat on the porch with my mother, snapping beans, saying hello to the few people in the Landing foolish enough to be out walking in the heat of the day. Got back to the farm in time to help with supper. H a little distant. Finally, she mentioned that my folks have a first-rate well and said she was surprised I hadn't brought back a few jugs of water. N overheard her and gave me a sympathetic smile and said we would go get some tomorrow. I wish he would speak up for me sometimes.

Caroline had drawn a line of six cows, or little clay statues of cows, at the bottom of the page, walking single file.

Virginia's memories of her grandmother at the farm were vague. Hurricane Hattie, they had called her, behind her back at first. Then Larry had slipped up once and said it in front of her. Virginia did remember the silence in the room, the horrified look on her father's face.

"Hurricane Hattie," her grandmother had repeated, a rare smile spreading across her face. "Well, it suits me, doesn't it?"

Not long after that, Hattie Rownd had a stroke that left her speechless. By the time Virginia was seven, her grandparents had moved into a house in Rownd's Point, where Hattie cooked and cleaned as usual and began to write messages in a Big Chief tablet. When they went to visit, Virginia liked to sharpen Hattie's pencils and line them up on the kitchen table. Once, when she was alone in the room, she had peeked inside the tablet and was surprised by the way her grandmother's handwriting had changed—the letters large and shaky, as if written by a child. "Need twine for morning glories," she read at the top of one page. And farther down, "Sorry broke the glass pitcher, wedding gift." Beneath that, in her grandfather Chandler's neat, back-sloping hand, "Not your fault, Hattie. Never liked it anyway." Virginia wondered if her grandfather had stopped talking, too, when he was alone with his wife.

At first, Chandler drove back to the farm nearly every day, but within a year he would come only to help with the big things, like planting and haying. Larry and Virginia had assumed regular chores of their own, and soon the farm felt like it belonged to them—their grandfather a polite, interested visitor from town. He didn't mind the town life, he told them. He could sleep as late as he liked, though he never made it past six-thirty. Behind the white frame house, he planted a small vegetable garden. He started carving birds. Herons, especially, fascinated him. He spent hours mixing paint, trying to capture the right shade of blue-gray for the wings. Some evenings he walked down the street to Andy Detweiler's, smoked a pipe on the back steps with his new friend, and listened to the loud voices of game shows on the television inside. Maybe that was the sort of life her father envisioned for himself. Himself and Lydia.

The phone was definitely ringing on the table in the hallway, and Virginia rushed to pick it up. "Rob," she said. "It's pretty late."

"Sorry. You know how these evenings go." He cleared his throat. "Jan and Steve say hello. That was a nice touch, having the flowers delivered to the restaurant. The waiter brought them right after we sat down."

"I thought Jan would like that."

"We missed you."

Virginia paced as far as the phone cord would allow while Rob described the anniversary dinner, his meeting with the head of orthopedics that morning. "Oh, and guess who I saw today. Your guy Eddie."

"Bisconi?"

"I stopped at Miranda's to get a coffee, and there he was behind the counter. He actually said, 'It's on the house, Doc.' He gave me extra foam."

"Extra foam? He must like you."

"Only because I'm married to you."

"Rob, I'm going to switch to the phone in my dad's office. Hold on a second." She stopped in the kitchen to fill a glass with water, then lifted the receiver and told her husband she hoped he was sitting down.

There was a long pause when she finished speaking, and then Rob said, "I have to admit I think your father's doing the right thing."

"Are you kidding?"

"Honey, give the guy a break. He's old, he's hurt, and now he has a chance to cash in and live his last years in comfort. Let him do it."

"He's not old." Virginia took a drink of water. "Not that old." Light flickered through the curtain, and when she stepped to the window, she saw a streaky brightness flashing across the sky. Heat lightning. "If he lost this place, he'd be lost, too. I know it."

"You are such a romantic, Virginia."

"But what do you think about my idea? The horses? He would be thrilled to have them. And then he could sell the cows and become a horse breeder."

Rob sighed. Virginia heard the rattle of keys, the clink of coins. She knew he was standing at the kitchen counter, emptying his pockets, dropping change into the clay pot Randall had made one summer.

"You should sleep on it," Rob said. "Consider what your father would have to go through if he actually wanted to breed horses. It would take time, especially if he started with a pair of yearlings. Even I know that much."

"Maybe I could get an older pair, too. Start him off with four."

"Listen. If you want to get away for a few days, come down here and visit me. I'm on call this weekend, but I can still show you a good time."

"You're not taking me seriously."

"But this horse thing is crazy. It's thirty years too late."

Neither of them wanted to get into a real argument on the phone, and so they said good night. At the window, watching how the lightning made the barn roof glow, Virginia was reminded of the house in Shaker Heights where Rob grew up. Its soaring lines and brightly lit windows had made her breath catch in her throat when he took her there to meet his parents. His mother, wearing a smoke-colored Chanel suit and black pumps, greeted her with a fluttery handshake and a quick, appraising glance. His father, a heart specialist with flashing white teeth, put his arm around her shoulder and offered her a Scotch. Everything about the house felt stiff and correct; even the antiques looked new. When they returned from the restaurant, where Virginia had mistakenly ordered a glass of "Pinot Georgio," she lay on the bed in the guest room, watching the watery reflection of a streetlamp on the ceiling, praying Rob wouldn't sneak in. Then, when he hadn't come, she had been disappointed in him.

Retired now, his parents owned two condominiums, one in Shaker Heights and one in Myrtle Beach. "It's good to travel light again." Virginia remembered Rob's father saying that, flexing his shoulders as if he had carried the huge house on his back all those years.

———

Winn Moffat sat stiffly on the edge of the bed in his narrow room, wearing a plaid shirt and a string tie, his hair freshly combed. He clasped his hands in his lap and watched them come in and sit down.

Winn's eyes were very dark. He claimed an Iroquois ancestor on his mother's side, and now that he was older, Virginia could see the truth of that. He seemed almost hawklike, quiet but alert there on the chenille bedspread. He had on a pair of running shoes with Velcro fasteners.

"Dad," West said. "Do you know who this is?"

"Yes, I do." He glanced at his son and then looked back at Virginia.

"She wants to buy some horses. She needs to ask your advice first."

"All right then." His voice was low, a little raspy.

"They're for my father," Virginia said. "You remember him. Nathan Rownd."

"No," Winn said. "I don't think so." He looked steadily at Virginia.

"My mother was Caroline."

Winn shook his head.

"Why don't we go outside?" West suggested.

Winn stood easily but kept one hand on his bed. He nodded toward the door of the closet, where a cane was hooked over the knob. It was an ugly metal cane like her father's, with a gray rubber handgrip and a rubber tip on the end. West handed it to him, and they followed him down the hallway to the reception desk, where West signed him out. On the wide front porch, two or three patients were dozing in rocking chairs.

"Go straight," Winn said when they got to the bottom of the steps.

Reaching the end of the lawn, they crossed a paved road and walked through a border of high grass onto a fairway. There was a putting green in the distance, a red flag on a metal pole.

"Who plays golf?" Virginia asked.

"The doctors," West said. "This is the country club. You can't see the clubhouse from here. It's on the other side of that hill."

"I like it here," Winn said. "They have ponds." He headed down the fairway, his cane leaving small, round imprints in the grass.

"I guess the old judge had it made." West looked back at the nursing home, once Judge Farley's mansion, situated above the long, sloping lawn. "He could roll out of bed in the morning and be on the course in five minutes."

"It's a nice home, anyway," Virginia said. "Not like some."

"Let's go," Winn called over his shoulder.

Approaching one of the ponds, a water hazard near the green, Winn stopped and told them to be quiet. He walked ahead stealthily, and they heard four or five loud splashes. "Damn," he said.

"He's always hoping to catch one of those big bullfrogs napping on the bank," West told her.

"I think they smell me coming." Winn led them on to the top of a small hill.

When the clubhouse came into view, they could see waiters in red jackets moving about the terrace, probably setting up the tables for cocktail hour. There were only two carts out on the course, a man wearing a yellow shirt bent over his putter on the ninth green. A whiff of chemical fertilizers hung in the air.

"This is his favorite spot," West said.

Virginia had passed West on the road, heading out of town, as she drove into Fayette. He had blinked his headlights at her, and she had pulled over, waiting for him to turn around. He'd just made a delivery to the restaurant, he explained, and then, when he found out where she was going, he said he would come along. He had warned her not to expect too much from his father.

"Do you think he really recognizes me?" Virginia asked.

"I can't tell. You must seem familiar to him."

When they got back to the nursing home, the porch was empty. They sat at a wicker table on the shady end to talk.

"Nice of you to come and see me," Winn said to Virginia. Before she could reply, he turned to West. "When are you two getting married, anyway?"

"I don't know." West smiled at him. "We haven't set a date."

"You're not getting any younger, son."

"Let me tell you about the horses," Virginia said, sliding her hands into her lap so that Winn wouldn't be confused by her wedding ring. West hadn't been wearing his lately, but there was a pale circle on his ring finger.

No, Winn had not heard of American Creams. It was a good name, though. He liked the name. He talked at length about the Shire horses they once kept on the farm, and Virginia realized then that Shire was a breed. Temperament and intelligence, those were the most important things to consider, he said, when you went looking for a draft horse. More important than size.

"People think your fancy horses are the smart ones. That isn't so. They only do what's natural to a horse—run, jump over a stream. It's the workhorses have real intelligence. They come to understand a job, what's expected of them." He chuckled to himself. "When to take a shortcut."

A nurse appeared beside them and held her fingers against Winn's forehead and then his cheek. "You're having a first-rate afternoon, aren't you?" she said. "But you're still a bit warm."

"It's from walking," he said. "We went to the ponds."

"I'll get you some Tylenol after your guests leave." She looked at West. "He's been running a low-grade fever for a day or so. The doctor says it's nothing to worry about, probably a little cold."

"They can't keep their hands off me." Winn watched the nurse going back inside.

"How do you know if a horse is healthy?" Virginia asked him. "Are you really supposed to check their teeth?"

"Only if you're buying an old nag. If you can, you want to get a good look at the mare and stallion both, the lines of them. Stand right up close and see if they're comfortable with people, lift their hooves. You can tell a lot right there, like with people's fingernails. Now the little ones, you want to have a good feel of them—their legs and bellies, see if there's any swelling or lumps. Talk to them. Watch how they respond to you." He stopped. "Son, are you going with her?"

"Well," West said.

"You don't want to send a pretty girl like this off by herself. Those horse traders are a terrible lot."

They were in the doorway of Winn's room, saying good-bye, when he decided he had better go, too. "I know how to handle a horse trader," he said. "When are we leaving?"

"Saturday," Virginia said.

"You tell them at the desk out there." Winn pointed with his cane. "You have to sign me out again. And don't forget. Otherwise, they'll think I've run away."

Chapter Fourteen

⸻

Winn was waiting on the porch of the nursing home, standing on the top step with his bag beside him. It was early enough that fog still hung over the valley. The golf course was deserted. They could barely make out the red flags hanging limply on their poles.

"He's been quite aware since you were here," the nurse said. It was the same one they'd seen before, and she was obviously curious about Virginia's presence. While West got his father settled in the truck, the nurse lined up Winn's medications on the desk and explained to Virginia when he should take them.

"Dr. Krausman wasn't in favor of this trip at first," she said. "But he's impressed by how Mr. Moffat has perked up the past few days." She handed Virginia a plastic bag containing the four bottles of pills. "As West knows, his father's state of mind is fairly unpredictable. I hope it works out."

"Thanks." Virginia decided to let it go at that. West had

promised to call the nursing home to let them know how Winn was getting along, to have him back by the end of the week.

Once they left the county road and turned onto the highway at little Washington, once they passed the first red and blue Interstate 70 sign, Virginia sensed a ripple of excitement in the cab of the truck. At last, they were on their way.

She was thinking of West's old pickup, the one that had taken them so many miles over the back roads. This one was deluxe. It had a CD player and padded seats that reclined, clean gray carpeting on the floor. Winn had made a nest for himself on the narrow backseat with the blanket and pillow West had brought for him and the jacket the nurse had pressed on him at the last minute. For now, he was sitting up, watchful.

"How about playing one of those little records?" Winn leaned forward, pointing to the plastic CD cases in the holder under the dashboard. "Have you got any Doc Watson up there?"

"Just for you," West said.

As the cab filled with the mournful twang of guitar and banjo, Virginia eased back in her seat and relaxed for the first time in days. They were passing by some of the older industrial towns on the western edge of the state, the sturdy two-story houses with their backs to the highway, the dark facades of churches every few blocks, some with the onion domes and ornate crosses of the Eastern Orthodox. They could see morning traffic in the streets, the shiny roofs of fast-food places, car washes, office supply stores. Virginia looked forward to getting past Wheeling, into the open farmland of Ohio.

They were planning to go as far as Indianapolis the first day. She had already made a reservation at a motel beyond the city, one room for West and his father, one for her.

"This trip is crazy," Rob had declared when they last spoke

on the phone. "Not to mention leaving a fourteen-year-old in charge of the farm."

"Randall is perfectly capable. And besides, Cody is going to stay and help out."

"Oh, much better. Cody's what . . . twelve?"

"Almost thirteen."

His wife, West had told her as they went to pick up Winn, was "skeptical."

"About what?" Virginia had asked.

"Everything."

She didn't tell him what Lydia had said to her, after she'd told her father she was going along with West to look at a Thoroughbred mare for Theresa.

"I know you people have different views," Lydia had begun when the two of them were alone in the kitchen, "but my advice to you is don't go traveling with a man unless you're married to him."

"You people?" Virginia was busy searching for a thermos in the cupboard.

"It can only lead to trouble."

Getting ready to leave that morning, Virginia had noticed her father and Lydia barely speaking to each other and guessed they'd had a disagreement about her. Only Randall and Cody, who knew the real reason for the trip, wished her well. They would take care of everything, the boys assured her. Not to worry.

"Did you know I used to be in a band?" Winn asked Virginia when the CD came to an end.

"The Grange dances," West said. "Remember?"

"Of course I do." She'd had a crush on Winn when she was eight or nine and went with her parents to the Saturday night dances. He was so handsome, up on the stage in his jeans and his shirt with the pearl snaps, fiddle tucked under his chin, his foot tapping time. She had wanted him to notice her when she and Henny held hands and swung each other, their skirts twirling above their knees. But Winn was always looking somewhere else, his head filled with music.

"That's how I met my wife," Winn said. "Playing at a dance over in Harmony. She came in with her fiancé. You didn't know that, did you, son?"

"Are you kidding?" West looked at his father in the rearview mirror. "That was your favorite bedtime story when we were growing up."

"My Gracie's gone now," Winn said.

West shook his head when Virginia turned to him. She had seen Grace Moffat at the market a few days before. "I'm sorry," she said. "That's a shame."

"We had a lot of good years." Winn's gaze wandered out the window but couldn't seem to settle on anything. Soon he had fallen asleep.

"It's sad," West said. "He thinks my mom died."

"What happens when she goes to visit him?"

"Sometimes he calls her Eunice. That was the name of a girl he knew when he was younger. We used to try to tell him it was Mom—Gracie—but that made him mad. One time she kissed him on the cheek, and he said, 'None of that. My Gracie wouldn't like it.' He thinks she's watching him from heaven, or somewhere."

"How awful for her."

"She says it shows how much he loves her."

"West," Virginia said, "you don't think this is crazy, do you? What we're doing?"

He smiled, his eyes on the road. "I believe your mother would be in favor of it."

"I wonder."

Caroline did relish a little adventure. When Hattie and Chandler were still living at the farm, there was a freak snowstorm, a blizzard that blew down from the mountains near the end of March. After the morning chores were done, Virginia and her brother set up the Monopoly board in the living room near the fireplace. Their mother brought them hot chocolate and sandwiches for lunch and joined them for a picnic on the rug. Each time they checked, they were thrilled to see the snow still falling.

By the time her parents went out to do the evening milking, there was no light left in the sky. Virginia watched them through the window, their bundled forms indistinct once they stepped away from the porch. Snow blew against the house, hard with ice crystals. Their grandfather said they had close to three feet.

Caroline and Nathan didn't come back when they should have. Virginia peered out into the storm, where she could see snow spinning past the floodlight on the side of the barn. Except for that, it was dark. The seconds ticked by on the kitchen clock. *Ink. Ink. Ink.*

"They'll come after twenty more," Virginia said, as the red second hand clicked and paused. And then she said fifty, a hundred.

"Something's happened," Chandler said at last, pulling his boots on, shrugging into his hunting jacket. "I'll go see." He shoved a flashlight into his pocket.

Half an hour later, they heard stomping on the porch. When Virginia opened the door, she saw her grandfather, alone, his bushy eyebrows stiff with frost, his cheeks bright red. He came in, brushing snow from his shoulders.

"They finished the milking, all right," he said. "But it looks like that damn heifer Pinky went off somewhere to have her calf. There was blood in the stall where I left her this afternoon, a trail of it leading up to the side door. She must have pushed it open. I'd say they went to find her."

Virginia touched the sleeve of his wool jacket, where the snowflakes were turning to tiny drops of water. "Did you see their footprints?"

"Next to the barn, I did. Then I lost them. The wind's blowing so hard it's covered them over." He started untying his boots. "I called and called, but the wind blew my voice away, too."

"I know where Pinky likes to go," Virginia said. "So does Larry. If you take us out with you, I bet we can find them."

Standing at the stove, Hattie shook her head.

"No need," Chandler said, returning his jacket to its hook. "They'll find their way."

Hattie dished up four plates of stew and nodded to them to sit at the table. "I'm not eating till they get back," Virginia said, sitting across from her grandmother. Hattie looked at her a long time before taking a bite herself.

The others had finished, and the dark gravy had congealed at the rim of Virginia's plate when they heard laughter outside and the scrape of boots on the steps. The door seemed to blow open, and there were her parents, as bright and vivid as if they had just returned from a party, their heavy coveralls coated with frozen snow. Their lips were blue, and icy wisps of hair poked out from under their hats. Virginia bolted from her chair but stopped when she saw the dark streaks across their shoulders and chests. She caught a whiff of it, something crude and briny mixed in with the clean, cold scent of them.

"It was Pinky," Nathan said, stepping gingerly out of his coveralls. "She was clear up at the hay barn."

"I figured something of the sort," Chandler said. "The cow barn wouldn't suit her."

"I knew that's where she'd be," Virginia said. "I wanted to go find you."

Her mother patted her arm, noticed her untouched dinner.

"Why are you all bloody?" Larry got up and folded their coveralls so that the smears were on the inside, tossed them toward the cellar door.

"She hadn't cleaned her calf yet." Nathan rolled up his sleeves and turned on the kitchen faucets, lathering his hands with the big bar of yellow soap, scrubbing up to his elbows.

Caroline stood beside him, reaching for the soap. "We had to carry it back down the hill."

"Pinky, too?" Virginia asked, hovering just behind them.

"No, silly," her father said, turning to smile at her. "She followed us because we had her calf. Complaining all the way."

"They're both fine," her mother said. "We've got them tucked into a stall and the door bolted."

"Bull calf," her father said.

"Figures," Chandler replied with a cluck of disappointment.

Virginia watched as her parents took the plates of warmed-up stew Hattie passed to them. Her mother's face glowed as she told about getting lost on the hillside, blinded by the driving snow so that they wandered into the woods. They had finally stumbled onto the dead sycamore, she said, the tree where the pileated woodpecker lived, and gotten their bearings. Eating her dinner cold, too stubborn to ask Hattie to heat it for her, Virginia shivered in her seat.

Winn stirred, sighing and yawning as the truck slowed and turned off the highway. When he sat up, he had the dreamy look of a child waking from sleep. Virginia wanted to reach back and brush the hair from his forehead.

"Stopping already?" he asked.

"You've been asleep for a while," West told him. "We're well into Ohio."

"Is that right?" Winn said, looking out at the cornfield beside the service road, the green stalks splashed with dust from the highway.

"It's lunchtime, Dad. Are you hungry?"

In their booth at the back of the diner, Winn took his glasses from his shirt pocket and studied the menu. The third time the waitress returned, tapping her pencil against the order pad, he asked for chicken-fried steak with mashed potatoes and gravy. "My Gracie stopped making that for me," he told the young woman, who granted him a reluctant smile. "She said it was bad for my heart."

When the food arrived, Winn concentrated on his plate, eating a bite of meat, then potato, then green beans in steady rotation. Virginia asked if it was good, but he seemed not to hear. He didn't look up until he had finished, and then he wanted to know if they were ready to go to the ponds.

"Ponds?" West put his fork down. "I'm not sure about that today. Would you like a piece of pie instead? They have coconut cream."

"You always take me to the ponds," Winn said.

"Unless it's raining."

Winn placed his hand in the square of sun that fell through the window onto the corner of the table. He turned his palm up, making a cup to catch the yellow light. "Tell him," he said to Virginia.

"There must be a pond around here somewhere," she said.

Virginia watched West talking with the waitress as she cleaned another table. She frowned and shrugged as her eyes traveled over his shirt and down to his shoes. He moved on to the older woman at the cash register. She might have been the waitress's mother—they had the same frown—but finally she pointed down the road.

"Thank you," Winn said, sliding closer to Virginia.

She took his hand and held it in hers on top of the table. It was warm, hard and callused, etched like an old chopping block with dark lines that would never wash clean. Years ago, she had watched him repairing fences and tractors, cleaning a shotgun. And then, too, bowing a fiddle, cradling a newborn chick.

"It's a creek," West said, back in the truck. "We turn when we come to the stone foundation, an old schoolhouse, she said."

When they found the dirt road, a mile or so beyond the diner, the foundation was a mound of rubble with a rusted iron hand pump standing beside it. Shaded by overhanging trees, the road grew rougher and narrower, until it petered out in a sandy turnaround, where a small blue car was parked. They heard voices and laughter before they saw the teenagers—two boys and two girls—splashing in the water. As West helped his father from the truck, the young people turned away, whispering.

"She said there was a swimming hole." West took his father by the arm. "Let's try down this way, where it's shallow."

"This isn't right." Winn planted his cane in the soft sand. "Where are we?"

"We're in a town called Reuben." West looked at Virginia. "And I'd guess this is Reuben Creek."

"Who are they?"

"Just some kids," West said. "Having fun."

"I don't like it," Winn insisted. "Too many trees."

"Look there." Virginia turned him gently by the shoulder so he could see the opening of a meadow at the water's edge. She persuaded him to sit on the running board of the truck, to let her remove his shoes and socks. Unlike his hands, his feet were white and tender. Rolling up the cuffs of his pants, Virginia thought of Winn's nurse and wondered if it was her job to clip the thick, discolored nails.

Refusing further help, Winn waded in and led the way, probing the creek bottom with his cane, telling them to be careful. He suddenly motioned for them to stand aside and be quiet. Hunkering down, he poked his cane beneath a flat rock, stirring up a cloud of silt. His hand darted out and snatched something.

When he opened his fingers, there was a crawfish in his palm. Its shell, oyster white and mud-streaked, reminded Virginia of the old man's toenails. Winn held it out proudly, stroking its back with his thumb, before letting it down into the water again. He laughed as it scuttled back under the rock.

"I know where to find you," he said.

That night, Virginia and West sat on an iron bench situated on the walkway between their rooms, sharing a beer and swatting mosquitoes. As the evening came on, they watched bats darting above the parking lot, diving into the clouds of insects that hovered around the light poles. West had left his father in the room, watching *Wheel of Fortune.*

"I hope he's all right," Virginia said.

"He had me worried this afternoon. But I think he'll be fine as long as we can locate water."

"The boys sounded good." She'd been struck by a new

quality in Randall's voice as he described their day over the phone. It was deeper all of a sudden.

"Cody couldn't be happier."

As they sipped their beer, Virginia was aware of the heat of West's body a few inches away. "Your wedding ring," she said. "You haven't been wearing it."

"It gets a little tight in the summer, with all the work."

He turned to watch a minivan with Missouri plates drive in and park nearby. A man and woman and three children got out, all wearing polo shirts and rumpled shorts. They stared at the fish decal on the side of West's truck, then started arguing about who would carry what. As they filed past the bench, the father nodded solemnly. The mother and children followed, each with a disapproving glance at the single bottle of beer and the plastic motel cups. Fumbling with the magnetic card, the father opened the door to the room next to Virginia's, and the children's argument started up again.

"Prohibitionists," West said.

They sat out until it was fully dark, listening to the ceaseless rush of traffic on the highway. To the east, the sky was lit up with the great arcing glow of Indianapolis.

Chapter Fifteen

"Oh, look," Virginia said, her heart lifting at the sight. Beyond the split-rail fence, in the green meadow beside the road, four mares stood with their foals—tentative, sniffing the morning air, as if they had recently been let out of the barn. As the truck approached, one of the foals leaped sideways, bounding away from its mother, and the others followed. The mares looked on, unconcerned, and began cropping the lush grass.

"I'll be damned," West said, slowing the truck.

The mares were the color of butter fresh from the churn, with sleek, muscular rumps and powerful shoulders. The foals were lighter, almost milky, and already she could see the strength of their young legs.

"What do you think, Dad?" West asked.

"It's a picture," Winn replied, pressing close to the window. "It certainly is."

Winn had appeared at breakfast with a two-day growth of beard and a wrinkled shirt, complaining about the noisy air conditioner that kept him awake all night. He was out of sorts because they had been chased off the golf course near their motel the evening before. They'd been strolling down the fairway, muttering about the foursome playing ahead of them. More than once, they'd had to stop and hold back while the men in their bright shirts searched for a ball in the rough. A sand trap had distracted Winn from the pond he had seen in the distance.

"We might find something good in here," he said, picking up the short-handled rake that lay beside it. He worked methodically, turning over the top layer. "One time I found a shell," he told them. "And then a half-dollar. That was another day."

They didn't hear the electric cart bearing down on them until it stopped with a squeal of brakes. A young man wearing a white visor hopped out. "What the hell?" he said, spreading his arms in a gesture of outrage.

"We're looking for shells and things." Winn glanced up briefly from his raking.

"Not here, you're not." The young man adjusted his visor, which had "Twin Oaks Golf Club" stitched across the band in green letters. "How did you get on the course, anyway?"

"We're staying at the motel." West nodded down the road. "We walked over."

"You have to leave." The young man motioned for Winn to put the rake down. "This isn't a public park, you know."

"It helps him," Virginia said in an undertone. "Something about a golf course . . ."

"Whatever," the young man said, his expression softening. "I can't let you stay here. Course rules."

They had tried to make it up to Winn by taking him to the motel swimming pool. The three of them sat on the damp concrete, dangling their feet in the water. Down at the other end, two children paddled back and forth on Styrofoam boogie boards as their mother watched from a deck chair. They could hear the big trucks thundering past on the highway.

All at once, lights the color of birthday candles winked on in the pool, creating pastel swirls in the water. The children shrieked delightedly. Winn pulled his feet out.

"I want to go home," he said.

"But we need you," Virginia said. "We're in Iowa now. We're going to see the horses tomorrow." She had reminded him again at breakfast, and he had finally eaten his eggs and toast as if it were a serious matter. Then he went back to the room to shower and shave. Now he was wearing a clean shirt and his string tie with the turquoise slide.

They turned in at a handsome sign at the end of a long gravel drive lined with trees. "High Gate Farm," the sign said, "Home of Silver Dancer."

"A highfalutin name for a draft horse," West remarked.

"I doubt he works much," Virginia said with a laugh. "Unless you count stud service."

"What's his fee?" Winn asked. He leaned forward in the seat, his dark eyes alert.

"I think it's fifteen hundred," Virginia said. "He's descended from a famous stallion of the nineteen thirties, Silver Lace."

"Silver Lace was a stallion?" West cocked an eyebrow at her.

"He started life as King," Virginia told him. "According to the story I read, the owner's son wanted to change his name to Silver, after the Lone Ranger's horse. The father added Lace. It had something to do with the name of the farm—which I honestly can't remember."

"But the farm was close to here, you said."

"Hardin County, not more than fifty miles away." Virginia

shifted in her seat to watch the foals running alongside the truck. "I do remember the stud fee for Silver Lace. It was fifteen dollars. They bred him for seven years, long enough to get through the Depression and save their farm."

Everything about the well-built shingled house at the end of the drive was reassuring. Lower and wider than the house Virginia had grown up in, it had a massive fieldstone chimney at one end and two dormer windows in the attic. A house that could stand up to a tornado.

West let out a low whistle, and Virginia turned to see the barn. Painted a rich cream color, with a gambrel roof that shone silver in the morning sun, it was three stories high, immense. On each level, windows in the long exterior wall gleamed as if they had recently been washed. Virginia wondered how they reached the smallest ones at the top.

A rhythmic clatter drew her gaze from the barn roof to the meadow beyond, where she saw a pair of horses pulling a mowing machine. Heads high, the big horses were magnificent, keeping up a steady, even gait through the chest-high grass. Braided with black ribbons, their white manes bobbed in time to the muffled thud of hoofbeats. Virginia felt the ground tremble when she got out of the truck.

"Putting on quite a show," Winn said as Virginia gave him a hand down.

They watched the grass falling away on either side of the mower, the revolving blades churning up a halo of dust and insects. The air smelled sweet.

"Welcome," a woman said, coming up behind them. "I'm Maggie Brower." She was short, with light freckles sprinkled across her face, even her lips, and curly auburn hair pulled back in a bow. She was smiling at Winn. "That's my husband, Tim, out there. I hope I didn't give you a start."

"It's all right." Virginia shook her hand, then introduced West and his father.

"I'm glad your husband could come after all," Maggie said.

"So am I," Virginia said. "Except he's not . . ."

She was interrupted by Winn, who pointed excitedly at a golf cart rounding the side of the house. "Don't tell me it's that young fool again. How did he get here?"

"Not a *young* fool." Maggie laughed and waved to the driver. "It's my father. He lives with us." She introduced him as Pat when he drove up beside them.

"How do you like it?" he asked Winn. "They gave it to me for my birthday last month."

Winn climbed in and sat on the seat beside him. "Very nice," he said.

"Hang on there. I'll give you a tour." Pat pulled away with a toot of the horn.

"He's crazy about that thing," Maggie said.

"We may not see them for hours." West grinned, watching the two white-haired men lean into the turn as they disappeared behind the barn.

"Don't laugh. Sometimes he forgets to charge the batteries. We've had to go out looking for him." Shading her eyes with one hand, Maggie squinted at the field, where her husband had turned the horses and started back the opposite way. "Come in and have a cup of coffee," she offered. "Tim will be along soon."

She rattled on pleasantly as she led them into the farmhouse kitchen. "Boys!" she called. "Go get your father. Tell him they're here."

A racket on the stairs followed immediately, and a pair of redheaded boys about eight years old surged into the room. Dressed alike in jeans and striped T-shirts, they regarded the visitors with identical expressions of curiosity.

They were so like Randall at that age, Virginia wanted to reach out and touch them as they shifted impatiently on their bare toes.

"Brendan and Steven," their mother said. "Put some shoes on before you go out."

The boys looked at each other and ran off again, their bare feet slapping on the porch. "Our feet are tough," one of them called back.

"They move so fast, even I can't tell them apart half the time," Maggie said, pouring the coffee. "Do you have children?"

"Five," Virginia replied. She meant to add "between us."

"All boys," West said.

Maggie's eyes widened. "God bless you," she said.

The coffee was good and strong, the way her mother used to make it, but Virginia found that she couldn't swallow. She hoped no one would notice as she took a deep breath through her nose and willed her throat to relax. It was a silly pretense— their marriage, their five children. Better to clear things up right away, she thought, especially since Winn seemed to think they weren't even married yet. She placed her hands on the cool surface of the porcelain tabletop, readied herself to say something about a misunderstanding, but the words didn't come.

Tim Brower appeared a few minutes later, mopping his face with a bandanna. His clothes looked freshly laundered, as if he had just been out for a stroll. He shook their hands warmly, asked about their trip. Everything about him seemed unhurried and confident.

"Bren and Steve are unhitching the team," he told his wife. "They'll be fine," he said quickly, as if she might disagree.

Virginia and West sat at the table with Tim, going through the stack of file folders he had ready for them. There was one for each of the twenty-four horses at High Gate Farm. In addition to the usual information about sire and dam, birth date and weight, Tim kept notes about their habits and personalities. "Will sell her soul for an apple," Virginia read in one. "A nipper, watch your back" in another. And this: "Won't eat grain until I scratch his ears and tell him what a fine fellow he is." All recorded in Tim's neat, tiny handwriting. There were pictures in the folders, too, taken at a week, six months, a year.

"Maggie's the photographer," Tim said.

"Bren and Steve tell me I take more pictures of the horses than of them." Maggie was standing at the counter, punching down a bowl of rising bread dough.

Maggie had already invited them to stay for lunch, and Virginia could smell the pot of vegetable soup simmering on the stove. "The pictures are wonderful," she said. "I can't wait to see them in person."

"I think you're going to like the yearlings I told you about," Tim said, pulling two folders from the stack. "We'll go out to the barn and have a look at them, but I wanted you to get an idea of our farm first, to understand where these horses come from."

As they talked, Virginia took in the details of the kitchen: the jars of wildflowers on the windowsill above the sink, the hooked rugs on the floor, the pair of green painted rocking chairs near the stone fireplace. She could imagine the Brower family here on a winter day, Maggie or Pat reading to the boys, Tim making his notes.

When they got to the barn, the twins, now wearing rubber boots, were mucking out a stall at the far end. The smooth, heavy planks of the barn floor had already been swept clean. Virginia breathed in the fragrance of fresh straw and grain, the unmistakable scent of horse. The yearlings thrust their heads over the stall doors when they heard Tim's voice, then shied at the sight of strangers, their hooves striking hard on the worn boards as they abruptly turned away. They were bigger than she expected and impatient from being held inside.

"Give them a minute," Tim said. "They're full of piss and vinegar in the morning. I'll give them a handful of oats, then I'll bring them out for you."

Virginia's heart pounded as she watched them circling the stalls. She hoped Winn would be back soon.

"They're a handsome pair," West said, and Virginia felt his reassuring hand on her arm.

"Yes," she agreed, wondering how her father might manage them on his own.

"He's the steady one," Tim said as he slipped a halter over the colt's head and led him out. "Aren't you, Jack?"

The horse pricked up his ears, pulling at the halter as he tried to turn toward the open barn door. "Mind your manners, now," Tim said soothingly, stroking the horse's neck. As he calmed, Jack lowered his head, nuzzling Tim's shirt. "You can touch him now," Tim said to Virginia. "Come up close."

Beneath her hand, his coat felt rough at first, and then she found the smoothness of his neck, the surprising heat behind the jaw. Jack's skin rippled with pleasure. "You are a nice fellow, aren't you?" Virginia said, running her hand over the taut muscles of his shoulder.

"That's right, talk to him," Tim said, giving her the halter. "You want them to get used to your voice."

"Look at that one." West nodded at the filly, who was bobbing her head as she watched from the stall door.

"Miss Jewel is jealous." Tim stroked her nose. "Jack and Jewel. That's what the boys started calling them, but it's not too late to change the names if you want."

"Those are good names," the boys said in unison. "The horses like them."

"They're the kind of names you want if you plan to drive them as a team," Tim said as he put a halter on Jewel and brought her out. "Short, with a strong sound at the beginning."

Jewel stepped forward boldly, then ducked behind Tim, rolling her eyes at Virginia and West.

"Well, Jewel," West said, approaching her. "We've come a long way to see you."

She stamped her foot and swished her tail but stood while West stroked her neck and murmured in her ear.

Handing her halter to West, Tim said, "I'm going to have the two of you lead them out to the yard, and then I'll hook on the long lines. You boys come along, too."

Winn and Pat returned in the golf cart in time to see Bren and Steve standing back to back, rotating as the horses on their lines trotted in a circle around them. The boys called out commands in their fearless young voices. "Ho up, Jewel." "Step lively, Jack." "Easy now."

"Are those the two you're buying?" Winn asked, stepping in between Virginia and West. His hair was windblown and his cheeks pink. He smelled like fresh air.

"What do you think?" Virginia asked him.

"They look fine, but I want to see them up close before I make any judgment." Winn combed his hair back with his fingers. "I like how those two kids can handle them. A yearling is a rambunctious creature, especially one that size."

Virginia watched as Bren and Steve let out more line, as the circle grew larger and the horses began a slow canter. Their coats were a shade between the milky white of the foals and the rich buttery color of the mares they had seen earlier. Buttermilk, Virginia decided, admiring the way their white manes and tails floated as they ran, the exquisite balance of beauty and strength. Yes, they were fine animals. And she would be responsible for them once she took them away.

By lunchtime, Winn had pronounced them "fit as fiddles." Together, Virginia and West had gone through their papers with Tim. Sired by Silver Dancer, Jewel was registered as Silver Dreamer (Maggie's idea, Tim explained). Jack, whose sire was a stallion from Michigan called Best Boy, was officially Brendan's Boy.

"That line from Michigan is a good one," Tim said. "They get a pretty uniform color and size. And you couldn't ask for a nicer temperament than Jack's. Give him a couple more years, and he'll mellow out real sweet."

"He's pretty sweet right now," Virginia said, recalling the way he had nudged her hand with his nose.

"Plus, with the Michigan line, you've got some new blood. If your father wants to breed this pair, I don't think he can go wrong." When Virginia didn't reply, Tim went on. "Jack would make him a nice gelding, too, if your father just wants a team for showing. Personally, I think it would be a shame, though. Those two would make some pretty horses."

"Take your time to decide," Maggie said. She had already started serving lunch to Winn and Pat and the twins, who were seated at one end of the table. "Maybe you'd like to look at some other horses."

"I don't need to look at any other horses," Virginia said. But the idea that she was about to plunk down seven thousand dollars of Aunt Ida's money made her queasy.

Listening to Winn and Pat making plans with the boys to go fishing, Virginia wished Randall and Cody could be here, to share the excitement of bringing the horses home. There was really nothing left to decide. It had been her father's dream to own these horses, and she was about to make it come true.

She wrote out the check to Tim Brower, signing her name with a little flourish. Maggie poured them fresh coffee, and again Virginia found it hard to swallow.

"Why don't you folks plan on staying with us tonight?" Pat stopped in the doorway as the fishing expedition was preparing to go. "Winn says it's impossible to sleep at that motel of yours. We have plenty of room, don't we, Maggie?"

"That's a grand idea," Maggie said. "We could all have supper together, and you could get an early start in the morning."

Virginia and West looked at each other. "That's awfully nice of you . . ." Virginia began.

"We've already paid for the rooms, though," West said. "And all our stuff is there."

"We'll have to decline," Virginia said. "But thank you."

"I'm staying here," Winn said firmly. "It's a damn sight better than the motel, if you'll pardon the expression."

"Are you sure you want to stay, Dad?"

"Yes, I'm sure," Winn said with a snort, following Pat out the door.

"This might not be a good idea," West said, explaining Winn's memory lapses. "He's doing well these days, but you never know."

"Why don't you bring his medications out?" Tim suggested. "And if he gets upset, we can give you a call."

"You two must never have a minute to yourselves," Maggie added. "You might want to go somewhere nice and have dinner."

"Yes," West said, smiling at Virginia. "I think we might."

Chapter Sixteen

———————◆◆◆———————

They hardly knew where to begin. After studying the menu for what seemed like a long time, they had ordered steaks and a bottle of red wine. Without discussing it, Virginia and West had rejected Maggie's suggestion, Chez Figaro. Too fancy. The restaurant at the motel wouldn't do, either. Too dismal. The only place left was Sally's, across the street from the movie theater. And now they tasted their wine and traced the flower pattern in the tablecloth with their fingers and tried to think what they might say to each other.

As the silence gathered between them, they watched the bartender mixing a martini in a silver shaker.

"He probably thinks we're having a fight," West said.

Virginia reached for a breadstick, broke it in half, and set it on the little white plate in front of her.

"Are you worried you made a mistake about the horses?" West asked her.

"No." She continued breaking the breadstick into smaller and smaller pieces. "My grandmother Hattie—I don't know if you remember, but she could be a sourpuss. Anyway, she had a saying: 'If wishes were horses, beggars would ride.' "

"And?"

"Wishes *are* horses."

"Well, then, I say we drink to Jack and Jewel."

"Silver Dreamer and Brendan's Boy." Virginia touched her glass to his, shaking her head. "My father's going to have his work cut out."

The waitress arrived with their food, the steaks smothered beneath mounds of French fries, a scoop of coleslaw on each plate. She asked them if everything was all right and hurried away before they could answer.

They fell to eating, talking about Winn and Pat, who had been out back cleaning catfish when West called to check in; about Randall and Cody, who had cheered out loud when Virginia told them she would be back with the horses in two days.

"What will Dad and Lydia think about your racket?" she'd asked Randall.

"They won't think anything. They're up at the chicken house, looking around. Something got in last night and took one of the hens. Granddad said a weasel, most likely."

He also had news, Randall said. His grandfather was teaching him and Cody to drive the truck, out in the field above the house. "We've had three lessons already. I could drive into town if I needed to."

"That's wonderful, kiddo. You can take me for a ride when I get home."

Neither Virginia nor West mentioned the calls they had made to their spouses. It had been hard work, coaxing Rob out of his sulk. She had told him about High Gate Farm as if it amused her, as if she weren't a little jealous of Maggie and Tim's life. Gradually warmed by the wine, she was glad that part of the evening was behind her.

The sun was setting when they left the restaurant, casting orange streaks across an ink blue sky. On the opposite side of the street, they saw a boy and girl in red vests standing close together, resting their elbows on the concession counter in the empty, brightly lit theater lobby. They could hear music in the distance and began walking toward it.

Thirty or so people had gathered in the small town park, seated on lawn chairs or blankets near the gazebo, where a band of mostly old men was playing a ragged version of "What'll I Do?" It had been a favorite song of her grandfather Chandler's, but Virginia could remember only one line.

"What'll I do," she sang softly, "with just a pho-to-graph to tell my troubles to?"

West leaned close to hear her and put his arm around her shoulder. Through the thin material of her dress, his touch felt warm and exciting and perfectly natural. They stood that way through two more songs before walking back to the truck.

Please don't say anything, Virginia thought when they reached her motel room. He didn't but went in with her and shut the door and kissed her. After so many years apart, the feel of his body was no longer familiar. She couldn't have said what was different, exactly, only that he was not a boy now. In the half dark of the small room, they held on to each other, and she slid her hands under his shirt to feel the muscles of his back, tensed and hard from work. When he kissed her neck and undid the buttons of her dress, she stepped out of her clothes and drew him to the bed.

They lay together in the falling light, exchanging the small graces of lips and hands until they were on fire, and then he began moving inside her, gentle thrusts that made her want to cry out. She clasped her hands behind his head, her fingers in the soft hair at the nape of his neck, and watched his face as she rose to meet him and draw him in deeper. Now every cell of her was filled with him; her blood hummed in her ears. It felt as if he were lifting her up and up, carrying her on a pure, deep current, until all her senses dissolved in one bright explosion.

He kissed the bridge of her nose; she brushed the damp hair from his forehead. When he rolled away, she felt a momentary chill, until he drew the sheet up and pulled her close again. The room came into focus slowly: the dusty green drapes, the hulking television set, the metal door with the chain hanging limply. It occurred to Virginia that she should get up and fasten the chain, but she didn't want to move. She could sense West falling asleep, his breath growing shallow and rhythmic.

When she woke in the night, Virginia slid out from under West's arm and went into the bathroom. She sat on the toilet, staring at her feet on the cold black and white tiles. In the harsh light from the bulb above the sink, they looked strange, as if they didn't really belong to her. It was hard to start, and then she thought she would never stop. Peeing like a horse.

It came to her that they hadn't taken any precautions. Since Rob's vasectomy, birth control wasn't something she'd had to think about. She tried counting the days since her last period and decided she didn't care. Whatever happened, happened.

She brushed her teeth quickly, avoiding her face in the mirror, and slipped under the sheet beside West. She thought he was still sleeping, but he reached out for her and held her and warmed her. They made love again, slowly and carefully, not so urgent this time, and fell into a dreamless sleep, vaguely aware of each other, of their bodies touching.

In the morning, West got up before she did, walked down to the motel lobby, and came back with paper cups of coffee and bagels with cream cheese and jam. They ate on the bed, Virginia sitting against the pillows with the sheet drawn up to her chin.

"Did you call your father?" she asked.

"Yes, ma'am." West wiped a smudge of strawberry jam from the corner of her mouth with his thumb. "He's not awake yet, Maggie says. I guess they had a high old time last night, frying up their catfish. They stayed up late, trying to play video games with the boys."

"He might be confused this morning. He might not remember."

"I told Maggie we'd be there soon." He stood up, gathering the cups and paper napkins, tossing them in the wastebasket. "I'll go next door and shower."

"Me, too," Virginia said. "Here, I mean."

"You're blushing." West bent down to kiss her. At the door, he stopped and turned around. "My God," he said. "You are lovely."

"Oh, stop it." Virginia smiled, waving him away.

"I mean it." He crossed the room and kissed her again.

———

This time, the meadow next to the road was empty. The white tents of spiderwebs glistened on the dew-soaked grass, as if a small army had come in the night. In the paddock they could see Jack and Jewel, who started running at the sound of the truck. When West stopped, they came to the fence expectantly.

At Virginia's hello, the horses skittered away again. "They know something's up," West said.

228

"I feel a little sorry for them." Virginia watched as they trotted some distance away and stopped, looking back. "Leaving home."

"Anyway, they have each other," West said, his hand on Virginia's back as they moved toward the house.

Tim came out to meet them and said he had made a list of stables along the way, where they could board the horses overnight. He handed Virginia a piece of paper with the names and phone numbers. It would be slow going, she realized, probably longer than the two days she had told Randall.

At the table, finishing his breakfast, Winn looked up when Virginia and West went in. "There you are," he said brightly.

"I'm not sure he knew us this morning," Maggie had whispered to them on the porch. "But I told him you were on the way."

After they had loaded the horses into the rented trailer and stowed the enormous lunch Maggie had made for them, Virginia hugged her good-bye.

"Too bad you have to leave so soon," Maggie said wistfully. "It's nice having another woman around for a change."

Virginia watched in the side mirror as Maggie stood with her family, waving good-bye, as the group in front of the house grew smaller in the glass and then slipped away.

That evening, Virginia and West sat in the empty bleachers of the Sheldon County Fairgrounds, two hundred miles west of Indianapolis. Down below, Jack and Jewel trotted gingerly around the equestrian ring, while Winn stood vigil at the fence. The farmer who was boarding the horses for the night had suggested they bring them here for exercise, as he had cattle in his field. No one would mind, the farmer had assured them. The fair was still a few weeks off.

They could feel the cool air rising as the shadow of the grandstand spread across the dirt track, edging over the fence, across the horses' backs. It was one of those evenings after a blue, cloudless day, when the air tastes of fall. They sat close, their legs touching.

"He hasn't mentioned a word about ponds," West said, brushing the back of Virginia's hand.

The day had gone well. They'd unloaded the horses once, in an open field near a service station, where they drew a small group of onlookers. Maggie had assured them the horses were "good loaders," and Winn had figured that things would go best if they put Jack in first. "You can see Jewel wants to be wherever he is," he'd said.

"Is it all right if I come to your room tonight?" West let his hand rest on Virginia's knee.

"I hope you will." She leaned closer, so that their shoulders were touching.

"Dad's tired. It shouldn't take him long to fall asleep."

All day, in the cab of the truck, they had been glancing at each other, smiling and looking away when their eyes met. They had kissed once inside the horse trailer, wedged between Jack and Jewel. Virginia had felt the horses' warm breath on her neck.

Their motel was down the road from the fairgrounds—a long, low building made of white stucco with rusting metal chairs outside. Once they got the horses settled for the night, they drove into the parking lot with the empty trailer rattling behind them and said good night outside Virginia's door.

Smelling of horse, Virginia decided she needed a bath. As she pulled back the shower curtain, a pair of earwigs tumbled into the tub, scurrying for the drain. Disgusted, she crushed them with a handful of tissue and flushed them down the toilet. Then she reached for one of the tiny bars of soap and a washcloth, got to her knees, and scrubbed at the mineral-stained porcelain until the soap dissolved completely. At last, easing herself into the steaming water, she lay back, trying to think of nothing.

It was no use. She was longing for West. She couldn't wait to lie down beside him, to feel his hands on her bare skin, his mouth. But she would have to call her son first. And her husband. What kind of person does this, she wondered.

———

The next day, in the afternoon, it began raining while they were still on the highway. Virginia was driving and West was dozing in the passenger seat when the first heavy drops hit the windshield. As the sky lowered and the clouds darkened, the rain came harder. She saw brake lights flashing as cars ahead of her slowed, and she touched the brakes cautiously, aware of the weight of the trailer behind. She clicked the wipers up to high. Just then a sudden gust of wind caught the horse trailer and sent them sliding toward the shoulder of the road. Virginia tapped the brake again and felt the trailer fishtail, pulling them back onto the pavement. West came awake as a car swerved past, the driver laying on the horn. Virginia tried turning the wheel the other way.

"Easy," West told her. "Don't touch the brake."

When the truck started to hydroplane, she flung an arm across the passenger seat and braced for a crash against the guardrail.

Then, mercifully, the truck slowed and straightened, and she was able to coast onto the shoulder and stop.

"Are you all right?" West asked her.

Her hands were shaking.

In the backseat, Winn had wakened, too. "What happened?" he said.

"We had some good luck," Virginia told him. "But I don't think I can drive anymore."

West got out. By the time he had gone back and checked on the trailer and come around to the driver's side, he was soaking wet. "It's really blowing out there," he said, sliding into the seat. "And the horses are spooked. I'm going to pull off at the next rest area."

"Here," Winn said, handing up his jacket. "Put this on."

It was already dark when they passed Columbus and reached the horse farm a few miles beyond, where they were expected. Neither of the horses wanted to leave the trailer. When Virginia untied her, Jewel tried to bolt. It took all Virginia's strength to hold her until Winn could get in to help. With Winn on one side and Virginia on the other, they backed her out, Winn crooning all the while, promising her a warm, cozy stall. The rain had turned to mist by then. Virginia and West walked the horses through the wet grass until they calmed and then rubbed them down and watered and grained them.

In Virginia's motel room, she and West lay on the bed in their damp clothes, talking about Winn. Getting Jewel out of the trailer had exhausted him. When they went to the motel café for supper, he had ordered a hamburger and taken only a few bites.

"We've traveled a long way," Virginia said. "Maybe it's too much for him."

"I want to ask you something." West turned on his side and looked at her.

"What?" She touched his cheek.

"Are you going to leave me again?"

From the parking lot, she heard the sound of a car door slamming. "I don't want to," she said.

They held each other, listening to the throaty rattle of the air conditioner in the window. When they finally undressed and got under the blankets, his question hung over them as they made love. Sleep came slowly, and in the melancholy night Virginia heard an occasional car hissing by on the pavement. When she woke, West was dressing in the thin light seeping through the venetian blinds.

"I'll get Dad up and about," he said. "And meet you at the café for coffee."

She stood and put her arms around his waist and rested her head against his chest, feeling the *boom, boom, boom* of his heart. They would, she calculated, be home in about five hours.

At the horse farm, they found Jack and Jewel had been let out to exercise. The horses were excited to see them, then turned and ran when West came near with the halters. Eventually, Winn climbed down from the truck and ducked under the fence with a handful of grain and held it out to Jack and talked to him as he edged closer. Winn got the halter on and led the horse clattering into the trailer, as Jewel crowded up against the fence on the far side.

"We're not going to have more trouble with you, are we?" West said, offering her grain. She eased over and licked his palm, then nuzzled his shirt pocket, in case he might have something hidden there, and he got the halter on her, too, and tied her in beside Jack.

"I don't blame them," Winn said, helping West close and latch the trailer doors. "I'd put up more of a fuss if it was me, having to ride in there."

Virginia insisted that Winn take her seat up front, claiming she wanted to stretch out and sleep in the back. West showed his father how to work the CD player and asked him to pick out some music. He smiled at Virginia in the rearview mirror, and they set off in a gray drizzle.

The rain kept up all morning, not hard but steady. It wasn't until they crossed the Ohio River on the iron bridge outside of Wheeling that the sky brightened. By the time they reached Fayette, the day had turned hot and muggy. They had planned for Winn to be with them when they presented the horses to Nathan, but he told them he was too tired. And besides, he didn't know exactly who Nathan was.

West parked behind the nursing home and opened the doors of the trailer to give the horses some air as Virginia gathered Winn's things from the truck and walked him around to the front. Inside, they heard the murmur of voices from the direction of the dining room and smelled the day's lunch.

"Good timing, Mr. Moffat," said a perky young aide behind the desk. "They just got seated." She asked Virginia if she would like to join him.

"I can't stay today," Virginia said, setting his bag on the floor, folding his jacket on top of it.

"Why don't you come with me, then?" The aide came around and offered her arm to Winn, who seemed confused.

"She wants to take you down for lunch," Virginia told him. "Are you ready to go?" She wasn't quite ready to say good-bye herself.

"I suppose," Winn said. "But first I need to have a word with this young lady here." He meant Virginia.

They stepped away from the desk, and Winn put his hands on her arms. "This is what I have to say: I want you to take good care of my boy, Ginny." He scanned her face. "You take good care of each other."

"We will," she said, and she felt tears starting up as she

hugged Winn. He felt small in her arms and wiry, too, and stubborn. "Thank you for going with us."

"I have to eat my lunch now." He stood back. "You'll come around in a few days, won't you, and let me know how you're getting on with those horses?"

"Yes," she said. "I'll do that." She watched him going down the hall, arm in arm with the aide in her spotless white uniform. Rumpled from the hours in the truck, he shuffled along in his baggy khaki pants, trying to keep up. He had called her Ginny. Until then, she wasn't sure if he knew her.

West was leaning against the cab of the truck, waiting for her.

"He told me to take good care of you."

West kissed her briefly on the cheek, cautious now that they were back among people who knew them. "We'll figure this out." He closed the trailer again and opened Virginia's door and gave her a hand up.

They had gone several miles along the river road before he spoke again. "Do you want to figure this out?"

"Yes, I do," she said. "Very much."

When they pulled into the dooryard of her parents' farm, Virginia was impressed by how neat everything looked. Cody and Randall had finished painting the porch and had mowed the grass around the house. Lydia had tidied the flower beds and hung up two baskets of pink geraniums, one on either side of the porch steps. Then she remembered. They were getting the place ready to sell.

She ran up the steps and went inside, calling hello, making sure no one was there. "How long have we been gone?" she asked West, coming back out.

"Five days," he said. "Five and a half."

"Everything feels different."

They moved quickly then, parking the horse trailer behind the barn, leading the horses inside, where they curried them and brushed their manes and tails, gave them water and grain. Henny had gotten her parents involved in the surprise, and they had invited Nathan and Lydia and the boys out for lunch that day. It would be Lydia's first time at the Eastman farm.

Jack and Jewel were restless from the hours in the trailer and skittish as they sniffed the strange cow smells. Virginia wished she could turn them out in the pasture for a good run, but she wanted them close by when her father returned. She had asked Randall to cut down the weeds in the old paddock beside the barn, which hadn't been used for years. She and West went to check the fence and, satisfied that it was sound, led the horses out and took their halters off. West unhitched the trailer and drove his truck around in front of the house. Then they went up on the porch to wait.

The horses stood at the paddock fence, watching them, pricking their ears at the slightest sound.

"They don't know what to do," Virginia said.

"Neither do I." West put his arm around Virginia's shoulder and kissed her hair. He froze when they heard a car on the road, but it went on past the driveway.

Twenty minutes later another car came along, and this one turned in. Randall and Cody were out of the back in a flash. They had spotted the horses right away.

"Ginny," her father said, easing himself out with his cane. "You're back." He took a few steps toward her and stopped. "Now, don't you two look like the cat that ate the canary?"

"That's because we have a surprise for you." She told him to close his eyes and then turned him around and walked him over to the paddock fence. "Open," she said.

"What in . . ." He swiveled on his cane, looking back at Lydia.

"Happy birthday, Dad," Virginia said.

"I don't understand."

"Their names are Jack and Jewel. Say hello."

"Your American Creams," Randall said, as he and Cody came over to pet the horses.

"They're pretty," Cody said. "And big."

The horses backed away, keeping an eye on the people outside the fence.

"Ginny, what did you do?" Her father turned to her.

"I got them for you."

"But why?"

RANDALL

———————✦———————

We're standing there looking at the horses, and it's not how I thought it would be. Granddad goes kind of white and stiff, and he's, like, What the hell? Lydia says my mom never thinks of anyone but herself. Then she goes inside and starts banging around in the kitchen.

My mom acts like everything's normal, but I can see she's hurt that Granddad isn't overjoyed about the horses. After he goes in to see about Lydia, West says, "Give him time."

While we're doing the milking together, she tells me about the Brower farm in Iowa, all the horses and the redheaded twins. She says I would have liked it. And then she tells me Granddad might sell his farm and that's what the horses are about, to give him a reason to stay. That's why Lydia's mad, she says. Lydia wants him to sell, because it's nothing to her, it wasn't her family who broke their backs here for two hundred years to keep it going.

I don't know what to think. I'd be sorry if the farm was gone, but I have to say her idea doesn't make sense to me. It's like a little kid's idea. The horses are definitely cool, but I don't see what one thing has to do with the other. Anyway, I go along with her and say yeah, when Cody and I start harness-training them, Granddad will get interested and maybe everything will work out. Her face lights up and she says that's just what she's talking about. By the time we hose down the milking parlor and get back to the house, I'm thinking, Who knows, it could happen that way.

When she's talking to Dad after supper, I can't hear what they're saying, because the door to Granddad's office is closed, but the way her voice is going, it sounds like she's trying to talk herself out of some kind of trouble. Then she goes upstairs, and I can hear her crying. Not loud. Maybe she's got her face in the pillow or something, but she's not even trying to stop. I count all the times I know of that she's cried. One. That was when Caro died.

Irene says my parents are going to get a divorce, wait and see. I know the signs, she tells me. Why do you think they're living apart this summer? Why do you think your mother went off with some guy? It's not some guy, I say. Besides, Cody's grandfather is with them. Ha, Irene says. That old man.

Every afternoon, while my mom was gone, Cody rode his horse back home to visit his family and I rode my bike to Irene's. The last day, Jodie and Lee go off in the car right when I get there and Irene says she's going to make me a drink. I say no thanks, but she says don't worry, it's vodka and orange juice. No one can smell it on your breath. She brings two glasses into the living room and we sit on the couch and she asks if I want a cigarette. I hate smoking, I say. Well, too bad, she tells me, and lights up.

I've had a beer with my friend Glenn before, but vodka is different. I get a buzz with the first sip, and I watch Irene smoking and don't really mind that much. I'm almost finished with my drink when she says, "Randy, do you even know how to act like a real boyfriend?" She wants me to kiss her, I know that much. She puts her tongue in my mouth, and I taste orange juice and tobacco. After a while, she says, "Kiss me here," and unbuttons her shirt partway. I sort of lick the little bird tattoo, and she likes that. When I put my hand on her breast, I'm surprised how soft it is and then her nipple, small and hard.

I have my hand on her thigh, which is so warm, and start edging my fingers up under her shorts, and I'm holding my breath. But she says, "No you don't," and pulls away.

I say sorry and try to kiss her again. I want to start over.

She stands up and buttons her blouse and shakes out her hair. "You have to do something for me," she says.

I say all right, and she says I better listen to what it is first. She sits on the coffee table and lights another cigarette and tells me that if I really like her I can help her find her father. She tells me he's living in Baltimore. She knows because she found an envelope with his return address on Jodie's dresser. His name wasn't on it, and the envelope was empty, but it was his handwriting for sure.

I say I really want to, but my mom needs me at the farm, especially now with the horses coming.

"We're not talking about your mom," Irene says. "We're not asking anyone."

"You mean like running away?"

"Smart boy."

I tell her I have to think about it, and she says you do that.

Irene is stubbing out her cigarette when we hear Jodie's car in the driveway. Irene picks up the glasses and the ashtray and runs into the kitchen. I go into the bathroom. I'm dizzy from the vodka and Irene. I think I might throw up. I wash my face with the nub of soap on the sink and squeeze toothpaste onto my finger and brush my teeth. I hold my head under the tap and wet my hair down and comb it with a pink comb I find on the windowsill and splash more water on my face.

"Are you all right, sport?" Lee says when I come out. He's looking me up and down.

Sport. Ha, ha.

Irene's sitting on the couch reading a magazine, and she says, "Have fun with the horses," when I start to leave.

What horses, Lee wants to know. He perks up when I tell him and says he worked with some of those big horses a few years back when he was a farm manager and maybe he'll come by one day and have a look at them. Jodie gives him a dirty look and says he managed a lot more than the farm.

Irene is holding her magazine up high so I can't see her face. I pedal home and Cody's there waiting and we do the milking.

Chapter Seventeen

⬤

The morning after Virginia got back, she found her father and Lydia mysteriously affable, as if they had discussed the situation overnight and come to an understanding. Let's humor her for the time being, she imagined her father suggesting.

She and Randall were returning from the barn when they met Cody coming down the hill on his horse. "How is everything?" Virginia asked him as they went inside together.

"Fine," he said. "My mom's excited to see Jack and Jewel. My dad's going to bring her over this afternoon."

"That's great."

It was already hot inside the kitchen. Lydia was setting up to can tomatoes, and she had two big pots of water boiling on the stove. After breakfast, when her father went out to watch the boys exercise the horses, Virginia helped Lydia carry a bushel basket of tomatoes up from the basement. As they were blanching the first batch, Lydia started telling a story about her brother Cooper, the youngest of her five siblings. She had mentioned him in passing once or twice, Virginia remembered.

Cooper was a sweet child, Lydia said, the way the youngest is sometimes. He was the only one of them who ever got close to their father, a gruff man who worked the first shift at the coal mine and then came home and tried to run their small farm. From the time he could walk, Cooper followed their father everywhere.

"My brothers used to joke that my father had Cooper because he couldn't afford a dog," Lydia said, peeling back the skin of a tomato she plucked from the ice-water bath. "They were jealous, you know. And it didn't help that he had a pretty face. Cody makes me think of him. Angel with a bit of the devil in him."

On a Sunday morning when he was five years old, Cooper followed his father out to the toolshed. While the old man's back was turned, he stood on tiptoe, trying to reach something on a shelf, and tipped over a jar of acid that splashed his face and shoulders. Lydia recalled the way her father had run into the house, how he had held the screaming boy upside down over the pantry sink while her mother furiously worked the pump handle, trying to wash the acid away.

"It was awful to see," Lydia told her, "the way Cooper's face turned purple. The skin started to blister before my father even got him in the car to go to the doctor. There wasn't much they could do for him. He was lucky he wasn't blinded, but he had terrible scars. Terrible."

"I'm so sorry," Virginia said. She had stopped coring tomatoes and was staring at Lydia.

Her parents started fighting over Cooper, Lydia continued. Her mother wanted to keep him at home instead of sending him to school, but her father insisted he get out in the world and learn to take his licks. Her father couldn't stand to have the boy near him anymore. Sometimes he yelled at him to keep away, to get out of his sight. When Cooper was fourteen, he took their father's deer rifle up to the hayloft and shot himself in the chest.

"He pulled the trigger with his toe," Lydia said. "The bullet went straight through his heart." She paused for a moment, gazing into the crockery bowl of peeled tomatoes, then turned and walked out of the room. Virginia could hear her in the downstairs bathroom, running water.

When Lydia came back, she was composed again. "Cooper has been on my mind lately," she said.

"That's a sad story." Virginia went to the door to let Cleo out and saw that Randall and Cody were leading the horses around to the cow pasture. Her father held the gate for them, and she could see him smiling as the horses plunged into the open field and sent the cows scattering. She was trying to think of something comforting she might say to Lydia.

"You won't get much milk next time," Lydia said, coming up behind her. "Cows hold it back when they take a fright."

———

In the early afternoon, Virginia was riding Randall's bicycle down the road past the farm, grateful for the fresh, cool air. There was a scattering of high clouds off to the west, as if a rainstorm might be moving in. She was heading east, toward Rownd's Point, to visit her mother at the cemetery.

She pedaled fast, determined to get away before West arrived with Theresa. It hadn't been his idea to bring her, Virginia was sure, but it would have been impossible to see them together. Lydia's story had unnerved her, too. It's always that way, she was thinking, the one misstep that changes everything, the hand reaching overhead, into the unknown.

Coasting down the gentle hill that brought her to the town's main street, Virginia noticed two boys sitting on the curb in front of Skoler's Grocery, one of the few businesses still operating in Rownd's Point. About Randall's age, they were dressed like suburban kids in oversize pants, white basketball sneakers, and baggy T-shirts.

"Nice bicycle," one of them said with a smirk as Virginia braked in front of the store.

"Thank you," she replied, searching her pockets for change. She managed to come up with enough to buy a bottle of water and propped the bicycle against a railing.

"Aren't you afraid we'll steal it?" the boy asked.

"Be my guest," she said. Inside, she took some time to look around. The floors were clean, but the shelves were dusty and the big front window flyspecked. The cashier, a girl of seventeen or so with several gold hoops in one ear, stood behind the counter, restocking the cigarette display. In the produce section, Virginia found a few overripe bananas and a wilted head of iceberg lettuce. Otherwise, Skoler's seemed to specialize in frozen pizza, chocolate milk, and air fresheners. There was no bottled water, but she discovered iced tea in the cooler. When she set it on the counter, the girl rang it up and took her money without looking at her.

In the street, the boy who had spoken to her was riding the bicycle. She sat down beside his friend.

"Don't worry," he said. "He's just goofing with you."

"He's going to get his pants leg caught in the chain," Virginia said. "You can't ride a bicycle in those pants."

"You're not from around here, are you?" the boy asked.

"I grew up right down the road." She turned to look at him. He had a thin face and dark eyes with thick eyebrows that nearly met above his nose, the hint of a mustache. He smelled like grape bubble gum. "You know what this town needs?" she asked him.

"A video arcade," he replied without hesitation. He laughed as the other boy rode past with his hands in the air.

She looked at the empty storefronts across the street. One of them had been a restaurant, another a drugstore. On a second floor, there was a light in the window and "Art Simms, Insurance for Home and Farm" stenciled on the glass. "So what do you guys do for fun?"

"Hang out," he said with a shrug. "Nothing, really."

"Don't you play any sports?" she asked, glancing at his shoes.

"We shoot some pool in Derek's basement. When his brother isn't hogging the table."

They watched Derek ride to the end of the street. When he didn't turn around, Virginia called, "Hey. Come on back here."

"Not a bad bike," Derek said, finally handing it over to her, hitching up his pants. "For an old clunker."

"I'll take that for you." His friend was reaching for her empty bottle.

She heard Derek making fun of him as she pedaled off. "Kyle, what am I going to do with you?" he said. "You are so effing polite."

Heading toward the river, Virginia considered that these boys would probably be Randall's classmates if he went to school here. Neither of them looked familiar. She had no idea who their parents might be.

Where the main road curved to the left, she stopped and got off the bicycle. Straight ahead, she had a long view of the river—wide and greenish gray under the clouds. On the far side, wooded hills rose up steeply. On the near side, a wide plain bordered the river for several miles. To her right, a narrow road led all the way to the tip of the Point, running through the farm Jonathan Rownd had started plowing in the spring of 1767. A Van Houten family from upstate New York had bought the farm the year after Randall was born. Where corn, oats, and alfalfa once grew, there were acres of flowers and shrubs. The original barn remained, but the outbuildings had been taken down and replaced with greenhouses.

In the field nearest the road, seedlings sprouted in pencil-straight rows, so small they were hardly more than a green fuzz. Virginia stepped closer and knelt in the damp soil, dark and fine as coffee grounds, and recognized the pungent odor of chrysan-themums. Beyond was a field of zinnias, their buds about to open, revealing faint smudges of the deep pinks, purples, and golds they would become. She and Rob had once brought Randall here during an Easter vacation, and they had marveled at the field of tulips, the lipstick shades of red and pink.

Standing to brush the dirt from her knees, Virginia let her gaze settle on the trellis of climbing roses at the side of the house, the white blossoms that nearly covered one end of the wide front porch. The house was sturdy, as her father used to say, three stories high and built of fieldstone. The new owners had painted the shutters pink. It was a nice effect, she thought, the soft pastel against the coarse, tan surface of the stone. The Van Houtens, she'd heard, sold flowers and plants up and down the East Coast.

Virginia was about to pick some of the zinnias to carry up to her mother's grave when she noticed a worker near one of the greenhouses, watching her. She picked up her bicycle instead. Rounding the curve, she felt the road beginning to climb as it gradually bent away from the river. Soon she turned off onto the narrow dirt road that would take her to the top of the bluff, and pedaling became too hard. As she walked along, pushing the bicycle, she discovered blue vervain and monkey flower blooming beside a stream and arrived at the cemetery with a small bouquet.

Leaning the bicycle against the black iron fence, she walked to the edge of the bluff to see the sweep of the valley. Up here, the wind was always blowing. When she was little, she used to believe that if she were brave enough, she could lean into it, spread her arms and fly above the river, follow where it disappeared between the hills.

The latch on the cemetery gate was stuck until Virginia remembered to lift up on it; then it opened with a sharp metallic rasp. Her mother's grave was near the fence at the back. "Hi," Virginia said, placing her hand on the cool granite, as if it were her mother's shoulder. She sat in the grass beside the stone, the space reserved for her father, and set her flowers down. Beyond the fence, the long, feathery branches of the white pines dipped and swayed in the air currents, like so many gesturing arms. They might have been a Greek chorus, lamenting lost loves and forgotten lands.

Virginia listened, but there was only the steady *shush* of wind in the trees. "I've been reading your journals," she said. The night before, she had skipped ahead, to September 5, 1979. "Our first day without V," her mother had written.

This afternoon, I heard the school bus going by in the road, and out of habit I stopped what I was doing to watch for her coming up the driveway. And then her place empty at the table tonight. When we left her in Greenfield yesterday, I could see her biting the inside of her cheek so she wouldn't cry. Tenderhearted V, good-byes so hard for her.

She was always sad when Ida left us at the end of the summer. And now a new life for her. The days ahead will be hard for Henny. And West. While V was here, I expect he still had hope.

Virginia had leafed ahead, trying to find a clue to her mother's hopes for her, but she found only details of farm life, an occasional mention of events in town, visitors, bad weather. Once her mother had written about missing her, but she followed with "V so bright. This little world of ours not big enough to hold her."

Her mother had nudged her away, Virginia reflected, scooping up a handful of pine needles. Moving through her teens, she had been vaguely aware of it, gone along with it. Her father had wanted her to stay. Another kind of love.

"You wouldn't believe what's happening to me," Virginia said, letting the dry needles fall through her fingers. She lay back on the grass and closed her eyes, clasped her hands on her chest.

Not far away, her uncle Herman's bones lay beneath the ground. She hoped there was no such thing as the kind of heaven he used to speak of, where she might meet him one day and have to explain herself. He had once preached a sermon on adultery, she remembered, when she and Henny were eleven or twelve. They had sat in a pew in the rear, giggling softly, not quite sure what adultery meant, only that it was something shameful grown-ups might do.

She recalled Uncle Herman's voice as he said the word— twice, with a deep breath in between. "Adultery." He had scanned the congregation, his face grim. "Adultery, my friends, is the worst form of treachery."

Henny had nudged Virginia. "The *worst* form of tretchery," she had printed on the back of the Sunday program.

"My friends?" Virginia had written beneath that.

There would have been one or two sweating out there in the pews, she reflected now, as the old minister condemned the recklessness that tore families apart. "And for what?" he'd asked them. "The pleasures of a moment."

Reckless. That much was true. But she doubted most affairs were begun purely in the interest of pleasure. The consequences loomed, even at the start.

Rob had made her cry the night before, not because he suspected her of sleeping with West—he wouldn't have thought it possible—but because he had accused her of living in the past.

"You can't stand it that your father has moved on," he'd said. "The same with West and Henny. You want to be right there in the middle of things so they don't forget about you. But the truth is, they don't need you anymore."

"Rob, that is so pompous," she'd said. "And hateful." She suspected he'd been drinking, something he normally avoided during the week.

He'd reminded her then that he would be going to a medical conference in San Francisco to give a talk on a new hip surgery technique. It meant another weekend that he wouldn't be able to visit them. He'd said it coolly, as if his absence were a punishment.

"Randall will miss you," she had replied.

Virginia sat up suddenly. It sounded as if someone had opened the cemetery gate, but it was only the bicycle sliding to the ground. The sky was completely overcast now. She buttoned her sweater and leaned forward, hugging her knees. Her mother had assured her once that she and Rob had a good marriage, the kind that could bounce back from a hard knock. That was a year or two after he had finished his residency and they had moved to Laurel Springs, after their first big argument. He'd wanted her to give up her teaching job, which she loved.

"And be a professional doctor's wife, like your mother?" she'd blurted. "No thanks."

Rob had come around, as her mother predicted. And from that point forward, Virginia had counted on their good marriage. They got along; they made things work.

"You wouldn't recognize me these days," Virginia said to her mother. It made her slightly uncomfortable, speaking to the dead. After rearranging the flowers she'd brought, she said good-bye and left.

Going down the hill on the bicycle, riding the brake, she watched thin rays of sun streaming through the cloud cover, their wan light reflected in the river. She looked for the worker in the Van Houten field, but he was gone. When she got to Rownd's Point, the boys were gone, too. A shaft of sunlight slanted across the dun-colored building next to the grocery and then vanished. It was getting late.

LYDIA

I t's the children from the first marriage that cause trouble in the second. They say so on all the talk shows. My sister Pearl, who left her perfectly fine husband to marry Deeter Jenks, says the same. It was a big romance until Deeter's two teenage girls came to live with them. Then it was pure hell, Pearl told me. She came around crying one day and said she wouldn't of minded going back to her old life, if it wasn't too late. "Pearl," I told her, "those girls are almost grown and gone. It won't last forever."

Then I learned better. Take Nathan's boy, Larry. It's true he let his father down when he washed his hands of the whole thing and moved out to South Dakota, but he called on a regular basis and sent Nathan a little something for his birthday and Christmas. And what more do you want? With girls, it's a different story. Seems like, if their father's halfway decent, they never will let go.

If I'd had any choice, I never would of asked Virginia to help us out. Truth be told, she was a hard worker. She and Randall were kind of fresh at first, but they didn't shirk a job, neither one of them. And Randall had a way about him. So did that Cody Moffat, who started coming around all the time.

Somebody should of put their foot down. First thing you know, Randall was going off whenever he felt like it to see that Irene girl, who was nothing but a disaster waiting to happen. And then seems like Virginia forgot she was married. I put some of the blame on her husband. What's the point of being a big-shot doctor if you can't control your own wife and son?

Nathan tried talking to her, but he had a soft spot for Virginia. He excused a lot on account of she'd lost her mother. Well, it wasn't like she was a ten-year-old orphan.

It was our own business—mine and Nathan's—if we wanted to sell the farm. I didn't put any pressure on him. I said what my own preference would be, pure and simple. And reminded him to think about his debt and his broken bones and his old age that was coming up.

My sister Pearl, when I had ten minutes to call her on the phone, couldn't believe it when I told her about Virginia running off with West Moffat and coming back with those two big horses. Maybe the woman is deranged, Pearl said. She's something or other, I told her.

"My advice to you," Pearl said, "is don't get between the father and the daughter. Step aside and let them work it out."

"What show is that from?" I asked her. Trouble is, I could see how all that foolishness started working at Nathan. It was plain, doubt had got its toe in the door.

"Could be guilt," Pearl said. "You know."

What was the harm in wanting a place of our own, a nice white house in town with a side yard and a front porch swing? Bernie Bishop knew of a couple places that would be just right. I wanted a wooden trellis over the front gate with those climbing pink roses. I had my heart set on it.

Chapter Eighteen

———————————

As the heat of August settled over the river valleys of southwestern Pennsylvania, the small streams ran shallow, the mud of their banks baking in the afternoon sun. The leaves of oaks and maples and sycamores felt dry to the touch. Birds that sang at first light vanished by midday, retreating to the cool shadows of the woods. On the roads, tar oozed through the cracks like shiny black resin.

At Second Farm, Lydia burned a pot roast; Randall stubbed his toe, sleepwalking one night. Otherwise, the days were long and slow and quiet. Virginia had seen West twice in the week since they got back, both times when he came to the farm to bring something for the horses. First it had been portable electric fencing they set up to keep Jack and Jewel separate from the cows and then a galvanized metal watering trough, both left over from his fallow deer. They had a few minutes alone as they carried pails of water from the barn.

"I miss you," West said. "I can't even think straight."

"I know." Virginia let her arm brush his as they walked.

"I need to see you."

They made a plan to meet at the Ridgeway house the following Monday. West would be returning from his restaurant deliveries, and Virginia could easily slip away on Randall's bicycle. She'd been riding it every morning. Meanwhile, it was only Friday. The weekend loomed, a mountain of time.

As Virginia and Lydia were clearing the supper dishes that evening, Jodie's car pulled up in front of the house. Lee Jameson got out, alone, and stood there waiting until Virginia invited him inside. He accepted Lydia's offer of coffee and, taking off his cap, sat down at the table. He wore a clean shirt and smelled of aftershave.

"I heard you got some horses," he said as Nathan came in from the hallway.

Nathan poured himself a cup and joined them. "Well, now, Lee Jameson. It's been a lot of years since you sat here with us."

"Yes, it has," Lee replied. "Maybe Ginny told you about Roger getting killed out there in Desert Storm."

"Worst news I've had in a while," Nathan said. "Roger was a good fellow."

"It's always the good ones that get it." He glanced at Lydia, who turned away and began running water in the sink. "What's all that noise, anyway?"

"The boys," Nathan said. "Randall and Cody. They're practicing in the living room. They've got some idea of putting on a concert for our entertainment."

"I didn't know Randall had a brother."

"He's recently acquired one." Nathan laughed, looking at Virginia.

"It's Cody Moffat," she explained. "He's been spending a fair amount of time here."

"One of those Moffat boys has been sniffing around our place lately. Hunter, I think she said. I swear, it's like having a bitch in heat." Lee drained his cup, suddenly embarrassed. "I'm sorry," he said. "That's no way to talk."

"Come with me," Virginia said. "I'll show you the horses. You can help me put them in the barn."

Cleo followed at their heels. "You'd best watch her, if she likes to get in amongst them," Lee said. "On the farm where I was working last, there was a real sweet dog, name of Annie, who loved chasing after the horses. One of them clipped her upside the head with his hoof, and it was all over for her." Lee reached into his pocket and removed a toothpick. "Mint stick," he said, clamping it between his teeth. "I'm tryin a quit smoking."

Virginia whistled for the horses, the way West had taught her, and saw them running up over the rise. The sight of them made her glad, as it always did.

"Jesus," Lee said. "That's a handsome pair."

When they noticed Lee, Jack and Jewel slowed and didn't come all the way up to the fence but stayed nearby, cropping the grass. "You start harness-training them yet?"

"Randall and Cody have been working with them, mostly on the lead lines, just so they can all get used to each other."

"You know anything about training a draft horse?" Lee propped an elbow on the fence post and looked at her.

"I got some books from the library."

"Tell you what. I wouldn't mind helping your old man out. But I'd need a get paid for my time."

"What do you know about it?"

Turning away with a half smile, he said, "You always was a sparky little girl." He picked at his teeth and watched the horses

257

and started telling Virginia about his job as a farm manager in southern Maryland, at a place near Pike's Creek, on the Potomac River.

"Lady that owned the place was about fifty," he said. "Nice looking, crazy as a loon. She had a husband that came and went—something up in Washington, I don't know. Anyway, she doesn't want a use a tractor, so she drags me over hell's half acre to the auctions and we buy up all the old-timey equipment she can get her hands on. Then she has to have a pair a Percherons. You know the size a them?"

"Not really."

"They make these two look like Shetland ponies."

"How was it, working with the horses?"

"I liked them, once I got use to it. That lady treated me fine. I stayed on almost six years. Then one night the husband comes home unexpected and finds me in his bathrobe, drinking brandy in the kitchen. Carla, that was her name, starts on some story how I got caught in the rain and she put my clothes in the dryer. Trouble was, it hadn't rained for a week. Hour later, I'm out on the road with my duffel on my shoulder and my thumb stuck out."

"Didn't her husband punch you in the nose first?"

"You would a liked that, wouldn't you?" Lee swung around, pointing an imaginary gun at Virginia. "Carla told me he carried a pistol in his car. Said he could be a mean bastard." Lee raised his hand above Virginia's head, pulled the trigger. "I didn't care to stick around and find out if it was true."

Virginia called the horses again, and this time they came up so she could get the halters on. She watched Lee with Jewel as he settled her in the stall. He knew what he was doing.

After Lee had gone, Virginia found Randall and Cody sitting at the kitchen table with her father. Cody was holding a carved wooden bird on his palm. "I saw it on the shelf in the living room," he said.

"Do you remember this one?" Nathan asked as Cody passed it to her.

"The woodcock," Virginia said, running her finger over the long, pointed beak and the plump, buff-colored belly, the dark spots on the wings.

"That was his first bird," Nathan said. "He made it for you and Larry."

"After my grandmother Hattie died," Virginia told the boys, "my grandfather started carving birds. She would've had a fit if she'd seen what he did to her kitchen—wood chips and paint everywhere." She recalled the clean smells of wood and turpentine, the smudges of rose and dun and blue on the table.

"We asked him if he didn't want to move back to the farm and live with us," Nathan said. "But he liked his little house. Snug, he called it. So he started in bird carving. He did more than a hundred—mourning doves, flickers, all kinds. That first one's kind of rough, but toward the end he was pretty good."

"What happened to the rest of them?" Cody asked.

"We kept a few," Nathan said. "The rest we put out at his wake so his friends could take them if they wanted. I wouldn't be surprised if your father has one or two."

"I'll ask him," Cody said. "I hope he has a flicker."

"I think Randall should have this one." Virginia handed it to her son. "Have either of you boys seen a live woodcock?"

"I've heard them," Cody said. "In the spring."

"So you know about the singing ground?"

Cody shook his head.

"You have to picture this bird," Virginia said, with a nod at the carving. "He's plump, with a big head. Walking, he bobs along from side to side, like a penguin. He can't even fly very fast. Normally, he's reclusive, keeps himself hidden in the woods."

"But he's a fool for love," Nathan put in.

"So, around the first week of April," Virginia said, "when the woodcocks return from the south, the males start their courtship display. Each one has his own singing ground." She described how her parents would take her and Larry up to the edge of the woods just before dusk and how they would settle themselves among the scrub pine, waiting for the male bird to appear in the forest opening. They could hear him before they saw him, his nasal *peent, peent* as he made his way into the open field, bobbing on his short legs. And then this shy bird, with his large, dark eyes, his feathers the color of dead leaves, would launch himself into the air, into a graceful, spiraling flight. He would spiral up and up and up, surprisingly high, and then make a dramatic downward plunge. Then he would strut around a bit more. *Peent, peent.* And up he would go again. It was the movement of air over the outer wing feathers that made the singing sound, more of a twittering, really. The woodcock would repeat this courtship flight for as long as an hour, and then do it all again the following evening.

"I'd like to see that," Randall said.

———

By mid-morning on Monday, dew still glistened on the grass as Virginia rode down the driveway. Jack and Jewel turned to watch her as she pedaled by. When she reached the road and turned left, Virginia felt her heart flutter against the cage of her ribs.

The Ridgeway lane was longer than she remembered, rough and rutted from neglect, nearly washed out in places. West was there when she arrived, standing near the front door, his truck parked off to the side. Letting the bicycle drop, Virginia moved into his embrace. They held each other tightly, as if they had been separated for months, as if all manner of things had conspired to keep them apart.

"I love it that you're here," West said.

"I love the feel of you." Virginia looked up at him and caught a glimpse of the house over his shoulder. "Oh, this is sad," she said. "Look at this place."

"I know." Still holding Virginia's hand, West stepped back to survey the damage with her.

The Ridgeway house, built of brick rather than the wood or fieldstone of its plainer neighbors, stood in a waist-high mass of sumac and burdock. The heavy mahogany door—now dented and sagging on its hinges—had been framed by narrow side panes. Like all the downstairs windows, they were broken. Remnants of Oona's lace curtains, tattered and stained, stirred in the light breeze. As West pulled the door open, the odor of the house spilled out: the bitter, sooty smell of chimneys mixed with the dust of peeling wallpaper and the leavings of small animals. In the kitchen, they discovered the cupboard doors had been smashed. The floor was littered with broken dishes and shattered glass.

"How awful," Virginia whispered, discovering the unbroken lid of Oona's brown teapot and setting it gently on the counter.

"Come on," West said, guiding her into the living room. "Be careful where you're stepping."

They found less destruction there, though the wallpaper around the broken windows was water-stained, and the upholstery of the maroon couch and chairs looked as if something had been gnawing at it. The rug, an imitation Oriental, was littered with bits of shell from the black walnut tree that grew near the back porch. In the fireplace, they found blackened metal cans and beer bottles.

"Someone camped out in here," West said, nudging one of the bottles with the toe of his shoe. "A while ago, I'd guess."

Both of them turned and looked down the dim hallway that ran through the center of the first floor, the open doorways on either side.

"Let's try the stairs," West said, taking her hand again and leading the way up the creaking but still substantial stairway.

"Amazing," Virginia said as they reached the upper landing, where it looked as if nothing had been disturbed. The windows were intact, the curtains drawn. Virginia opened a door at the end of the hall and peered in. Despite the cobwebs and the musty smell, it was an ordinary girl's room—a painted iron bedstead with a faded quilt folded at the end, a chest of drawers and a small chair, a framed picture of a shepherdess and three lambs on the wall. The room next to it was nearly the same, except for a doll wearing a white cotton slip, both eyes closed, sitting on the chair. Down the hall in the bathroom, the heavy porcelain fixtures were stained with rust, the roll of paper in its holder dry as old parchment.

They stood together in the doorway of what would have been Oona and Taylor's room. The bed was made, a yellowed chenille spread tucked neatly over the pillows. On the dresser, Oona's hand mirror sat atop one of her crocheted doilies, along with a bottle of dried-up lotion and a scattering of desiccated moth wings.

With his hands on Virginia's shoulders, West kissed her forehead, the top of each cheekbone. She held him around the waist, rising to meet his kiss full on the mouth. After several minutes, he pulled away, drawing his thumb down the side of her face. "You kiss the way you did when you were sixteen," he said.

They sat on the bed and removed their shoes and lay back, side by side. The room was filled with dull yellow light, the papery scent of years gone by.

"It feels wrong to be here," Virginia said.

West lifted her hand and held it against his chest. "I want to marry you," he said.

She felt his breathing stop for a minute. "I want to marry you, too," she said.

"Would you?"

Virginia thought of Randall, of how he would look at her when she told him. "Yes," she said. "I would."

They lay together on the bed in the Ridgeways' half-ruined house, watching the dappled light on the ceiling, not talking anymore. To Virginia, it felt as if they were contemplating murder. And yet she had never wanted anything so much in her life.

———

When he called that evening, Rob sounded refreshed, even though he had taken the red-eye from San Francisco the night before and then spent nine hours at the hospital. His talk had gone well. San Francisco was a grand city, he told her. They would have to make a trip there together, the two of them.

"Sorry, old buddy," he said, as if Randall were on the line with them.

Rob had traded his on-call weekend with another doctor and would be able to come up that Friday, after all. He was anxious to see them, he said, and the horses, too. "How's your dad getting along with them?"

"I'd say Jack and Jewel are doing a good job of stealing his heart." Virginia hoped her husband wouldn't hear the quaver in her voice. "It helps to have Lee Jameson around. He and the boys put the harness on today and had the horses pulling a two-by-four. It was kind of funny." Except for Lydia, all of them had been out in the pasture when she returned from the Ridgeway house. They hadn't noticed her.

"Maybe Lee's a better guy than we thought."

Virginia didn't mention that she was paying him.

"I had a visitor," Rob told her. "Right after I got home tonight."

"Not Eddie Bisconi, I hope."

"It was the gardener, from across the street. He wanted to know what happened to the lady with the rake. He said, 'More than eight weeks now I don't see her.' "

"I've never even talked to him."

"He was checking on you, in any case. I'm not sure he understood, but when I explained that you'd be back soon, he gave me a flower for you. It's a very pretty white something or other in a pot. He said it likes not too much sun."

"That was sweet of him." This gesture of friendship saddened her. "Did you plant it?"

"I'm sure I'd put it in the wrong place. I'll leave it for you."

"Don't forget to water it, all right?"

Chapter Nineteen

———————

"Henny, keep your chin up," Virginia said.

"How much longer?"

"A few more minutes."

"At least let me sit where I can see the horses."

Virginia waited until Henny had swiveled her wheelchair around before moving her own chair and sitting down again with her sketchbook. "Not like that," she said. "Look more toward me."

"Bossy, aren't you?" Henny said.

"Be still. Please."

When Virginia had brought Henny over to see Jack and Jewel, they had come right up, interested in the wheelchair. Each of them had taken half an apple from Henny's open hands and then nuzzled Virginia, even though she had nothing for them, pushing at her with their shaggy foreheads.

"They love you," Henny had said.

Virginia had then insisted they sit in the shade while she made a few sketches. She wanted to get started on a portrait of Henny. It was way overdue, she'd said, and Henny hadn't objected.

"One thing, though," Henny said after a few minutes. "Don't make me weird, like those paintings you did at college."

"I promise."

"Whatever happened to them, anyway?"

"Someone actually bought the Bob Will painting. It could be hanging on a wall somewhere." Virginia frowned, rubbing at the sketch with her thumb. "I think the other two are still up in our attic, buried in all the junk."

"It's strange, when you think about it, that you painted Bob Will back then."

"I should have painted you. Or my dad."

Virginia began another sketch from a different angle. Though the afternoon was hot, there was enough of a breeze to make it pleasant. They shooed away the occasional fly and hummed along with the music coming from the house.

"Now that Agatha's playing with them, they sound better," Virginia said. Chick had brought over his daughter's electric keyboard and set it up in the living room of the farmhouse. "Are you coming Friday night?"

"And miss the debut performance of the Smoke Rise Trio? My mother's still deciding what to wear."

"Agatha Mason is such a pretty girl," Virginia said. "She plays a mean keyboard, too."

"I don't suppose Randall has noticed—that she's pretty, I mean."

"Well, the last couple of times he's gone to see Irene, he hasn't stayed long. Lee Jameson said something about Cody's brother Hunter hanging around." Virginia turned to a new page and shifted her chair once more. "I'm rooting for Hunter."

Concentrating on the planes of her friend's face, the high forehead and cheekbones, the wide, full mouth, Virginia considered how well Henny looked. She had put on a few pounds over the summer, and she seemed happier. Virginia thought of Randall and Henny laughing together when the three of them had gone to Fayette a couple of nights before to eat at the old Twin Twister drive-in. They had scoffed when Virginia ordered a salad instead of chili dogs and onion rings, when she said she was too full for dessert, the famous soft-serve cone with chocolate and vanilla stripes.

"What about Rob?" Henny asked.

"Hmm." Virginia was trying to catch the way Henny's hair curled behind her ear. "I've never been good at ears," she said. "Could you maybe bring your hair forward?"

"I suppose he'll be here Friday night."

"I'm making a mess of this." Virginia fumbled in the pocket of her shorts until she found the gum eraser and methodically erased the ear and part of Henny's jaw. She blew the eraser crumbs away.

"He won't?"

"You have to help me," Virginia said at last, closing the sketchbook. "I'm going to leave him. I've decided."

"Don't tell me that."

"Rob *is* coming this weekend. I don't know what to do."

Henny turned her chair to face Virginia. "This isn't because of West, I hope."

"I know how this might sound, but we love each other. We want to be together."

"Is that what you're planning to tell Rob?"

"Essentially, yes." Virginia squeezed the soft eraser in her palm. "I made a mistake all those years ago, and now I have a second chance. How often does that happen?"

"What's wrong with the life you already have?"

"It's just that I see what West and I could have together." She couldn't tell Henny that she'd been noticing slight swellings and tenderness, signs of early pregnancy. The possibility frightened her, and yet she longed to believe it could be true.

"I wonder if you do." Henny let her gaze travel across the fields. "Look, you need to think about this. You can't let Rob come here this weekend and spring it on him."

"Maybe I should go down to Laurel Springs for a day. Or meet him somewhere, halfway."

"I wouldn't be in such a hurry to throw everything away, if I were you. At least think about Randall."

"I know. That's the part that kills me."

"Not to mention Theresa. Do you have any clue how rough she's going to be? By the time she gets through with West, he won't have a nickel."

"That doesn't matter."

"You might see things differently, when you're not a doctor's wife anymore." Henny came closer. "That day you came by and told me you were going off to buy horses for your father, I should have stopped you. I should have said something."

"Henny, my mind was made up."

They heard Nathan calling hello and turned to see him walking toward them. "I hope you girls are enjoying this lovely afternoon," he said. He stood behind Henny, resting one hand on her chair, and pointed with his cane toward the horses. "Look at those two," he said. "Aren't they something?"

Thunderheads built up along the river, gradually moving westward over the hills. By three o'clock, the sky was dark. At five, when Virginia and Randall went to the barn, no rain had fallen, but the clouds were holding steady. Randall had just switched on the milking machine when the first drops hit the metal barn roof, followed quickly by a downpour.

"Too bad Dad can't be here tonight," Randall said. "We're going to play some of the songs he likes."

"He wanted to be. I'm sure he told you that." Virginia was surprised at how little Randall had reacted to the news that Rob wouldn't be coming after all.

"It seems weird that you're going home tomorrow." Randall pushed at some fallen hay with the toe of his boot.

"Only for a day. We have things we need to talk about."

There was an abrupt letup in the rain and then the clatter of hailstones.

"Irene says you're going to get a divorce."

"Irene said that?" Virginia listened to the deep rumble of thunder that echoed from the hills. "She's just blowing off her mouth."

" 'Blowing off her mouth'?" Randall smiled at her. "That's a new one."

When they left the barn, the rain had stopped and the sky was brightening. The ground was covered with ice crystals.

"Look," Virginia said. "It's going to be nice for your concert." They were planning to use the front porch for a stage and had already set up chairs on the lawn. "I'll get a towel and dry off those chairs."

"We're going to be awful," Randall said. "I hope no one comes."

"You'll be terrific." Virginia rested a hand on his shoulder as they walked toward the house, and he surprised her by putting his arm around her waist and giving her a squeeze.

Two hours later, it had turned warm and steamy. Handing

out the programs, Virginia watched her father and Lydia, dressed in their good clothes, take their seats in the front row. Behind them, Chick and Bonnie were chatting with Jodie and Lee. Jodie had greeted her in a friendly way and cracked a joke about Lee being a farmhand again. Irene, keeping an eye on Agatha, made a point of straightening Randall's collar.

The moment Virginia had been dreading—West's arrival with Theresa and the boys—passed in a blur, so many people came at the same time. Sissy and Jere had come, too, and other friends of her father's who hadn't been out since the wedding. Most of them were there because Nathan had called and invited them. She had thought of going to get Winn until she considered how confusing it might be for him.

"I can't believe Cody's wearing a tie." Theresa was suddenly beside her. "They look good, don't they?"

The boys were both wearing white shirts and black ties. Agatha had on a sleeveless black dress, her light hair drawn back with a ribbon. "Yes," Virginia said. "They do."

"Cody's going to miss Randall so much when you go back home."

"I think they're ready," Virginia said. "We should probably sit down."

As she joined Henny, Virginia recognized the first notes of "My Funny Valentine." She remembered dancing to the tune when Rob had taken her to a nightclub on their first date in Cincinnati, the thrill of the smoky room and the dark, glistening face of the saxophone player. After playing it through twice, Agatha stepped away from the keyboard, took the microphone from the stand, and began to sing in her husky, untrained voice.

When they finished the few songs they had practiced, the children bowed and blushed as the audience clapped. Then someone called for an encore, and they looked at each other.

"Just do 'Funny Valentine' again," Chick called out.

Before the applause died down, Virginia and Lydia started bringing out food. Lydia had baked two cakes. Virginia had made the punch she always made for school events, with fruit juice and ginger ale and a floating ring of ice. She stood off to the side as the gathering on the front lawn became a party. West caught her eye and tapped his heart, a quick gesture. She steadied herself on the back of an empty chair.

"I don't suppose you have anything stronger than this kiddie punch," Jodie said, sidling up to her.

"We don't. My dad hasn't been drinking since his accident."

"In that case, I think me and Lee are going to shove off. You won't mind giving Irene a ride home later, will you?" She handed Virginia her half-empty cup.

Later, saying good-bye to the last of the guests, Virginia realized she hadn't seen Randall and Irene for some time. She walked through the house and then checked out front. Someone had folded the chairs they'd borrowed from the church and stacked them on the porch. She bent down and picked up a crumpled paper napkin.

"I don't know what's become of Randall and Irene," Virginia said, returning to the kitchen, where her father was helping Lydia clean up. "Have you seen them?"

"I wouldn't be surprised if they were in the barn. This would be Randall's first chance to show her the horses," Nathan said.

Sliding open the heavy door, Virginia stepped into the warm, dusky space and called their names. She heard Jack and Jewel moving in their stalls and went to them. "Aren't you good?" she said, giving them a pat. "Yes you are." A pigeon flapped down from the rafters and landed on one of the grain bins.

"Randall," she called again. "Irene."

Walking out behind the tractor shed, she saw that her father's pickup was gone. She had parked it there earlier to make room in the driveway, and now there were tire tracks in the grass where someone had backed it out. She looked up the hill, expecting to see headlights. A joyride, she was thinking, Randall showing off. But the fields were dark.

She hurried back to the house. "Dad," she said, standing in the doorway. "Randall's taken your truck. He and Irene."

"That's nervy." He was in a good mood.

"He's out on the road, I mean. Can he even drive?"

"He does all right. That old truck isn't too complicated."

"But he's never driven at night before. I'd better go find him."

"Irene's house isn't that far. We'll give him hell when he gets back, and in the meantime, why don't you sit down here and take it easy? You've been nervous as a cat lately."

"Nathan," Lydia said. "Randall shouldn't be alone with that girl at night."

"True. Do you want me to go with you?" her father asked.

"Help me finish up here," Lydia said to him. "We'll have everything shipshape by the time they get back."

Virginia went to Irene's house first, but there was only Jodie's car, a single light in the living room. She passed the house and turned around, preferring not to get Jodie and Lee involved. As she began to search, following one dirt road after another, alert for places to pull off, she was stunned by the audacity of Randall's taking off with her father's truck. It wasn't like him.

More than an hour went by, her headlights picking out nothing but trees, an occasional farmhouse, one lumbering raccoon. Circling back to the Landing, Virginia stopped at Mason's Garage to call her father. No, he said, worried now, Randall hadn't come back. Speaking to him, she watched the lights in the upstairs windows of Bonnie and Chick's house going out one by one. With the town asleep, Virginia could hear the murmur of the river, the gentle slap of water against the shore.

She thought of Durgin Hill. On the way back from Fayette, they had stopped there at Henny's suggestion, to show Randall the river at night. They had stayed in the car, watching the lights of coal barges below, moving slowly along the channel. Randall had said it would be a nice place to build a house. That was where he would be now, she was sure of it. She could get there in twenty minutes.

Approaching the top of the hill, she saw someone parked there, but it was only a small black car. Disappointed, she continued down the other side and on into town. She slowed at the Twin Twister, intending to turn around, and there at the back of the lot was her father's truck. She drove straight for it, her headlights on high beam. No one appeared to be inside. Parking beside it, she tooted the horn, expecting to see their heads pop up.

When nothing happened, she got out and knocked on the truck's fender. "Randall, just say something." Virginia waited a couple of minutes before pulling the door open. The truck was empty.

Climbing into the seat, she felt behind the visor. The key was there, the way her father always left it. The engine started easily, and she watched the needle of the gas gauge float up to the halfway mark. She switched on the overhead light and looked around the cab and checked the glove compartment. Everything seemed to be in order.

The drive-in was closed, but there was a rusted station wagon parked near the back door. When Virginia peered through one of the big windows, she saw a young man wearing a brown and white striped hat, mopping the floor.

"Hello," she called, but he didn't seem to hear her. She banged on the window, and his head jerked up.

"We're closed," he mouthed.

"I know. I need to talk to you."

He reached over to turn down the radio on the counter. "Closed," he said again.

Virginia went to the glass door and made a key-turning motion. "Please," she said.

Still clutching the mop, he edged closer. "We can't let anyone in after hours."

"I have to ask you something, that's all."

"Go ahead," he said, standing close to the glass.

"That truck parked in the lot. Do you know anything about it?"

He craned his neck to look where Virginia pointed. "I didn't see it before," he said.

"My son was driving it. Maybe you saw him? Tall, red hair? There was a girl with him."

"Nobody's been in here since about nine o'clock."

"What time is it now?"

"Close to eleven. I have to finish up." He turned away.

She replaced the key above the visor. Finding a scrap of paper and a pencil in the glove compartment, she left a note on the seat. "Call right away," it said. "Call collect." She wrote down the number at the farm, in case he had forgotten. She decided to drive through town. They could be out walking.

Even on a Friday night, the streets of Fayette were mostly deserted. The movie theater and the Miss Fay Diner were dark; only an occasional car passed by. Finally spotting the bright lights of a gas station and convenience store on the far side of town, Virginia stopped. Inside, she walked up and down the aisles, as if Randall and Irene might be hiding behind a shelf of crackers and cheese spread. Aware that the clerk was watching her, she picked up a pack of gum, and as she was paying for it, she described them, asked if they had been in. The clerk shook his head.

"It's my son," she explained. "He was having trouble with his truck. Maybe he came in to use the phone."

"Haven't seen him."

Returning to the Twin Twister, Virginia parked beside the truck again. The young man she had spoken with came out of the building, looking at her curiously before getting into his car and driving out of the lot.

"Randall," she said to the darkness. "Please be safe."

Now she would have to go to the police, to the station across the street from the courthouse. And she would have to call Rob.

Chapter Twenty

The house was dark when Virginia drove up behind Jodie's car. The sheriff, summoned from home by the deputy on duty, had blinked and yawned in the fluorescent brightness of the station and asked her if Randall or Irene had left a note, if any of their things were missing. She didn't know.

Virginia knocked several times before a light came on. Jodie opened the door, wearing a man's pajama top.

"What?" she asked, peering over Virginia's shoulder. "It's after one o'clock."

"They're gone," Virginia said.

She followed Jodie inside and described her search, the empty pickup in the lot. "The sheriff is guessing they ran away," she said. "He wants us to make a list of anything they might have taken with them, people they might contact."

"Irene had her backpack with her tonight, but I didn't think twice," Jodie said.

"Could you look and see if there's anything else? Maybe she left a note."

While Jodie was gone, Lee wandered into the kitchen, dressed in a pair of jeans. He was surprisingly thin, his chest nearly hairless. "Irene's not the kind a girl who leaves notes," he said.

"That damn bear." Jodie came back with a lit cigarette. "Fluffball, or whatever she calls it. That's gone. I know because it's always sitting on top of her pillow."

"Snowball," Virginia said.

"Now what?" Jodie sank down on the couch.

"Tom Ratliff, he's the sheriff in Fayette. He wants to get a statement from you, so you'll have to go see him in the morning. Meanwhile, we have to think."

Lee sat on the arm of the couch next to Jodie and took a drag on her cigarette. "This isn't the first time," he said.

"You don't need to go into that." Jodie waved his smoke away.

"I'm just saying. Irene's run away before. Last time, she ended up at her grandmother's house—her dad's mother. That lasted about three days, then the old lady drove her home. Irene was getting on her nerves."

"Did you have a fight or something?" Virginia asked.

"She's been mad ever since her dad took off," Jodie said. "Like it was my fault."

"She told Randall you know where he is."

"Yeah, well, I don't. Once in a blue moon he sends me some cash. One time I got an envelope from Baltimore with forty dollars. That's what a big man he is." She ground out her cigarette in the ashtray. "Last time it was Richmond. Another forty. What in hell am I supposed to do with forty dollars?"

"What about that friend of hers?" Virginia suggested. "Shelly."

"Shelby," Lee said. "Them two girls were tight. You wouldn't get nothing out of Shelby."

———

The farmhouse looked like a beacon in the distance, light pouring from every window. Virginia wondered if her father thought Randall would see it and find his way back. She had called him from the sheriff's office to let him know she'd found the empty truck. Cleo was sleeping on the porch and woke with a start when Virginia got out of the car. In the kitchen, her father and Lydia were at the table, drinking coffee.

"Would you like a cup?" Lydia asked. "It's decaf."

"I have to look in Randall's room first. I'll be back."

Cleo followed her upstairs, her toenails clicking on the worn wooden steps. The glass jar on Randall's dresser, the jar he had been saving money in all summer, was empty. Besides his regular allowance, Virginia had been paying him thirty dollars a week for his work on the farm, and Nathan usually let him win a few dollars at poker. He had about four hundred dollars, Virginia calculated. Opening his closet, she saw that his backpack was gone, too. So was his denim jacket with the gold lacrosse pin on the pocket. She sat on his neatly made bed—a clue in itself; Randall never made his bed. So the two of them had planned this. He must have stashed his things in the truck while everyone was busy getting ready for the concert.

His barn clothes lay in a heap in the corner of the room, the heavy work pants still bent at the knee, holding the shape of him. The little carving of the woodcock stood next to the empty money jar and, beside that, the black necktie.

Virginia heard her father working his way up the stairs, the bump of his cane on each step. "I'm going to try to get some sleep," he said. "You should, too."

She nodded.

"Is Rob coming?"

"I haven't called him yet."

"He was expecting to see you tomorrow." Her father looked at her questioningly, and when she didn't reply, he said, "It was the girl who talked Randall into this. You know that, don't you?"

"You think she had to twist his arm?"

"Don't let Rob convince you it's your fault. That's what I'm saying."

"Okay, Dad." She kissed his cheek and went back downstairs. She had to take a picture of Randall to the sheriff's office. There was one in the living room she could use, his eighth-grade graduation picture, Randall scowling at the camera in his white shirt and sport coat. Her father had put it in a frame and placed it on top of the bookcase, as her mother would have done.

"It's so late," she said to Lydia, glancing at the clock in the kitchen. "Almost three. I don't know if I should wake Rob now."

"He'd want you to." She took Randall's picture from Virginia and studied it, absently rubbing the glass with a dish towel. "This will come out all right," she said.

———

Rob called her early Saturday morning, right after she and her father had finished milking. He was on his way to the hospital for an emergency surgery. A young man had been smashed up in a car accident, and it would probably take most of the day to put him back together. They decided that Rob should stay in Laurel Springs, in case Randall showed up there. Virginia would call the Maryland state police to alert them. She would also call Randall's friend Glenn Oakes. Her plan was to drive down to Beckley, she told Rob, and look up Irene's friend Shelby. She had an idea that was where they were headed. She didn't mention that West was going with her.

He and Cody arrived soon after breakfast, followed by West's older boys in Weston's truck. Weston followed them into Fayette, where they stopped at the copy center and made up two hundred flyers with Randall's picture. West talked Cody into going with his brothers to distribute the flyers, convincing him that he should stick around because he was the one person Randall might try to contact.

"He's incensed," West told Virginia as the two of them walked toward the sheriff's office. "He can't believe Randall didn't say anything to him."

"The same with Glenn," she said. "I'm really surprised Randall hasn't been in touch with him." That fact made it seem more serious, somehow.

Her father's truck had been moved and was now parked next to the police cruiser in the lot behind the station. "What's it doing here?" she asked.

"We'll dust for fingerprints," Tom Ratliff said, looking at West. "You can take it home later today."

"Fingerprints?"

"Routine." Ratliff rubbed his hands over his face. He looked as if he hadn't slept much, either. "We don't suspect foul play at this point."

Randall and Irene had not purchased a bus ticket in Fayette, he told them, which meant they were probably hitchhiking. He moved aside a mass of papers on his desk and started writing on a yellow pad. "Tell me anything else you can think of," he said. "Sometimes the smallest thing turns out to be the key."

They didn't have to make the trip to Beckley, he assured them. He would contact the sheriff down there. Of course, it helped to be doing something, he understood that. He had placed Randall's picture on his desk, next to a family photograph, and told Virginia she could have it back when she came for the truck.

"You aren't related, are you?" he asked West as they were leaving.

"We're old friends," West said.

"Well," Ratliff said, shaking hands with him. "Tell that pretty wife of yours I said hello."

"He and Theresa are cousins," West explained when they were on the street again.

"He wasn't very encouraging," Virginia said. "He scared me, talking about fingerprints. Why would he bring up foul play?"

"Here's what I think," West said as they drove out of town, heading south on Route 19. "Randall didn't want to steal your father's truck, he just wanted to get a head start. So he left it where it would be found easily. Then they took off with their packs and hitched a ride."

"Anyone might have picked them up."

West patted her leg. "I'm guessing your hunch is right. They're probably in Beckley already. We'll have them back home by suppertime."

"I'm glad you're with me. I couldn't handle this alone." She thought of Rob, awake since her call in the middle of the night, in surgery now, working over a broken body. She thought of the day that lay ahead for him, the fitting of pins and plates, the tiny sutures, the nurse who would squirt water into his mouth and wipe the perspiration from his forehead.

"I can't believe Randall would do this to us," he'd said on the phone. He had wanted to start for the farm when Virginia first called, but she had persuaded him to wait until daylight and, later, to stay there.

She picked up one of the CDs they had listened to on the trip with Winn. "How's your dad? I told him I would come and visit."

"He's pretty good. He remembers going to get the horses, but he thinks it was a long time ago." West reached over and brushed Virginia's hair from her cheek. "That's what happens to him. Everything gets shoved back into the past, all jumbled together. 'How is our little Ginny?' he asked me."

"Look," Virginia said, pointing ahead to the left side of the road, where a woman was placing letters in her rural delivery mailbox. "Let's stop and talk to her."

The woman had just raised the little red flag on the side, and she stepped back when West pulled into the driveway, keeping the box on its sturdy post between herself and the truck.

"I'll ask," Virginia said, getting out with one of the flyers in her hand.

"What is it?" the woman said. "You're not from that church, are you?"

"This is my son." Virginia held the paper up so the woman could see Randall's picture. "He's missing, and there's a good chance he came this way."

"How old is he?" The woman glanced back at her neat, ranch-style house with its orderly hedge and flower beds. A small child was standing inside the front window, holding on to the curtain.

"Fourteen. He's tall, though, so maybe he looks older."

"I haven't seen anyone."

"There was a girl with him. We think they ran away together."

"I'm sorry," the woman said, looking at Virginia and then at West.

"Take this." Virginia thrust the flyer at her. "My phone number is at the bottom."

"I hope you find him," the woman said, moving away.

"Do I look scary?" Virginia asked, getting back in the truck.

"Maybe a little." West smiled at her. "Your eyes are all red."

They reached Beckley in the early afternoon, a string of disappointing encounters behind them. No one had seen Randall, but now at least his picture was tacked up inside every small business along the highway. Most people they talked with had been sympathetic. Some told stories of other teenage runaways. One of them had turned up in Akron, another in Memphis. One had never been heard from again.

Though she hadn't been there often, Virginia had always liked the town of Beckley, the seat of Raleigh County, for its genteel bustle. It was the sort of place where someone could make a movie about small-town life in the 1950s. West parked the truck on the street, and they approached a pair of elderly men drowsing on a bench near the courthouse.

"Nope," one of them said when Virginia asked if they knew of a family named Garret.

The other man hawked up a gob of tobacco juice and turned away to spit. "Not one of the old families, anyway," he said, wiping his mouth with the back of his hand.

"This boy, Randall MacLeod," West said, showing them a flyer. "We think he might have come down here with Irene Garret. She used to live here."

"Run off, you mean?" the first man asked.

"Well, yes," Virginia said.

"Hell of a thing," the second man said. "Ask around in the courthouse. Someone in there might know."

Spotting a pay phone, Virginia stopped in the big open hallway to call the farm, tapping her foot impatiently as she counted the rings. "What took you so long?" she asked when her father picked up.

"I was outside with Lee. He came over to work the horses."

"Where's Lydia?"

"She had to go into the Landing to pick up a few things. She'll be back soon."

"Someone should be in the house. What if Randall tried to call?"

"You're right, Ginny. I wasn't thinking." He told her Lee had offered to stay and help with the evening milking.

She then called Rob's number at the hospital and left a message on his voice mail. He would be exhausted by now, going on adrenaline.

Virginia and West found the county clerk's office on the second floor and asked the receptionist, a young woman with sparkly blue fingernail polish, if she knew where a family named Garret used to live. She looked at them doubtfully, shaking her head.

"The girl had a small tattoo right here," Virginia said, touching herself above the right breast. "A bird of some kind."

"I know the people you mean." A balding man wearing a tie and a short-sleeved shirt came out of the nearest office, polishing his glasses. "Donny Garret's family."

"He might be the father," Virginia said. "I don't know his first name."

West gave each of them a copy of Randall's picture as Virginia explained why they had come.

"Donny Garret rented a mobile home from a friend of mine, out on the Porter Road," the man said. "Donny was a decent guy, but a couple months after he left, his wife had some new guy living with her. Lots of drinking and partying going on. They didn't pay the last month's rent, either. Skipped out in the middle of the night."

"Irene has a friend here, Shelby Carter. I was hoping we could talk to her," Virginia said. "Maybe Irene's been in touch."

"Shelby Carter," the receptionist said. "Her dad runs the hardware store."

"Right down the street," the man said. "Shelby's working for him this summer. I'll give Carter a call and let him know you're coming."

Seated on a high wooden stool in her father's office, Shelby Carter looked frightened. She could be Irene's sister, Virginia thought at first glance. She had the same pouty face and pudgy hands.

"They don't even have a phone up there," Shelby said when her father asked if she had talked to Irene lately.

"Does she ever write to you?" Virginia was leaning against the desk, close to the girl, trying to sound friendly.

"Couple times." Shelby watched a customer walking past the open door.

"This is no joke," her father said. "If you know anything about it, you need to tell us."

They heard the *ding* of the metal bell beside the cash register, and her father said he would be back in a minute.

"You must know something," Virginia said. "Irene told me you were her best friend."

"I already told you," Shelby said, whining. "I don't."

"When was the last time you heard from Irene?" West asked her.

Instead of answering, the girl slipped off one of the silver bracelets she was wearing and began sucking on it.

"Would you stop that?" Virginia said. "Talk to us."

Shelby shook her head.

"I mean it." Virginia took hold of her wrist.

"God," Shelby said, trying to pull her hand free.

Virginia gripped her tighter, and the girl looked up, her eyes filling with tears.

"Ginny," West said.

"All right." Virginia released her. "But you're not doing your friend any favors by keeping quiet."

"God," Shelby repeated, rubbing at the red marks on her arm.

"You'll call us, won't you, if you hear anything?" West tapped the photocopy on the desk. "The number is right here. It's not safe for them to be out on their own. You understand that, right?"

"Sure," the girl mumbled, slipping the bracelet into her mouth again.

Leaving the hardware store, Virginia and West made their way through the town, talking to the other shopkeepers, to people on the sidewalk, passing out Randall's picture. Eventually, they got back in the truck and went looking for Porter Road, because they couldn't think of anything else to do.

It snaked up a steep hill, not far from town, a gravel road with an occasional house perched forlornly beside it and barking dogs that ran out behind the truck. Coming to a trailer, West stopped. Virginia got out and knocked on the door. Shading her eyes, she peered in a window and saw a kitchen and a sparsely furnished living room. All the surfaces were clean and bare. She tried the door, but it was locked. They drove to the end of the road, but there was no other trailer.

"We should probably head home," West said. "We can stop in Fayette, if you want to get your dad's truck."

"I suppose." Virginia took off her sunglasses and rubbed her eyes. "I'll bet you anything that girl Shelby knows where they are."

"She might. But you're not going to squeeze it out of her."

Virginia kept a sharp watch on both sides of the road as they started back on the highway. "They could be on this same road right now, riding in somebody's car."

"They could be a lot of places." West switched on the head-lights.

"At least more people will be looking out for them." West's boys had spent the day driving the back roads near Fayette, putting up flyers, asking around. The last time Virginia had called her father, he'd told her the boys hadn't turned up any-thing, either.

"What about Rob?" West asked.

"He's going to wait at home for now. We thought Randall might end up there, or try to contact him, at least." Virginia sighed, finally closing her eyes and resting her head against the seat back. When West took her hand, she returned the pressure briefly and then crossed her arms over her chest.

A few minutes later, West pulled into a gas station. Virginia studied him in the side mirror as he filled the tank and then as he went inside to pay the cashier. She had never loved him more. And because of that, she knew, she was being punished. She knew it as surely as if the old minister were there beside her, whispering in her ear.

"Half a sugar," West said, passing her a foam cup through the window. "Lots of milk."

She tasted the coffee as he started the truck. "Thank you," she said. "It's just right."

"I'm really sorry, Ginny," West said. "I thought we'd be bringing them home tonight."

Miles later, they both turned to look as they passed the house where Virginia had spoken to the woman beside the mailbox. The curtains were drawn, and there were lights inside. Virginia imagined the woman sitting down to dinner with her husband and child. Perhaps she had shown her husband the flyer and said what a shame.

"Randall didn't run away because of us," West said.

"I'm not so sure." She told him about Irene predicting a divorce, the way she had tried to make a joke of it. Maybe Randall had understood more than he let on. "Whatever it takes," Virginia said suddenly, "I'll get him back."

Chapter Twenty-one

That night, Virginia took the cushions from the couch, made a bed for herself in her father's office, and placed the telephone on the floor beside it. Cleo curled up next to her, sighing with contentment. Virginia put an arm across her belly and pulled her closer, letting her forehead rest on the soft fur of the dog's neck. She drifted off to sleep that way, and when she was wakened by the twitching of a dog dream, she was thinking of West. He had kissed her tenderly in the parking lot behind the police station and waited for her to start up her father's truck. He followed her most of the way home, blinking his headlights when he turned off on the road to the Moffat farm.

She and Rob had talked for more than an hour after she got back, in the way they used to, going over every detail of the day. She told him about Shelby and the empty trailer and all the stops along the way. This time, she said that West had gone with her, but Rob didn't seem to notice. He told her about the young man he had operated on, only twenty-one, driving too fast. The father, he said, broke down and cried when Rob assured him that his son would recover, that he would have only a slight limp. They kept circling back to Randall, assuring each other he would get in touch with them. Finally realizing they were tying up the phone, they said a hasty good night.

Randall. She fixed on the image of him playing the saxophone, just the night before, the way he had closed his eyes and bent over his horn. It had amused her then, her boy pretending to be a real jazz musician, a grown-up stranger with a life of his own.

She woke to a faint pink light, the sound of footsteps upstairs. Someone, it must have been her father, had looked in on her during the night and covered her with a blanket. Her back ached, and as she got up, she felt a familiar cramping in her stomach. Virginia nearly cried when she stood up from the toilet and saw the bloody streaks in the water. It's for the best, she told herself, but she felt as if something precious had been taken from her.

Still dressed in the clothes she had worn the day before, she went out to the barn with Cleo and heard the heavy sounds of the horses moving about in their stalls. "Hello, beauties," she said, kissing each of them on the nose before leading them out to their pasture.

Cody came in while Virginia and her father were still milking. "I had an idea," he said. "Richard's Falls. Irene liked it there. Maybe they're camping out."

"We can look," Virginia said. "As soon as we finish here." It didn't seem likely, given the distance Randall and Irene would have traveled from Fayette to get there, but looking for them anywhere was better than sitting around waiting for a phone call.

"Have something to eat first." Her father switched off the milking machine, and she started unhooking the cows. "You need to keep yourself up."

———

As they neared the falls, Virginia began to hope again. It was a plan two teenagers might come up with. Leave the truck somewhere to confuse the grown-ups, then double back and hang out in a nice spot for a few days—long enough to make Jodie worry.

"Cody," Virginia said. "Was Randall mad at me?"

"I don't think so. Why would he be mad at you?"

Even so early in the day, the rocks were hot from the beating sun, and they paused in the spray from the falls. It seemed to Virginia that years had passed since she and Rob had stood in the same spot, watching Randall struggle to lift Irene onto his shoulders. She smiled, remembering the way Rob had waded in and lifted her off. When they worked their way down to the lower pool, she and Cody found one of the small stones he had brought up and given to Henny. They stood with their hands on their hips and looked around. There was no sound except the roar of the falls.

"Maybe over there," Cody said, pointing toward the clearing where they had eaten their picnic lunch.

Four or five crows flew up as they entered the opening in the trees, cawing and circling overhead. There was a bad smell—the sweet, putrid odor of rotting flesh—and they spotted the carcass at the same time.

"Coyote," Cody said.

One side had been torn open, the ribs picked clean. The fur of its neck was matted with dried blood and bits of leaf. It was old, with a gray muzzle and clouded eyes.

"Don't look." Cody took Virginia by the arm and walked her back to the pool, where she knelt and splashed water over her face, trying to wash the smell away. He picked up the small, glittery stone and studied it for a minute before tossing it in the water.

"It's all right," Virginia said as they climbed up to the car. "It was a good idea."

They drove back through Tenney's Landing as church was letting out. Spotting Chick and Bonnie and their girls on the sidewalk, Virginia pulled over to the curb.

"Any news?" Chick asked, leaning in her open window.

"No," she said, aware of his spotless Sunday shirt.

"Reverend Gleason prayed for you this morning," Bonnie told her. "For Randall and Irene to come home safely."

"Did he?" Virginia hated the idea of Reverend Gleason speaking about her troubles. The three Mason girls, she noticed, were whispering with Cody.

"We were just sick when Henny told us," Bonnie said. "I can only imagine what you're going through."

"Randall will call you," Chick assured her, laying his hand on her shoulder.

"What did Agatha say?" Virginia asked Cody as they drove on.

"Well, you know, she kind of likes Randall." He sighed, put his window partway up and then down again. "She didn't know he was going out with Irene."

"Ah," Virginia said. "And you kind of like Agatha."

When Cody shrugged in reply, she suggested they stop by and visit with Henny for a few minutes. Maybe she'd heard something.

They found her sitting out on the porch with a man Virginia had never seen before. Parked near the wheelchair ramp was a car with a Kentucky license plate.

"That would be Marcus," Cody said.

"Who?"

"You'll find out."

Reaching for Virginia, Henny held her tight and kissed her on the cheek before introducing Marcus Frazier. Virginia hadn't noticed at first, but he was in a wheelchair, too—a lightweight chair with a nylon seat and back.

"I wish we were meeting under different circumstances," he said. "Henny has been telling me about your son."

Sitting with Cody in the porch swing, Virginia went over every detail again, from the tire tracks in the grass beside the barn to the dead coyote at Richard's Falls. Distracted as she was, she couldn't help noticing the way Henny and Marcus looked at each other from time to time, as if they were friends.

"Kids do wild and foolish things every day," Marcus said when Virginia stopped talking at last. "They scare the hell out of us. But most of the time, things turn out fine." His speech, the measured gentleness of his Kentucky accent, was reassuring.

"Marcus is a lawyer," Henny said. "So he knows a thing or two about wild and foolish."

"Is that right?" Virginia was waiting for an explanation, and Marcus obliged.

He had, he told her, inherited a house in Tenney's Landing when his great-aunt Dorian died the year before. He'd finally stopped procrastinating and come up to have a look at it, intending to sell quickly and be done with it. But he'd forgotten what an appealing house it was; he hadn't seen it since he was Cody's age, one summer when he visited with his mother. "It has a grand view of the river from the back porch," he said.

He and Bernie Bishop had spent a day cruising around in Bernie's Town Car, and Marcus had started wondering what it would be like to live up this way, especially when Bernie told him the nearest lawyer's office, in Fayette, was run by two geezers overdue for retirement. He didn't have any family back in Lexington; his parents had both died in the plane crash that crippled him twenty years before.

"His father was a pilot," Henny said.

"He had a little four-seater," Marcus continued. "We were coming back from a wedding and ran into bad weather. But what I meant to say was Bernie brought me over here to get Henny's advice. He said he wouldn't be in business today if it wasn't for her."

"Marcus drives, too," Cody said. "That's his car."

"I do get around." Marcus smiled at him. "The car's fitted with hand controls."

"So you're thinking of staying here?" Virginia asked.

"Yes, I am. Thinking about it."

"My mom says he's handsome," Cody remarked a few minutes later, when they were back in the car.

"You've met him before."

"He was here one day when we stopped by. My mom says Bernie is trying to fix them up."

"I think he's succeeding."

"But my brother Weston says just because two people happen to be in wheelchairs, that doesn't mean they're going to like each other."

"He's right. I have a feeling those two like each other, though." Virginia was remembering a Christmas party at Dorian Frazier's house years ago, the way snow had started falling as she and Henny and the others stood around the piano while Marcus's great-aunt played carols. "Why haven't I heard about Marcus before this?"

"I don't know," Cody said. "Here's another thing: Marcus's fiancée was in the plane with them. She died, too."

When they got back to the farm, Jodie's car was parked in front of the house, and Virginia's father was standing at the fence, watching Lee with the horses. Lee was trying to hitch them to a small cart he'd made with the wheels from her mother's old garden cart, but Jewel wasn't standing still for it. Virginia heard the sound of splintering wood as Jewel tried to kick her way out of the harness.

"I'll help him," Cody said. He ran across the driveway and ducked through the fence. The horse calmed at the sight of him and let him take hold of her halter.

"Try her on the left-hand side," Virginia heard her father say. "I believe she prefers that."

Jodie was seated at the table, morosely watching Lydia as she stirred a kettle on the stove. The air in the kitchen was steamy, with a tangy fragrance.

"Green tomato relish," Lydia said. "I needed something to do."

"Any calls?" Virginia asked.

"Your husband, twice. He said to tell you he'll be at the hospital. That boy he operated on yesterday had a bad night. Rob went to see about him."

"You find anything?" Jodie had taken off one of her earrings and was twisting it around her little finger.

Virginia shook her head.

"West, too," Lydia said. "He has to do some work on the trout ponds today, but he'll check in later."

"She's really gone too far this time," Jodie said. "Taking Randall with her."

Virginia couldn't think of anything to say in Irene's defense, and so she started washing the jars Lydia had set out on the counter. When Jodie and Lee left in the afternoon, Virginia went upstairs and took a long shower and dressed in clean clothes.

———

Virginia and Lydia were putting away the supper dishes when the phone rang.

"This is Officer Piaseki, Baltimore Police Department," a young but official-sounding voice said. "I'm trying to reach Virginia MacLeod."

"Speaking."

"We have your son Randall in custody."

"Custody? What happened?"

"We picked them up about an hour ago, ma'am. Irene Garret and your son. They were on one of the I-495 entrance ramps, trying to hitch a ride."

"Into Baltimore?"

"Yes, ma'am. The officer who stopped asked what they were doing, and your son told him they were running away from home."

"I can be there in four hours."

"We have him in the juvenile detention facility. We'll keep him overnight, to make an impression. You can sign him out after oh-eight-hundred tomorrow."

"Eight o'clock?"

"That's right, ma'am. I'll give you directions."

When Virginia hung up, her father and Lydia were standing in the doorway. "He's fine," Virginia said, laughing and crying at once. "Randall's in Baltimore."

"Well," Lydia said, putting her arm through Nathan's. "Thank God."

The sun was setting when Virginia finally got on the highway. She had hastily packed an overnight bag, then called Rob to arrange to meet him at the motel Officer Piaseki recommended, near the detention center. Though their house in Laurel Springs was only an hour's drive from Baltimore, she wanted to be as close as possible. She had asked her father to call West and Henny and the others to let them know, and then she had stopped at Jodie's house.

"I think me and Lee will go down sometime tomorrow," Jodie had said. "Leave her ass in juvie for a while. See how she likes that."

Lee was chewing on one of his mint sticks. "Quite the little mother," he'd remarked. He told Virginia he would go to the farm in the morning to help her father with chores.

Virginia reached across the seat and unwrapped the sandwich Lydia had sent with her. She had, as Lydia pointed out, only picked at her supper, and now she was hungry. Handing her a thermos of coffee as she was about to get in the car, her father had said, "I'll be happy to see that rascal. You tell him I said so."

By the time she reached King John's Mountain, it was fully dark, the highway nearly deserted. It had been a little more than two months since they crossed the mountain, Randall sulking in the seat beside her. Passing the rest area at the top, she thought of the log truck driver who had come to her rescue. She poured coffee into the stainless steel cup and switched on the radio.

The motel, a Cozy Inn near the highway, was a nondescript building surrounded by gas stations and fast-food restaurants. At the desk, the clerk gave her the room number and told her Rob had already checked in.

Virginia didn't know how she would face him, certain her betrayal would be obvious in every word and gesture. And then, before she reached the room, Rob opened the door and stepped out into the fluorescent hallway. He looked drawn, but he smiled and held his hand out to take her bag.

"I heard you coming," he said.

He followed her through the door and put his arms around her and held her. "Thank God, it's over," he said.

Heart pounding, she stepped back and touched his cheek. "I know."

"Have a seat. I'll fix us a drink."

Virginia sat on the edge of the bed and watched as he fished a bottle out of his bag, filled two plastic cups with perforated cubes from the ice machine, and then poured Scotch over them. "How is your patient doing?" she asked.

"Pretty good. We've got him stabilized."

Rob propped pillows against the headboard, and they pulled the bedspread over their legs to keep off the chill of the air conditioner. Too tired to talk, they found an old black-and-white movie on the television and fell asleep with their clothes on, slumped against each other.

The juvenile detention facility looked very much like the Cozy Inn, except that it was surrounded by a chain-link fence topped with three strands of barbed wire. On one side there was a basketball court with chain-mesh nets and, on the other, an overgrown strip of lawn with two picnic tables. When Virginia and Rob went in the front door, they were met by a Mr. Stott, who had been expecting them. As he led them to his office, Virginia was aware of cooking smells and a sort of clanging racket beyond a set of closed double doors.

"Breakfast cleanup," Mr. Stott said. "The boys are nearly finished."

Sitting in front of his desk, Virginia and Rob answered questions as he typed their answers into a computer. At last he stopped and peered at them over his glasses. "Your son seems like a nice kid," he said. "I don't want to see him in here again."

They signed the release forms and then waited in the office while Mr. Stott went to get Randall. At the window, Virginia saw a side door open, and a dozen boys came spilling out. Dressed in shorts and T-shirts, like ordinary boys, they called to each other, their voices sharp. The sound of basketballs bouncing on concrete and the rattle of chain echoed against the side of the building.

When she heard Randall's voice—he was saying something about his ankle—Virginia was out of her chair, and there he was in the bright corridor. He was still wearing the black pants and white shirt from the concert, the shirt filthy. He had a scrape on his left cheek that had been painted with iodine. When he rushed toward Virginia, she saw that he was limping. She held him tightly, aware of the scent of perspiration and woodsmoke.

"Hey, Dad," he said after a minute. Embarrassed, Randall wiped his eyes with the back of his hand and hugged his father.

"What happened to your leg?" Rob asked.

"I fell down an embankment and sprained my ankle. It's not too bad."

"We had the doctor look at it last night," Mr. Stott assured them. "He put ice on it and taped it."

Virginia took Randall's backpack and let him walk ahead with his father. "I was wondering about Irene Garret," she said to Mr. Stott. "Maybe I could see her."

"The girls are in a separate facility."

When he didn't offer any further information, Virginia decided to let it drop. She caught up with her husband and son, and in the parking lot the three of them stood awkwardly between her car and Rob's.

"Why don't I drive Randall home?" Rob said. "I need to get to the hospital, but I want to have a look at that ankle first."

"We're staying here?" Randall asked his mother.

"Well, for a couple of days, anyway." Rob turned to Virginia. "Don't you think?"

"We do have Lee helping at the farm," she said. "And Cody. I guess we don't need to rush back." Trying to imagine what it would be like to walk into their house again, she thought of the schedule she had taped to the side of the refrigerator before Lydia's call—the summer so thoughtfully blocked out. She had no idea what she and Randall would do for the next two days.

Rob opened her car door and held it for her. "You know the way from here, in case we get separated in traffic?"

"Yes," she said. "Sure."

VIRGINIA

I sit in Aunt Ida's room at the little desk, a cool breeze coming through the windows. From the hillside, I hear Randall on the tractor, though it is nearly dark, the days noticeably shorter now. We have finished the second cutting, but he wanted to take the tractor out one last time. He hasn't been allowed to drive the truck, and so he has spent hours on the tractor instead. I often wonder what he is thinking about. He has said nothing about Irene since we got back.

He has kept himself busy, though. Besides haying and helping Lee with the horses, he has been working on what he calls his community service projects. One of them was building a wheelchair ramp for our porch, in time for my father's birthday dinner. Henny and Marcus came together, in his car. Once upon a time, Henny wouldn't have objected to being carried up the steps, but now she won't hear of it. When I asked her the other day if she thought she and Marcus might get married, she said stranger things have happened.

I will have to finish packing soon. Randall and I will be leaving in the morning, going home. I have my mother's journals in a box to take with me. We—my father and Randall and I—went to visit her grave today. I took a bouquet of her pink roses, tied up with a ribbon. She always liked the second, late-summer blooming. Even though the roses are smaller and not as fragrant, they last longer, all the way to the first frost. In the quiet cemetery, we could hear the needles of the white pines beginning to fall, the faint rustle as they drifted down.

When I went to see Winn, he called me Caroline and asked how Hattie and Chandler were getting along. The two of us had a nice stroll on the golf course. He told me about Mack and Molly, the Shire horses he raised as a boy. He said it's best not to be too hard on them because you don't want to take away their pride. "If they make a mistake, let them try again," he said. "You want to end their day on a good note."

West and his boys helped us finish the haying, but West and I have not been alone together since our second meeting at the Ridgeway house. The day after I got back with Randall, we sat and talked in the ruins of Taylor and Oona's living room. When I told him I had sworn to give him up, West said it sounded like a deal with the devil, trading away our happiness for Randall's safe return. We could have had both, he said.

I am not superstitious enough to believe one thing caused the other, but if I had been offered such a deal, I would have taken it. I will go home with this ache in my heart and be grateful.

My father and Lydia have decided not to sell for now. They will see where things stand next spring, they say. Perhaps Jack and Jewel had something to do with it. Now that my father is feeling stronger, he is able to spend more time with them. When they see him, they rush to the fence to be petted and admired. Also—to Lydia's dismay, I suspect—Lee has moved into the farmhouse. He appeared on the porch one evening with his duffel bag and told us Jodie and Irene were gone.

When Larry came for my father's birthday—alone, because his wife couldn't get time off from work—the house was crowded. Walking around in his khakis and loafers, my brother seemed remote. When I showed him the horses, he laughed and said, "American Cream. How do you remember all that stuff?"

I think of Aunt Ida, the way she would grow melancholy on her last day, gathering the things she wanted to take back to the city—a stone she'd found in the brook, a sycamore leaf, a blue jay's feather. And her box of preserves. Lydia has packed one for me, too.

When I was a teenager, I halfway envied Ida as she drove away. I would try to picture her classroom and the second-graders at their desks, freshly scrubbed and eager on the first day. She sent me postcards during the school year and wrote about the concerts and plays she attended. The first time I went to visit her on the bus, she took me to the Buhl Planetarium, where we watched the star show, and to a Greek restaurant for stuffed grape leaves.

Now I am sorry to think of everything that will happen here while I am gone. I will not see Jack and Jewel learning to be draft horses instead of pets, or my father driving them for the first time, or Cody riding down the hill in the morning, or Henny finding her way with Marcus. I will not be here when the woodcocks come back in the spring. I will not see West, even at a distance, or hear his voice.

But one person can't live two lives. I am trying to practice the difficult art of taking one day at a time, looking ahead only far enough to anticipate the changing seasons. It helps to keep in mind my parents' journals, their patient noting of the year moving forward, of events both expected and unforeseen.

This morning, I walked down into the cornfield. The stalks have grown above my head, as green as they will be. My father and Lee won't attach the four-row picker to the tractor for another few weeks, when the corn starts to look like autumn—the yellow silk turning brown and the leaves beginning to lose their color. They will get it in before the first hard frost, before the snow clouds blow over the mountains. Before the earth settles into the long, slow wait of winter, my mother's favorite time of year.

Acknowledgments

This book would never have been written without the persistence and care of my agent, Nat Sobel. And it would have been a diminished thing without the kind attentions and fortitude of my editor, Alexis Gargagliano. I thank my lucky stars for both of you. Thanks, as well, to Nan Graham and to everyone at Scribner who had a hand in producing it. I am grateful to the friends who not only read and commented on early drafts, but urged me to believe I could make something of it: Andrea Doughtie, Ed Doughtie, Mary Hays, and Steve Long. For their generosity and help of all kinds, I thank Leslie Epstein, David Huddle, and—most especially—Margot Livesey. For making the time away from my desk a lot more fun, and the time there a lot more productive, I am indebted to many dear friends, including five of my oldest: Susan Boehmer, Susan Brison, Carol Krausman, Paul Krausman, and Lynda Roseman. For their love, faith, and everything else, thanks to my family—scattered across the country, but close to my heart.

About the Author

CATHERINE TUDISH is the author of the acclaimed short story collection *Tenney's Landing*. Tudish taught writing and literature at Harvard for eight years before moving to Vermont to work as a journalist and fiction writer. She now teaches at the Bread Loaf School of English and Dartmouth College.